Free Her

Emma Ellis

This book is written in British English.

This is a dark novel. Sexual assault on a child is mentioned. Compared to the first book, there is more violence including graphic descriptions of gore.

Chapter One

Isobel

The therapist's sofa is the same as it was years ago when I was a kid and came here. The dust poofs up like it's not been sat on since, the lumpy springs telling the opposite story. It smells like the same air freshener Katarina would use to disguise the beer permeating her clothes when she worked in the bar.

I still mentally refer to her as Katarina, as if she is somehow separate from me.

Doctor Cottrell looks as moth-eaten as the upholstery, his salt-and-pepper beard denser than his comb-over. His voice is what I remember the most. He always sounds one breath away from a cough, his pitch only ever trudging out the lowest frequencies, like he thinks he's conversing with an elephant rather than a human. The fifteen years since our last session means each word now sounds like it could be his last.

At least his old-fashioned ways mean he doesn't check my IMAtech. A hormone readout is not going to help me get through this.

'Relax, Isobel,' he says. 'I want you to shut out the rest of the room, to believe nothing outside this room exists anymore.'

From my position lying on the sofa, it's only the ceiling I can see. White wood-chip, nicotine stains showing where the latest lick of paint failed to get into the corners, combined with yellowing patches from sun bleach around the window reflections. It's hardly the type of view to send my thoughts into overdrive, but I shut my eyes anyway, allowing the blackness to be my imagination's canvas.

I wonder how hormones are meant to change with the mild hypnotic state he's aiming for. What are the happy hormones again? I forget, but trying to remember only elevates my heart rate. Relaxing isn't as easy as it used to be.

'Concentrate on your breaths,' he says. 'Slowly in. . .and out. Listen to nothing but my voice.'

Did this crap ever work? It must have done once. Years ago, when the sofa was more comfortable and smelled better. When I was more determined to forget.

'Try to visualise that safe. You remember the safe we built in your mind years ago? Can you see it?'

'Yes,' I say. Visualising is something I can easily do. Succumbing to hypnosis, not so much. 'It's navy blue with a large chrome lock.'

'And the room around you. Is it comfortable?' There's the sound of him drinking some water, to likely clear the rattle from his voice. Loud, echoing swallows.

'The safe is in my bedroom at home,' I say. 'The carpet is pink and my bed is tidy. My games console is off. It's peaceful.'

The slightest clink from the glass being placed back on the desk. 'Good, Isobel. That's excellent. Do you have the key?'

On the shelf in my imaginary bedroom, the chunky brass key lies, dust-free next to the books on wildlife and gerbil welfare. 'I do.' I imagine taking the key. Its weight is more than I expected, it's cold to touch. Somewhere outside of my bedroom, my mum is cooking dinner, reminding me that all of this is fake. She's been dead for years.

'Excellent,' he says. 'Now, in that safe are a lot of bad things, and we want to keep them in there. So, do you remember how we do that?'

I cast my mind back to the mental techniques he taught me over a decade ago, fingering through reams and reams of instructions I've built for myself over the years, peeling away each instruction until I find the original mention. 'I shove the new memories in there without looking, and I shut the door quickly, then lock it.'

'Very good. Now, in your free hand, are you holding the memory you wish to put in the safe?'

My mind's eye looks down at my left hand. In there, I see a minuscule version of what happened. Adam Ward and the other board members just before they die, the flames after the explosion, the building collapsing around me before I get pulled out. Peter Ward's face as he reaches for me before I—or rather,

Katarina—pushed him to his death. The severed hands. All of it glows in a ball in my hand, waiting to be thrown.

'I do,' I say.

'When you're ready, and take all the time you need, I want you to open that safe and throw those memories in there. All the fear you felt, all the anger, throw that in the safe, then lock the door.'

There's nothing to be afraid of in my old bedroom. It's where I spent hours and hours as a girl playing computer games to take my mind away from reality. It's the only place I ever felt free.

I squeeze my closed eyes and wait a moment. Concentrating on my breaths is harder when they're accelerating. I haven't visualised my mind safe for years. It's a Pandora's box of my past. I lock those memories away for a reason, and even thinking about it knots my stomach. They are part of a previous life, when there was even more pain. When I was a different Isobel.

Those memories could leak out. I'm too close. The memory I hold in my hand isn't as bad as what's in there, I'm sure.

I wait for a few painful minutes as Doctor Cottrell carries on talking about my breathing or something. I don't know. I'm not listening. In my imaginary bedroom, my back is pressed up against the wall, my eyes wide as I wait for the safe to fling open and its contents to pounce in an ambush.

The key is heavy and cold in my hand. I swallow, step forward, then put it in the lock. I look away a moment, tense and bracing, before I put the key back on the shelf.

'Done.'

'Good. Now, concentrate on your breath a while longer, and when you're ready, you can open your eyes.'

I open my eyes straight away. That white painted wood-chip ceiling comes back into view, and the tension in my arms dissipates. I sit up.

Doctor Cottrell is smiling at me. His sparsely-toothed mouth lingers in that shape for a moment as he peers at me over the brim of his glasses. 'Well done, Isobel.'

I nod. 'Thanks.' I hop off the sofa, and with my feet on the ground again, I'm a little giddy, my first couple of steps stumbling as I leave.

There's no receptionist to talk to as I go. Doctor Cottrell's office is in a downstairs room of his home. The decor is as dated throughout. Textured wallpaper peels at the edges, patterned carpet with stains mostly hidden under the dim light from bulbs cased in nicotine-tinged shades.

'I'll see you again soon.' He has the narrowed eyes of someone who thinks they know best, but I've appeased my dad's wishes by coming here once. The therapy was his idea. I'm sure I'm fixed enough.

'Thanks again.' I say.

The blast of fresh air is a welcome change, and I stretch my arms up as I exit onto the busy street.

Katarina is waiting for me, propped up against a neighbour's rickety fence. Her weight against it doesn't make it lean any more. Her attire seems fitting for once, since the day is so warm and she shows more skin than fabric, as usual. That black lacy top has a sheen under the sun, her skin as tan as always. She walks in step with me as I make my way towards the train station.

'That doctor is a cowboy,' she says.

I take out my phone, then put a headphone in, hoping everyone around me will assume I'm talking on the phone rather than to myself. Well, one of the other people who shares this body.

'My dad likes him,' I say. 'He wanted to help.'

'I know you didn't put anything in that mind safe.'

Of course she knows. I glance her way only for a split second, giving a subtle shrug.

'And I know *why* you didn't put anything in that safe.'

I bite the inside of my cheek, keeping my gaze straight ahead this time. There're some pigeons on the pavement in front. I pause a second to watch them, their bobbing heads, the male one's neck iridescent in the sun. They're such underrated birds, I always think. Beautifully colourful and spend their lives cleaning up our mess. No one likes them because they're so common. People only like what's rare or unusual.

'It's not because you don't want to forget,' Katarina continues. 'I know you do. It's because you're afraid to open that door.'

I take the headphone out, not willing to justify this with a response. She'll go away, eventually.

'Those memories won't stay in that safe forever,' she says, with more determination in her voice now. 'No mind safe is that strong. And you know as well as I do, all those bad memories are bursting to get out.'

I shake my head to disguise the chill trickling over my spine, and I walk again, the pigeons flying out of my path, not satisfying her with as much as another glance.

Katarina fades away. It's just me walking to the train station now. Alone.

Just Isobel.

Chapter Two

Isobel

My dad insisted on the therapy. My burns healed with some scarring but the mind suffers more, he said. Mental wounds run deeper than skin. Best to put it all behind me so I can move on. He suggested my old therapist. I didn't feel I need it, not really. I'm stronger than he thinks I am. But I guess with my new job, it's good to have a mental detox.

It's been two months since the explosion. Seven weeks since I left the hospital. Harry, well, his treatment is ongoing. Luckily, his family's billions can spring for the best doctors in the country. Half of his body is covered in welts and scars. Four skin grafts down his right side so far and counting. It's like there are two different sides to him.

I can relate.

In the hotel room, I stand and check myself. The green dress plays down the redness from the scars, but the sleeveless design means they're on show, as the Baxters requested.

'Don't hide what happened, Isobel,' Hugo Baxter told me when he first offered me the promotion, when he first started preparing me for social functions. 'You survived a great ordeal. Your scars are a badge of honour. They show how far you've come.'

How much the company has helped me, is what he really means.

He and his wife, Malorie, mollycoddle me more than they do their son. With the Baxters being the only surviving board members at Ward Innovation Technologies, they have the company's reputation to think about. They only offered me the office manager role to butter me up, to stop me suing WIT for the CEO apparently blowing up the pub. The explosion was written off as Adam Ward messing up an insurance job. No one ever suspected the guilty one was this body I share.

The salary is far higher than the job dictates. It's all bribes, but still, I accepted. Well, Layla accepted. She gleamed with pride at the job offer, whereas I bristled under Katarina's disapproving glare.

The social functions are an extra. At least I get paid overtime.

'Two-faced,' Katarina said when I was on my first day back at work. I'm sure she meant it as an insult rather than an accurate statement. 'You should have sued them. It's what they're expecting.'

'They have millions to spend on lawyers.'

'Still, it gives them bad press.'

I laughed at her comment. Bad press was Layla's aim, Katarina's was blood. She was trying to appeal to that side of me, the compassionate and reasonable side. She was playing a game, as always.

And me? I want what Katarina wants—the end of IMAtech and the Clarity Directive. I just want it the right way. Without killing people.

'What you need is more important than what you want,' Layla reminds me every time my thoughts go to Katarina. 'We need to eat, to pay rent. We don't need to fix the world.'

Try telling that to Katarina.

We approached the door of the WIT building on my first day back and went inside, just as my IMAtech app buzzed to indicate the start of my working day.

'We should be in prison for causing the explosion,' I said to Katarina as she huffed next to me. 'And for killing Peter Ward.'

'Look around you,' Katarina said as she glanced around the office. The building had an atmosphere less jovial than a funeral. 'We already are in prison.'

In the hotel room now, prison seems pretty far from the truth. Its five-star rating barely does it justice. Though, what would I know? Fancy hotels are hardly my usual turf. The furnishings all look hand carved from solid wood. The carpet squishes between my toes, forgiving and plush, and the light fittings refract and jingle like they're made of genuine crystal. The bed is so huge, I could sleep like a starfish and there would still be room for a person on either side.

Room for three? In this body, that's handy.

There's a knock at the door, and Hugo Baxter comes in before I've said a word. My shoulders tense at the sight of him. For the first second after the door opens, I swear his posture slumps a little, like he's disappointed he didn't catch me in a state of undress. Perhaps I'm being paranoid.

He puts his hand on his hip and one corner of his mouth curls up. 'Oh, Isobel. You look lovely.'

'Thanks.'

'What a star you'll be tonight. A real example of how WIT and Baxter Pharmaceuticals care about its people.'

I give him a tight smile. 'Of course.'

'Just be your sweet and lovely self, and I am sure we'll have investors lining up.'

'Great.'

'Five minutes? I'll see you in the lobby.'

He closes the door, and my tension dissolves. The heat that was rising up my neck cools, and I can breathe normally again. No man should unnerve me so. No boss should chill my bones. It's Katarina's influence, I'm sure. Her man-hating defence mechanism putting me on edge. In the mirror, behind my reflection, is Katarina, inspecting me with narrowed eyes, her pillowy lips twitching.

'You look gorgeous, by the way,' she says.

'You saying that is quite narcissistic.'

'Well, you know me.'

I do. Too well.

I tried to shut her out, her and Layla, to take ownership of my entire body and mind again. I missed so much while the two of them took over. It should be my turn to live, my turn to try to do some good. But being in control all the time is impossible, like cutting off a limb. Plus, I'd be alone again. Bad friends are better than none. Imaginary or not.

'The prison has had an upgrade, I see,' she says, glancing around at the fancy furnishings before eyeballing me again and stepping so close, her body brushes against mine. It doesn't matter how much I know she isn't really there, her warmth still touches my skin. 'Let's break out.'

I stiffen and shake my head. 'No.'

'Think about it. A fancy hall filled with a ton of rich and powerful men who want to be even more rich and powerful.'

My eyes widen, and I step away. Away from her scheming and influence. 'Don't. Whatever you've got on your mind. There are other ways to make a difference.'

'The only difference you'll be making is diverting their eyes. Leave the rest to me.'

My chest tightens, and where her warmth was is now itchy. Whatever Katarina touches becomes an irritation. She's a wasp, buzzing, unnerving, ready to sting.

Layla needs to be here, to reason, to have my back. But she's so often absent these days, like this body no longer wants to listen to her kind of logic.

Katarina takes a while to disappear, but she does, and the image of her gradually fades into nothing. I turn and leave the room. My heart dips, as from the edge of my vision, there's an image of Layla, watery eyes, brow knotted with worry. Her presence is lacking in my life, as she has no purpose being with me. I'm not the one she's screaming at. To me, her voice is silent.

Her screams are for Katarina.

Chapter Three

Katarina

The champagne is real at least. One massive perk since that weedy prick Adam Ward burned to death and took his sobriety with him. My only regret is I couldn't witness his death personally. I'd love to have smelled his flesh singe, to have seen his skin glowing like embers before it turned black and blistered off. I hope it was slow, that the drugs in his system kept him conscious long enough to see his bones show as the tissue melted off.

This body is on champagne number two, though it was Isobel who got to enjoy the first one. She hasn't learned yet that she's a lightweight, and it doesn't take much booze before I'm able to take control.

I've left my phone upstairs, since it's not like this dress has pockets, and my handbag is too small. It only holds a lipstick. It's a pointless accessory, but Hugo insisted on buying it for me, along with the dress. He'd sent his wife, Malorie, out shopping with me, though why we needed to go together was beyond me. She didn't say a word to me the entire time and chose the outfit without listening to my opinions at all.

It's important to look the part, Hugo said. To look like someone those rich pricks would like to spend time with, instead of trashy old me, I guess.

Suits me fine. I'm like one of those angler fish, and this dress and the pointless little handbag are my lure. Don't those fish have the sharpest teeth?

Like I said, suits me.

From the lobby, I glance into the hall. There are as many wait staff as there are guests, such are the endless demands of these pricks.

I fidget in my dress as it tightens and rubs. Isobel fighting for her space in this body is more than just a mental game. She stands differently, her shoulders roll forward, she itches at even the slightest irritation. Manipulating this body is her way of reminding me that she's in charge. She likes to think so, anyway. It's a little tickle up my arms and neck, like I'm about to shed my skin. Layla's moans are a near constant tinnitus, like the drone of traffic or humming air con. I can block her out as easily as background noise. It's my turn now.

They're both too tired for this shit, too happy to go along with it, to drift down the river and wait to smash into rocks. They'd rather that than the effort of trying to swim upstream. They never want to create the ripples.

It's better I'm here. They'll see that soon enough. Neither of them can work a room like I can. Like a lioness stalking her prey, I go in.

I've learned many of the attendees by name now. I spent hours studying these people online, their social media profiles, business statistics, dredging up personal information, and whispers of scandals. There's always something. No one sits at the top of the corporate tree without trampling some saplings. No one gets that rich without ensuring others are poorer.

As I inspect every one of them, I picture what they'd look like naked, whipped, and hanging from a noose. A flush of heat spreads over me and I sip some more champagne, letting the bubbles linger on my tongue a moment, the cool sharpness quelling the thrill.

The one thing they all have in common is their enthusiasm for *#behave* when that was doing the rounds. It still is, of course, just not trending so high. If it were up to these arseholes, us women would have it tattooed on our foreheads. The top bosses' brainchild to get women to know their place and stop 'bleating on about every bit of touching,' I believe was how they put it. It escalated and led to the Clarity Directive passing, to protect their own wandering hands above protecting women's rights. Requiring consent was too much of a puzzle for these pricks. Apparently, every word and action besides no is ambiguous.

All these wealthy pricks with their air of importance take advantage of the Clarity Directive now, since this is the bell tower of dickheads the Directive was brought in to protect. Let the greedy boys touch their dessert and worry about sticky fingers later.

I salivate as I look around the room, heart humming in my chest. There's so much here for me to feast on. So many men on my kill list. So much flesh to slice and burn. Heat wells up inside me again and I grab another glass of champagne from the waiter. It's such a temporary fix, as when the booze kicks in, my excitement will only multiply.

The hall resembles something regal, with textured walls covered in paintings in thick frames, of people who look like they were posh enough to dine here once. They all have deadpan faces and neck ruffs. They're probably all related to the wealth in attendance tonight. Money like that doesn't travel down the food chain very far. There are big pharma bosses, tech CEOs and socialites, men who made their money from mining the rainforest and collecting personal data. All with a history of underpaying staff and prioritising their company's stock market status over workers' rights. Doing their bit to keep the wealth gap inflated, their egos ballooning with it. Any of them could be my prey for the night. Taking down one of these rich pricks would create enough ripples to be seismic on the Richter scale, to create a decent enough dent in the stock exchange, and to nudge investor confidence down a peg or two. I stand a little straighter, hold my cool glass of champagne to my chest to take some of the heat off.

And of course, they're all here to learn about the ever-increasing benefits of IMAtech.

'This is an opportunity the corporate world has never seen before,' Hugo bangs on time and time again, whenever some sycophant is within earshot. The trial at WIT is almost over, and the sales pitch spills out of his mouth like constant verbal diarrhoea.

Whenever he talks, I want to cut his tongue off and stick it up his own arsehole.

There's a man I only vaguely recognise at one end. He's somehow oozing even more arrogance than the rest. He's better looking than the others certainly, younger, with his broad shoulders and defined features, a hairline that appears natural, rather than plugged with implants. Even his torso is taut, none of the indulgent podge that's almost unanimous among his older peers. He'll be a great target. I make a mental note to try to speak to him later. That shouldn't be hard. He's been staring at my tits for a full minute.

I lick my lips, the drink not quenching my thirst. I wish vampires were real and I was one. Some fangs or talons would be so satisfying to gouge out neck tissue. Instead, I have to opt for more traditional methods.

'Isobel!'

The call comes from behind, and it takes a moment to register they're calling me, or who they think is me. The sound of his foot scraping along the polished tiled floor from his limp tells me it's Harry before I've turned to face him. He's casually dressed, though his joggers and T-shirt probably still cost a month's rent. He's not meant to be attending this soiree, as per Mummy and Daddy's instructions, since he's not fancy-function-and-boardroom material with skin cratered like that. He's supposed to be hiding his face away, no longer the pinup boy that pleased the cameras.

'Hi,' I say.

'Oh.' He steps back. 'It's you.'

It irks me that he can tell who I am. He always seems to know. For a man with all the intelligence of a potato, it's a wonder how he can tell. Isobel probably gives off some frigid vibe I can't mimic. Whether he can distinguish between Layla and Isobel, I've no idea. Perhaps it's because I've seen his cock so many times it's impossible to hide from him now. I've had him inside me as much as out.

'Who were you expecting?' I ask with a grin.

I know the way he feels about Isobel, like she's all the good bits of me he used to like. He was a good fuck once. Now he's good for nothing.

'Funny.' He smirks. 'What are *you* doing here?'

I take another glass from a waiter's platter, then give him a wink. 'Enjoying the fizz.'

'Isobel and I have talked about this. IMAtech—'

'IMAtech will continue as long as there are people rich enough to create the demand. The Clarity Directive also won't go away until we take proper action.'

'Maybe your actions made things worse. Have you thought about that?' He says this with a glint of tears, the sort of emotion that would have Isobel pawing at him for forgiveness. Pawing at his left side of course, not his right. The right half looks like gnarled tree bark. Shame.

'That was just stage one,' I say. 'My plans are bigger than that dick Adam Ward and his friends. There's a lot more wealth in London that needs taking down. An entire bell tower of dickheads to destroy.'

The colour drains from Harry's cheeks. Even his scars grow pale. 'What are you planning?'

I wet my lips. 'The gap between the richest and poorest in the country has never been bigger. I'm addressing that gap from the top down.'

His chin trembles like a toddler's on the verge of a tantrum. 'Don't, Kat. I mean it.'

'Just get out of here before I find a way to scar your other side.'

'Get Isobel back.'

'No.'

I turn my back on him and plaster on a relaxed expression, wistful, smooth brow and alluring eyes.

'I mean it. Stop whatever you're doing.'

'Or what?' I put my glass down on the table to face him again, then fold my arms and front up to him with raised eyebrows. The sight of his pleading face makes me think he still would be a decent fuck. I'd chain him up and make him beg. He'd be even more pathetic than he is right now. 'What exactly are you going to do about it? Get me locked up, and your darling Isobel gets locked up too. We're a package deal, as you know.'

His eyes give away his feelings. I know he's sweet on that prude. With this body and her personality, I'm surprised his dick isn't hard at the mention of her name.

'I would never harm Isobel,' he says.

I pick up my glass again. 'I absolutely know that. And it fits my plan perfectly.'

'You can't just murder every CEO on the FTSE.'

'Fine. I'll kill every board member on the S&P500 as well.'

His sharp intake of breath makes me chuckle. How did I ever put up with him before, all his babbling and whining? The sex was good, but nothing is good enough to make him tolerable.

'I'll do whatever it takes to stop IMAtech and get that damned Clarity Directive consigned to history,' I say, as my arm twitches, an itch radiating up from my spine. It's Isobel. I thought I could have her with me for this, to observe, to learn. But she needs shutting out. I tense every muscle, crack the knot in my shoulder, and send her to limbo. I smile through my gritted teeth, and with the rigidity that comes with the strain, even Layla is gone. I hold my glass a little tighter, in complete control.

'I'm meeting with some, you know,' he says, his voice wet and pleading. 'I'm going to put them off IMAtech.'

'You going against what Mummy and Daddy say?'

'Piss off. I'm doing what I can. We can't change things overnight.'

'The Clarity Directive came in overnight.'

He huffs, then purses his lips. 'Going on some murder spree won't change anything. Talking to people might.'

'Eurgh. You sound just like Isobel.'

'Harry!' Hugo's voice rings out like the bells of Big Ben. He looks so much like Harry, only rounder all over and with the ruddy complexion of raised blood pressure. 'Son.' He laughs now, a quiver of a laugh to hide the alarm in his voice as he takes a handkerchief from his pocket and wipes his forehead. 'You should be resting.' The glare in his eyes doesn't imply the concern of his words. It says, *Fuck off back to your hole, you hideous mole rat.*

'Dad, I just wanted to say hello to some people—'

'Well, that's what social media is for. Now, go home. Your mother will walk you out.'

I hadn't noticed Malorie behind Hugo, her thin frame so easily concealed. She steps around him, emerging from his shadow, her pale face as expressionless as always. Though she's dressed for the night in a gold gown, she has all the enthusiasm of a piece of furniture. She raises her chin a second to look at Harry, yet her pallid watery eyes almost stare straight through him.

Harry's posture slumps, and he links arms with his mother. I give him a slow wave as he walks away. His head hangs low, his bottom lip even lower.

'Now, Isobel, dear,' Hugo says. 'There's someone I'd like you to meet, who would like to hear all about how Baxter Pharmaceuticals and WIT have supported you during your ordeal. His name is Andrew Dawson, and he's very important in the tech world.'

I nod as if I'm just now learning about this man, but of course I know. He's been on my hit list for a while. Inherited wealth made all the greater through his unscrupulous business practices. The same as all the rest.

Andrew Dawson wears the same expression he does in every photo and video clip I've seen: a hard smile with a jutted-out chin. Probably trying to give the impression of the chiselled features he lacks. His ex-wife, Faye, was meant to release her biography last year, but his well-paid lawyers put a stop to it. Since then, whenever she's been questioned, she replies with a standard, 'Normal divorce. We grew apart' spiel. She's moved into a huge house by Sandown Beach with premiership footballers for neighbours. The book has never seen the light of day.

It's hard to hide my excitement at the prospect of meeting him. I clench my jaw and subtly wipe my clammy hand on my dress. He's just the person I was hoping to be introduced to. I eye him from afar a moment while I finish my drink and Hugo drones on about the guy, bigging him up like he's royalty, but his voice is just background noise. My attention is on Andrew Dawson's body, mentally locating all of his arteries.

We walk over to him and I avert my gaze, playing the demure poor little lady Hugo expects me to play. It's an easy role, one all women can play. The put-up-and-shut-up role. The don't-speak-unless-spoken-to role. We've all been rehearsing this since we could talk. It's been drummed into us since the year dot.

Hugo's hand is on the small of my back as we take our final steps towards Andrew Dawson, and I tense as I pretend not to be bothered by this. I look up at Andrew Dawson through my eyelashes, quick glances to confirm I have his full attention. With this amount of cleavage on show, I don't really need to look to check. Testosterone presents in a series of stages:

Stage one. Pervy glance: check.

Stage two. Rolling shoulders back, generally trying to look bigger: check.

Stage three. Pervy glance number two: check.

Stages four and five. Compliment, followed by nonsensical, thinly veiled personal brag: let's see, shall we?

Hugo introduces us, then walks away to speak to someone else, leaving me standing a foot or two from Andrew Dawson and his wandering eyes.

'So, you're the famous Isobel Harrison, the legendary woman who survived the blast that took out Adam Ward.'

I flinch, as if the memory upsets me more than excites me, while mentally ticking off stage number four.

'I'm sorry,' he says, leaning in closer. 'I didn't mean to upset you.'

'It was such a tragedy.'

'I'm not sure if you're aware, but I own a large company with considerable investments in tailored medical care. If there is anything I can do for you.'

Stage five, done. So predictable. Next will be digging into my personal life to see if I'm likely to accept advances.

'That's very kind,' I say. 'I have a therapist, since I still struggle to sleep some nights.'

His gaze goes lower, all the way down, then back up again, his double chin flopping even lower when he does. He's so close, I can detect the different notes of his aftershave. No doubt he paid hundreds for a bottle of that assault on my nose. 'No one at home to make you feel safe?' he asks.

I suppress a sigh. I wish I was wrong about these men, I really do. But still, if he's being a testosterone junkie, I'll take a shot.

I shake my head and look at the floor a moment before meeting his eyes. 'Sadly not. And now with my scars, I fear there never will be.' I reach my arm across to show my scar, tilting my head away. This angle adds volume to my cleavage, and I stroke the contour of my neck. The scar there is barely perceptible, but it keeps his eyes going right where I want them.

He says nothing for a moment, transfixed. He might as well be dribbling before he clears his throat and steps so close, his breath brushes my ear. 'Well, that's just a tragedy. A beautiful young woman like you all alone.'

Pervert. 'Thanks. That's kind of you.' I smile and keep my gaze low. God, I can be so fucking meek when I want to be. If I saw someone else behaving like this, I'd probably throw up.

'Perhaps I could make sure that tonight, at least, you are safe. Staying in a strange hotel must be frightening.'

I fight my reflex to retch or thump him. He's a hideous specimen, must be twice my age and definitely married, and as far as he knows, I'm scared and vulnerable. Predators always pick out the weakest, so that's what he's doing. Luckily, I'm not the timid little rodent he thinks I am. I am venomous. I can bite.

'It really is,' I say, almost in a whisper. 'All these people are quite intimidating. It's hard for me to talk to some. Not to you, though. You seem much nicer than the rest.'

He steps closer, I can hear his tongue moving in his mouth. 'Well, if all these people are a bit intimidating, why don't we go somewhere a little quieter—just the two of us?'

I smile, a genuine smile, because of my achievement in the task I set myself, although my insides hollow with the bitter aftertaste of disappointment. I was quite up for a challenge. But this is too easy.

Chapter Four

Layla

Whenever I'm not awake, it's like a dreamless sleep. The kind I wake up from still heavy with lethargy, my brain taking a while to register I'm conscious, my limbs taking even longer. The dreams are there, little snippets of reality lost in some mind fog that takes an effort to tune in to, like trying to make an old TV work. It's because the memories aren't mine, I'm hijacking them. These eyes saw them, but it wasn't me who acknowledged it all. The colour is off and the sound crackles. I turn the dial a little and the crackle changes pitch but doesn't go away. The grainy screen flickers the other way. I don't know the day, or where I am, and dread sits heavy in my stomach. What's happened while I've been away? What mess am I going to have to clear up? Often, it's a literal mess. Neither Isobel nor Katarina seem capable of tidying the flat, nor stocking the cupboards.

It's difficult to know why I go away, though I feel it's mostly about congestion on the conscious plane. There's only so many minds one brain and body can cope with. I've been reading when I can about dissociative identity disorder, if that's what my, our, diagnosis would be, and its associated amnesia. Or schizophrenia. They say it's often linked to childhood trauma. Perhaps whatever Isobel shut away behind Doctor Cottrell's imaginary safe is to blame.

'Open the door,' Katarina has said so many times. 'Let it all out.'

If whatever is in there is enough to cause our current predicament, then who knows what confronting it would do. I vote to keep it shut, if indeed, my vote counts for anything.

I worry it's Isobel shutting me out, favouring Katarina over me. Katarina is more fun, those two have some weird chemistry. Sometimes all three of us are present, though it's like interacting through water, my thoughts are sluggish, everything I touch feels cold. Isobel being the primary has more say in who is around, at least I think so. All I know is, however much I try, I can't shut out Katarina, nor can I get her attention when I need to. I scream and yell, but it's as if she's hermetically sealed off.

As I wake now, I snap into reality within a room I don't recognise. The first thing I notice are the heavy curtains made of thick gold fabric and a French style ornate table in front. The sky outside is black. There's no light from other buildings, so I must be somewhere remote or high up. I look up at the high ceiling, a swirly pattern styled into the plaster, crystal light fittings giving a soft glow.

It's there, somewhere in these shared neurons—a recollection. I've seen this room before. Recently, but I wasn't in control then. It looks so different without the mistiness of suppression.

Searching my brain is slow, one cog turning at a time. My head throbs from the effort, a splitting pain like this shared brain being ripped into three, but it's there somewhere. I keep turning the pages to find what I should remember, for what this body has done. If whoever did it will allow me to remember.

Staying on the conscious plane is harder than usual, as all three of us are here. Katarina's face is blurred to one side, Isobel's to the other. Neither are clear in this shared space, though Isobel is further from reach. It's impossible to tell who's in charge during these times, it's almost like it's a group effort.

Tactile memories surface quickest. My hands are hot, there's a clamminess around my neck. The dent of carpet fibres on my knees. An ache across my shoulders. This body is tired, adrenaline lingering, a slight tremble to its limbs. As the room comes into sharper focus, I grow heavier, more lucid as I sense they're handing control to me.

Then I look at the floor and realise why.

'Is he. . .' I say, my voice trailing off. He's still. Too still. His chest isn't rising or falling. His face is purple like his capillaries are overstuffed. His eyes are open, the red lines criss-crossing the whites as if scorched.

'Yep,' Katarina says, too smug for being in the presence of a dead guy.

'How?'

'You know.'

And I do. Somewhere locked inside this brain partitioned into three, there's a gate they've left open, allowing me a mental walk-through and assess the damage from the other side. I squeeze my eyes shut and try to think, to access that part usually closed off to me.

The movie plays as I find the right channel; the scene rolling in a sequence of frames I wish I've never seen.

Erectile dysfunction medication.

Cocaine.

A lot of both.

All consumed on a promise of some fun outcome.

Katarina playing the damsel in distress. 'I just wish I could remember what it was like to have a good time.' The last words she said to him. Encouraging him. Knowing that he has heart disease.

This body I share, its mouth smiled, watching him as the pain ripped through his chest and left side, eyes bulging in panic. In my hands, I still feel the soft pillow forcing down on his face just to make sure he's finished off, and the vibrations as his heels kick the floor.

I still feel the aftermath of her arousal.

I nudge the body with my foot, his fleshy arm jiggling with the touch. No rigour mortis has set in yet. The only stiff part of him is his exposed cock.

'Who was he?' I ask.

'Some dick,' Katarina says. 'You know he owns a mining company that is literally destroying the Amazon.'

'Right.'

'And he pays his employees in the UK less than minimum wage, shared umpteen times *#behave*, and he's a pervert.'

The pervert bit is unnecessary. The fact he's naked in our hotel room makes that clear enough. My arms hang to my sides as I stare blankly back at her. Isobel has moved around so she's just behind Katarina, fainter, an ambivalence about her.

'And why am I here?' I ask.

Katarina smirks. 'Because you play Miss Innocent better than anyone.'

They're gone. As suddenly as I appeared, they vanish. I can't sense them next to me or hear them talking. There's none of their rationale or twisted reasoning. It's just me and the body of some man who these hands have just killed.

The room is tiny with them gone, small and closing in, getting smaller by the second. Hot waves of panic rise within, every pore breaks out into sweat, and I scream. My hands to my mouth as my body bends double, shaking all over.

I'm trembling too much to hold the phone, dropping it several times before I can speak to reception. 'Please,' I scream and wail. 'He's not breathing. Help!'

It's then I realise I'm only in my underwear.

I crouch on the floor in the corner, hugging my knees as security and reception come in, paramedics arriving moments later. They speak to me, put a blanket over me, but I can't hear what they're saying. I am somewhere else, behind a wall of shock and fear, willing the other two to come and take over, or at least keep me company. There is so much commotion around me, yet I am alone.

I watch as the paramedics try and fail to resuscitate the man. There's an emptiness to a corpse. What was once a human being is now a shell. When the soul leaves, the room around them is colder, any warmth they shared has gone.

I shiver as my own thoughts rattle in my shared mind. I can relate. With only me here, this body also has an emptiness about it. I am hollow without them, all worry and self-doubt. Abandoned.

Chapter Five

Isobel

Hugo has the sort of 'there-there' voice that wouldn't even work on a toddler. It certainly didn't work on Layla and rather than risk our shared heart exploding, I kicked her out and took over. I wonder how it must have been for Harry as a child, to have a father as comforting as a brush with a pine tree.

I'm dressed now at least, in the casual clothes I wore here, not the fancy dress I'd been wearing. My contacts are out and I've left my glasses off, preferring some mild blur for the moment. My T-shirt clings to my body, still clammy from sweaty panic, and I squirm from my itching back.

'Don't you worry about a thing,' Hugo says. His rubbing my shoulder is unsolicited, but I don't tell him no. Causing a scene won't help me now. 'You won't be in any trouble. No one will be gossiping. The public will never even know you were here.'

As if I give a toss about gossip. I just care about getting away with it. After all, it wasn't my fault. This is once again Katarina's doing. The handshakes shared between Hugo and the detectives, and their hushed conversations interspersed with louder snippets mentioning cash donations as a thank you, let me know that getting away with it shouldn't be a problem.

Hugo's PA is in the corner on the phone. No doubt pulling strings with every press person he knows to make sure this doesn't get out and doesn't reflect badly on WIT or Baxter Pharma.

I tug my sleeves down, crumpling the cloth in my fists. The police have questioned me and may want to question me more later, but they aren't suspicious, I don't think. They've been looking at their notebooks and the scene, taking photographs rather than eyeballing me. Layla's authentic hysteria worked a charm, and they've not even taken a pillow to examine. The heart attack following the mixture of drugs and his unfavourable BMI will be enough to satisfy the coroner.

It shouldn't be so easy.

It niggles me. Killing people is meant to take more planning, especially wealthy, high-profile people. Not killing, *getting away* with killing. Did he have a family? I'm not sure and not about to zone out hacking into Katarina's memory banks to find out. I should be wretched with remorse, regret, guilt, but instead, I feel nothing. Or close to nothing. My shivering has stopped, I am neither hot nor cold. There's the dimmest flicker of worry for myself and my job, but that's all. The dead guy. . .I think maybe Katarina is right, and the world is better off without him. It's one less person propping up the Clarity Directive.

There's a police officer writing some notes in the corner, and I stand a little straighter, hoping to see but no such luck. She has gorgeous red hair pinned neatly back and her arse looks great in her uniform. Asking her out would be inappropriate. I'm meant to be in shock, not horny, and I avert my eyes. Outside, the whirr of passing air traffic distracts me, while from the hallway a maid pushes a trolley. I wonder where I'll sleep tonight.

She makes her way over to me and I fixate on the here and now, to source an inner pool of regret and trauma so I can at least pretend to be upset. I've seen a dead body before, so I imagine that one instead. The sight of my mother's dented head on the kitchen floor, the blood pooling beneath and seeping into the cracks in the tiles. It doesn't summon the tears I need, but gives me a slightly more glazed look. I can't focus on this dead man and look the part of shocked mistress the more I recall the facts about him—his cruel business practices and the fact he was trying to fuck a vulnerable person half his age. My sympathy wanes until it's imperceptible. I ram my knuckle into my eye, inducing a few tears while making it look like I'm wiping them away. Katarina could pull this off more easily. She has the acting skills. Layla would be genuine in her distress but would risk tripping over her words. Really, I just want to pass the buck.

The police officer says something. Her voice has a mellifluous, hypnotic quality, not stern or authoritative at all and I stare into the mid-distance. I don't hear what she says, thinking about the rest of my weekend plans instead. There's a two-for-one on white wine at Sainsbury's Local down the road. I need a haircut, and there's that new walk-in place I could try since I haven't booked anywhere. They'd be less snooty, I hope, since I colour my hair myself.

'Now,' Hugo says, after the officer has left. I hadn't noticed her leave, such was the power of my daydream. 'Let's check your levels, see what we can do.'

He takes my phone. I don't resist as he loads up IMAtech. 'Cortisol is a little high, that's to be expected. Adrenaline of course, also elevated but not too bad. Just some good hydration and you should be fine. I'll have a mild sedative and a beta-blocker delivered to help you unwind and sleep this whole nasty business away. How does that sound?'

I swallow, then nod.

He steps close, the side of his body against mine, and I manage not to flinch as he rubs my shoulder again. 'There, there.'

Prick.

Chapter Six

Isobel

I'm moved into a new hotel room by overly fussing staff, escorting me like they think I'm about to jump out of the window—or sue. The room is identical to the last, minus the corpse and police tape. There's a collection of pills on the art déco table waiting for me as Hugo Baxter promised, which I flush down the toilet. I've spent enough time on various medications when I was institutionalised to ever want to take anything like that again. My mind is altered enough.

After an hour of tossing and turning, I think maybe I should have at least taken the sedative. Every muscle refuses to relax, my body insisting on remaining poised and ready. But ready for what? Whatever Katarina has planned. It's not the first time she's killed. Even if I exclude the pub explosion, there have been more.

She doesn't tell me this. It's something I know. The sight of that body on the hotel floor unfazed me. This shared brain is accustomed to such a view.

Dead guy. Rich. Cock out. Standard.

I sit up and get a glass of water, feeling my way in the dark rather than putting a light on. I've a creeping anxiety of what I'll see if the light shines, dreading experiencing the aftermath of Katarina's antics. Everyone has bad thoughts about people they hate, only most don't have someone manifesting all those secret imaginings into reality.

I know this hotel room is fine. I know there's not a body on the floor. There's no blood on the walls, or severed hands about to rain down on me. But it's like the tired feeling after a load of exercise, like blotchy vision after looking at the sun. There's memory in our neurons. Some aftereffects. What these eyes have seen can't be unseen.

She should be stopped. That's what Layla says, over and over. I hear her now, some background noise keeping me awake, her voice a mosquito in my ear. As if I don't know how bad Katarina is for us. Was she ever this whiny when it was the real Layla? No. The real Layla was kind and reasonable. This one my mind has conjured is different, more of a nag, like the time she had in control has left her with a constant air of disapproval.

Layla likes to remind me big companies' balance sheets have never been fatter, the gap in wages between CEOs and the lackeys never wider, the Clarity Directive shows no signs of going away, so what good is Katarina doing?

Justice. Revenge. An eye for an eye.

For kicks.

That's exactly what Katarina would say.

After I get back into bed, sleep still won't come, so I reach for my phone, the glare from the screen turning the rest of the already dark room into total darkness.

There's a dodgy batch of cocaine going around London, so the news is reporting. Several city men dead. Mix some potent fentanyl with anything and it becomes dodgy. Mix Katarina in with anything and the result is the same.

I should stop her. I really should.

I bite at the skin around my nails and read on. There are warnings from health experts and drug helplines, but there's no helpline to rid me of Katarina. How do you stop a part of you like that? Tell a smoker to quit in an instant, take the sugar cravings away from someone with a sweet tooth. That's what Katarina is in this body. All the bad habits and desires rolled into one. The part that functions on urges alone.

There are unread messages on my phone. Harry asking if I'm all right, if Katarina has gone for now, reassuring me we can put things right.

We. Me and him. It's got a nice ring to it.

He's always reassuring me, talking me off the edge when Katarina takes over and blows up buildings.

'We can fix things together. I know we can,' he said to me one night when we went for drinks at a bar fancier than any I'd been to before. Looking around at the clientele there, it seemed hard to imagine the city could be anything besides broken. Each drink cost more than half a day's wages.

The red lump on his collarbone shows Harry also has an IMAtech chip. Monitored, scrutinised, his blood makeup and vitals now reduced to metadata. He pointed to it and said, 'I'm just like the rest of you now.' His Rolex dangled from his wrist, his other hand holding his crystal glass of champagne.

It's good to have him on board, but I know even without his help, from the inside, I can do some good in WIT and Baxter Pharmaceuticals at least. You need to be part of something in order to change it. Katarina will claim it's a waste of time, a prison, or whatever, but it's my best hope. I can try to reason with the bosses regarding IMAtech, to be a voice for the staff. That would be one thing off the tick list sorted.

I reply to Harry and tell him I'm fine, then idle away time on my phone, waiting for the all-elusive sleep to take hold. A glance through my bank statement tells me Katarina's thirst does not come cheap. She has to look the part, I suppose. At least I earn a decent wage now. Well, Layla does. I do minimal hours at work. When the IMAtech starts buzzing, I just zone out and Layla is there to tune into work mode. Not every day, but this mental delegation works well. It keeps her entertained and keeps the bosses happy. And my dad, as he reminds me how proud he is of my work ethic these days, how Mum would be proud too. At least someone is pleased. I'm the good girl he always wanted, making the big man happy, so he always says.

I lost track of time a few weeks ago, and scanning my bank statement tells me Katarina enjoyed a cottage break in Surrey.

No way would Layla be so frivolous or sociable. I groan when I see the amount. Even on my new wage, that's a sting.

Everyone always says there's not enough hours in the day. Now imagine your time is even less. How am I meant to stop Katarina on her vendetta and try to fix things the right way when this body is shared?

It's hard to shut out Katarina as she's everything I once wanted to be. Layla is everything my parents wanted me to be, which makes her so much easier to ignore.

I switch off my phone, then toss and turn again. The bed is so perfectly comfortable, but my mind won't let me rest. I have too much to think about and who knows how much time to mull it over before Katarina or Layla barge in and take their share.

The only way to stop Katarina is to somehow stop IMAtech along with the Clarity Directive before she does any more harm. I roll over again, rearranging my pillow as my mind turns the thought over and over. A hopeless cause is still hopeless, however drastic her methods. She's trying to alter the tilt of the earth, like trying to convince everyone the sky isn't blue, that down is up.

Don't anger the big man. Keep my head down. Be a good girl, so my dad always said. Yet if I don't fix things, Katarina will. And I can't even imagine the lengths she'll go to.

Chapter Seven

Isobel

I escape any mention in the papers, as Hugo promised. The weekend news and Monday morning's papers cite natural causes, same as Dead Guy's company website, neither mentioning the drug binge on the coroner's report. The company will prevail, it says. They'll find another CEO. A little niggle creeps up my spine as I imagine which prick will take his place. I blink that thought away. Katarina doesn't need any more encouragement.

I'm late for work, but being a little late won't matter. Since they're still waiting for the pub blast to blow over, I'm basically invincible. I rarely bother checking my own IMAtech. They're hardly going to sack the person the old CEO almost killed. Layla insisted the promotion was due to her, my, our—God, I don't even know which pronoun to use for us—our work, mostly keeping up with IMAtech seconds before the explosion and getting the coding and designing done. Layla's the part of us that is good at timekeeping and being organised, but there's no way the promotion was due to that alone.

I bite my nails on the tube, a habit I share with Layla, biting so close to the quick it hurts. Katarina loathes our habit and spends a significant portion of her time undoing the damage and a significant chunk of our paycheck on nail extensions. I try to limit my chewing to the skin around my nails to help out the manicurist. An even worse habit, but at least I'll feel less of the tightening agitation of Katarina's disapproval.

As much as I try to shut them both away, their influence clings to me almost constantly, little whispers in my ear and a moral tug or push. Only this morning, Katarina is totally absent. There's a quietness in my head I am so rarely able to enjoy.

Then it dawns on me. Why am I late? Why did I oversleep? Was I asleep last night, or did Katarina wake? I'm tired, which is nothing new, but I'm really tired. My feet ache like I've been wearing high heels, my shoulders throb like I've been lifting something heavy. Perhaps I slept funny, or too little, and that's causing my symptoms. But the lack of Katarina trying to surface is only explainable one way: Katarina is too worn out to bother me.

I keep biting at the skin around my thumb until I draw blood. It tastes good.

I sip from my water bottle, rinsing that taste away with a shudder. Blood doesn't taste good, not at all. Liking the taste of blood sounds all-too Katarina. She may not be scratching her way onto the conscious plane, but her influence remains, tainting me, leaving her mark.

Her arousals and kicks aren't mine. I fight for what is right. She murders what is wrong. That's the difference between us.

I sip some more water, then tighten my jacket around me. Katarina would hate this jacket. It's pale grey and unflattering. *Good*.

I think I dress better than I used to, or what the company would consider better. After hospital and recovering at my dad's, I got back to my apartment, and I had a bedroom of clothes that didn't belong to me. Dowdy items, plain colours and poorly fitted items, all so Layla. Some of my stuff remained, some old favourites that are so uniquely me, but mostly it was functional and drab. Layla had enjoyed almost complete control for two months, and little of my stuff was left.

My first day at work after my sick leave finished, I considered wearing my floral Doc Martens and a bright dress, to really embrace the real me being back. But there was something about knowing I'd be delegating, managing people with some semblance of authority that took any desire for individuality. I am now a suit, wearing the same corporate stuff as the board, only from a cheaper shop and not as well cut. And flats. There's no way I'm resorting to wearing heels. Katarina spends enough time in them to cripple my feet.

Joel smiles at me as I walk in and I make a beeline to speak to him, but he's sitting at his desk typing before I get close. Everyone is. The typing never stops. Only about a third of the staff are taking the Baxter pharmaceutical supplements as prescribed by their IMAtech, but even those surviving on their own steam barely look away from the screens. I remember when office staff used to converse a bit, laugh. Now they might as well be robots.

I walk through the office, asking if everyone is okay, though I get minimal responses back. The odd nod or mumble is the most I can expect. Still, at least I've asked. At least they know there's someone looking out for them, even if it's someone as powerless as me.

Just as I get back to my desk and sit, I startle. Someone's choking and chair legs scrape against the floor, followed by some yelps of surprise.

Breaths pant out of my lungs as I stand and scan the office. From the far end, someone stands for a second, then his head dips below the desk. By the time I reach him, he's flat out on the floor, his body convulsing. There's foam collecting at the corner of his mouth and the convulsions make his whole body rigid. His face is turning blue.

'Oh, my God!' I grab his shoulders. 'Simon? Simon! Can you hear me?' The rest of the room melts away. All I see is Simon, fitting on the floor and unresponsive. I call his name again and shake his shoulders. His tense body jerks and I lay him on his side, adrenaline giving me the extra strength to do so. His leg jerks out and knocks the table, a coffee cup crashing to the ground, spilling its hot contents everywhere.

Shit! 'You're going to be okay, Simon. You hear me?' The words are for me as much as him as my shaking hands grab a phone to call an ambulance.

A lot of the staff don't even notice, too dosed up on whatever the dispensary has given them. The few that do are mostly too shocked to move. Joel's beside me now, then takes over, reassuring him and keeping him on his side while I talk to the emergency services.

I can't take my eyes off him as I call and speak to the operator. My voice rasps as I state the office address, my vision misty with tears.

It takes an age for the ambulance to arrive, central London not exactly known for speed of travel. I clean up the spilled coffee as Joel stays with Simon, then I pace from the desk to the front door a hundred times before the blue flashing lights come into view. I sigh with relief at the sight of them, then I wipe my sweaty hands on my trousers as I hold the doors open for the paramedics, the rattling wheels echoing through the office.

Simon is semi-conscious and lying still, the foaming spittle crusted down his chin, his breaths shallow.

'What has he taken?' the paramedic asks me as he crouches next to him.

'I. . . I don't know.' I look at the dispensary staff and point him in their direction.

They load Simon onto a gurney with a breathing mask on his face. He's less blue now, his eyes half-closed, his chest rising and falling with regular rhythm. I cover my mouth with my hand as they wheel him away. My knees go slack and I slump into Simon's chair.

'What the hell is going on?' Hugo's voice booms as he arrives in the office. Several members of staff milling about is hardly the sight he's used to. His eyes go to the IMAtech tally on the wall as soon as he sees Simon.

'Maybe an issue with the supplements, sir,' I say as he barges past the gurney and towards Simon's desk. His phone is still there, his app displayed.

Hugo picks up Simon's phone and laughs, the sort of laugh a child makes when they get caught with their hand in the sweetie tin. My hands grasp the edge of the chair, my arms tense and knuckles blanching.

'I see the problem,' he says, as if the problem is something as trivial as dodgy WIFI. 'His IMAtech app isn't synched correctly. He must have changed phones and not reloaded the app properly.' He holds the app up to the remaining paramedic at the dispensary. 'Back to work then, everyone. Remember to sync the app correctly if you have a new phone and download all updates.'

The response from the staff who helped is lacklustre, and we all drag our feet back to our desks.

'Come on. Nine minutes down today!' Hugo claps as we walk, and I fight the urge to slap him. The staff need a break, some time to unwind after such a shock. Nine minutes is all he cares about.

I swallow my groan and sit at my desk, watching out the glass doors as the ambulance drives Simon away.

'Thanks for your help, everyone,' I say when we're all back at our desks.

Hugo scoffs at my gratitude, glances up at the seconds tally once more, then shakes his head as he walks through to the staff room.

***

'This way now. Up the stairs.' Hugo's hand nudges my elbow, gently but implied with all the force of being hit by a truck. He leads me up the stairs and into the glass-walled office that looks down on the so-called Powerhouse of Productivity below. The well-lit room houses a huge square table of glass over burnished metal and shows every smudge and speck of dust. The woman who cleans the office, 'the maid girl' as Hugo calls her, attends with her bottle of polish and cloth before and after every meeting, just to give it the shine Hugo Baxter insists upon. Probably so he can gaze at his own reflection.

'Management meeting,' Hugo says as we enter the office, then shoos her out. 'We need to go over the stats. Isobel, take notes.'

I am unprepared for note-taking and Malorie passes me a tablet, her usual deadpan face as subservient as ever, and I wonder what her IMAtech data reads. A flatlining heartbeat and not a single hormone in her system, by the looks of it. Thirty-five years of being married to Hugo Baxter has left her as brain dead as the dead guy from the hotel room.

There's a man sitting at the table who I don't recognise. He's all greasy hair and glasses and is poring over his laptop.

'Well?' Hugo says to him, his voice resembling a bark. 'Come on. It's gone ten. What are the results?'

The man's face twitches before he speaks. 'The hormone data for the last two months indicate low levels of endorphins in the staff who are not taking their tailor-made supplements. Endorphins do rise towards the end of the day, particularly Fridays.'

'So the staff are happy to be going home? Ha! Lazy shits.' Hugo snorts and leans back in his chair. 'Still, I don't pay them to enjoy themselves. I don't give a shit if the staff are miserable. We don't need them having a lovely time at work. We need them to get the bloody job done.'

As much as I am trying to listen, I'm standing right by the window and on the office floor below. Someone tripped and spilt coffee on their shirt. It could be hot. They may have burned themselves. I should be there to check they're okay. I need to make sure everyone is okay, given the morning we've already had. Their welfare is my responsibility. Hugo is quite capable of taking his own notes.

'Well, dopamine is associated with improved task performance,' Greasy Guy says, and my ears prick up.

Dopamine, the happy hormone. It doesn't matter how much I say to the staff they're doing well, the hormone data shows they're still miserable here. My back curves forward as my muscles go weak. However much I try to perk the staff up, IMAtech hammers them back down.

'And along with endorphins, that's pretty low,' Greasy Guy continues. 'The two kind of go hand-in-hand.'

'What about this morning?' I ask. 'Poor Simon. Should we not be discussing a failsafe to stop that happening again?'

Hugo waves a dismissive hand at me. 'He'll be fine, and the rest of the staff can make up his lost seconds, so there's nothing to worry about.'

Katarina is waking. That side of my brain is now alert and angry. My heart rate picks up, and my cheeks flush as my tightening jaw aches. I concentrate on my breaths, slow, in and out, keeping her at bay. If she takes control here with Hugo Baxter being this much of an arse, I don't know what she'll do. I zone out their conversation as much as I can, focussing on the mundane things around the office.

Hugo grunts at Greasy Guy. 'What else?'

Next to Greasy Guy, there's a cup of tea that looks like it's been there since the dawn of time with scum swirling around the top, crusty evidence of spillages around its base. I wonder how long Greasy Guy has been in this room.

'Again, in the staff not taking their tailor-made supplements, cortisol is elevated throughout the day, which indicates stress.'

'We don't want the staff chilled out at work.'

'No, but too much stress is counterproductive. All in all, it's a grim outlook on the staff.'

I wish I could shut my ears as easily as my eyes. However much I try to zone out, their conversation punches through.

'And the productivity?' Some spittle flies from Hugo's mouth as he talks, catching the light. 'In the two groups, are the supplements making the staff more efficient?'

Greasy Guy's mouth twists a moment before he finds words. 'There are three groups to compare, the ones on the tailor-made supplements, the ones on Texi alone, and the ones taking nothing.'

Texi. I remember when that came out and I thought it was a bad thing, some legal stimulant to increase concentration. Now with the rest of the cocktail IMAtech is prescribing, Texi seems no worse than sugar.

'Well?' Hugo barks. 'Don't suck eggs. Just tell me.'

'The supplemented staff are about thirteen per cent more efficient than the staff on nothing. Texi lies somewhere in the middle.'

Hugo grunts and folds his arms. 'Thirteen? I want more than that. Perhaps the supplemented staff are still distracted by the others. We must need an all-or-nothing situation. Isobel, what do you think?'

My name snags my attention and I look his way. Hugo's expectant face is all raised eyebrows and pursed lips. I clear my throat. 'Oh. Well—'

'You're on the office floor. Are supplemented staff still being distracted?'

I swallow and search for the right words. Diplomatic words. This is where I can make a difference and be a voice for all the overworked staff. I should have been practising this instead of trying to zone out. 'I think the amount of pressure is having a negative effect.'

'Well, a negative effect doesn't matter, as long as the share price isn't negative.' He belly-laughs at his own comment, and my insides heat up.

'A negative effect on productivity as well as mentally.' I project my voice a little louder this time, making eye contact and standing up as straight as I can. With him sitting on the chair, a little height advantage gives me a swell of confidence. 'IMAtech isn't making people work harder, it's only making them exhausted. Any benefit will be short-lived if they all end up off sick with repetitive strain injuries, stress, and exhaustion.' I over enunciate each syllable of the last few words, forcing them out clearly, despite how dry my mouth is.

When I finish, the rest of the air in my lungs escapes in relief and my limbs feel lighter. I did it. I stood up for the staff. Layla would never have said that. How long has she been going along with Hugo's plans? How compliant and goody-two-shoes has she been? I shouldn't have let her spend so much time at work.

Hugo plants all four chair legs on the floor now and pauses before he replies. 'All right, sweetheart,' he says to me, and I force myself to maintain eye contact. 'Well, that is brilliant news. We'll make the supplements compulsory immediately. If they're stressed, they can take a fucking pill. If they're exhausted, there's a pill for that too. It's for their own good, right? If the staff want to be fucking happy, we make it compulsory that they're all fucking happy. All the drugs have been trialled with Texi to show they work well together. Those paper-pushers health and safety nutters at the DSA have even approved it. So we'll have a delightfully happy and motivated workforce. Sound good to everyone? Good.'

I tuck my chin in, keep my mouth shut, and wring my hands.

He pours himself a coffee from the pot and glowers around, as if daring any of us to speak.

After calling our bluff, he sips, then plonks his cup down on the table with enough enthusiasm to splash some over the rim. 'Now. . .' He faces Greasy Guy. 'What do ethics say?'

Greasy Guy pushes his glasses up and keeps his gaze on his laptop. 'They say you can't force the staff to take medication.'

Hugo scoffs and lifts his chin. His top lip recoils as if this lack of power is something unseemly. He swivels on his chair and peers down on the office floor below while Malorie continues to stare at nothing at all. I wonder how strong that glass window is. He's not a small man, but one little push and he would faceplant into that glass. Katarina chuckles in my ear. She's wide awake now, rested, and she wants Hugo impaled on a spike. My hands tense as if I'm getting ready to make that push, as if Katarina is bracing herself.

Hugo swings his chair around and I jolt back. Looking him in the eye is a sudden reminder he's a human being, not something I should be pushing out of windows. He eyeballs me for a moment with such a steely gaze, I submit and look at the floor. Surely he can't know what I was just thinking.

'But we can insist on levels being within a certain range, right?' he says to Greasy Guy, though his eyes flick between the two of us. 'We can hardly have women jacked up on hormones once a month, isn't that right? That's not bloody fair.'

My cheeks heat, and I angle away to hide my reddening complexion.

Greasy Guy taps away at his laptop a second before responding. 'Well, discriminating based on hormone levels—'

'I don't think there's a law for that, is there?'

'Hormone discrimination, n. . .no. Not specifically. I don't think so.'

'Right. Well, that's our angle. There is no point in us knowing this data if we're not planning on actioning anything. IMAtech ensures productivity by keeping the staff at the top of their game. We don't have to worry about "hormone levels" with AI.' He actually makes air quotes. 'Fucking snowflakes and their feelings. Fuck that. This is what we're doing. All in agreement? Good. Let's get this press briefing done. It's time we started telling the world exactly what we can do.' He gets up, the chair flying across the room behind him as he does. 'And get my PA to chase up that meeting with Christopher Morely.'

Hugo walks out the office, heavy footsteps resounding over the whole floor, then plods down the stairs, leaving via the front door before I've even taken a breath.

In Hugo's absence, I can think clearly again, like I've been released from a pressure cooker. Christopher Morely. I know that name, but I can't place him just yet. I look down at the blank tablet. What are my notes meant to say?

'Erm,' I ask Greasy Guy, 'can I get that all emailed to me?'

He nods and I walk downstairs to my desk, treading lightly so as not to make a noise and disturb anyone.

The office whirrs with keyboards tapping and little else. No conversation, no breaks. Computers ping with emails stating deadlines and more work that needs doing. The collective IMAtech seconds are displayed, down as always.

'You're all doing really well,' I say to the staff, and as much as I mean it, I'm sure I sound like a patronising arse. They must see me as some corporate suck-up. Going up into that office means I've crossed the line into traitor territory.

Every face in the office is drawn, red-eyed and puffy. I can't remember the last time I saw one of them smile. The hormone graph underneath the IMAtech tally shows the staff are in the red, despite almost half making use of the dispensary.

Katarina comparing it to a prison seems more and more accurate. A woman, Ellen, sits straighter and stops typing for a moment to stretch her neck, her adjacent colleague tutting her way. We're still arranged in alternating genders—an attempt to keep women's synchronicity at bay. There's a sign on the staffroom door, saying multiple women cannot spend more than three minutes together in there. All but one of the female toilet cubicles have been shut off.

'We can't have one hormonal woman making the others the same. It's not productive,' Hugo said at that particular board meeting. 'We'll shut the men's toilets too, then they can't moan about discrimination.'

It was a busy day at work and so Layla was leading then, and she was nodding along, bowing to this bullshit.

Perhaps making the supplements compulsory won't be so bad. Perhaps that will mean gender restrictions will be lifted. Perhaps they'll open the toilets again, and I can pee without there being a queue in the morning.

All that is what Layla would say. Katarina would smash the furniture and Hugo's kneecaps.

My IMAtech app buzzes, my hormones showing I'm agitated, as per usual. Consider an endorphin booster, it suggests. The dispensary will have it ready for me.

I sit, put my phone facedown on my desk, then opt to flick through employee files instead, to check their data and find ways to motivate them. I read through the notes Layla's made: capping bonuses, earlier start times, mandatory silence.

Yeah, because the conversation around here is so deafening.

I add a few notes of my own: fresh fruit and juices, rewards, more working from home, flexible hours, make sure the app syncs properly. The big bosses are all about the punishment and iron fist. Someone has to be the voice of reason and tame them.

Walking around the office is like trudging through a thick soup of annoyance. Fingers slam on keys with more force than needed, while the only vocalisations are sighs.

I spoke up for them today and it didn't work, but I will figure out more ways to be their voice. My skin tingles when I think of this, like Layla is crawling over me, telling me to just do my job, be a good girl, to think of our paycheck. Yet my heart races, nerves and dread making my stomach cave. Katarina is itching to do things her way.

Being their voice isn't going to be enough.

Chapter Eight

Isobel

My first kiss was when I was seventeen, with some girl who visited my college briefly. She held me so tightly, it was as if she was about to fall off a cliff. She told me I was gorgeous, that my eyes sparkled like the stars. It was as corny as hell, but I lapped it up. I was in awe of her. She was all colour and sunshine. When we kissed, it was as if we were breathing life into each other, as if she was putting the sunshine in me.

She left the college right after that. I never saw her again. A fumble in the school field was as far as it went. I dyed my hair soon after, bleaching it first even though it was already light, just to make the colour really stick. I slathered it in pink goo that stained the brittle ends. Bit by bit, I swapped my usual clothes for ones that reminded me of flowers and meadows. Of her.

That was my first reinvention. It seemed harmless enough at the time.

I sit at home now in my flat, listening to a fox screech outside. They probably have cubs this time of year, so I left some food out for them on a plate.

I'm wearing my comfies and necking a glass of cool white wine. It helps temper the stuffy heat of London. Nightly drinking is becoming a habit, but I need something to take the edge off and to help me sleep. Weed, years ago, used to help, but now with IMAtech monitoring everything inside me, that's no longer an option. I look through my IMAtech readouts. A little sedative in the evening, something with less calories than wine, better for my liver, maybe it won't be so bad. I know from my time in a mental institution, living with a part of me permanently suppressed is foggy and confusing. Although, with Layla and Katarina sharing my headspace, that doesn't sound so unfamiliar.

On the TV, *The One Show* has a feature piece on IMAtech. The BBC forever in its quest to be unbiased tries to imply the thing isn't all bad.

'Well, it's for safety, really,' the presenter says. She's doing a good job of showing she believes it. Perhaps she really does. 'It's only right to know if someone enters a public building all hyped up on adrenalin that perhaps they're up to no good. People looking after children too. If you've nothing to hide, then what's the problem? What's the harm in suppressing bad emotions with some supplements? Not to mention, it should reduce suicides if we know and can stop people from being low on endorphins.'

Layla is with me at the moment, and she hangs her head with the news, though she tries to keep her voice proud and persuasive, like she thinks she can fool me. 'It isn't the worst idea though. I mean, what if from IMAtech they could tell if a man was about to rape, for example?'

She can be such a suck-up sometimes it makes me want to scream. If Katarina is all impulse, Layla is all over-thinking and over-worrying. If she was still alive, I wonder how different my life would be. Would we have fallen out over IMAtech? Would real Layla have disputed any plans to stop it?

Real Layla would see my side. She would understand. Wonderful, inoffensive Layla. I miss her so much. Her warmth, her rationale, her encouragement. The Layla in my head is a poor projection. Sometimes there seems little similarity between her and the woman I grieve for. She's more nagging and critical.

'It's not for that reason, though, as we both know it,' I say. 'It's so employers can check we're working at maximum output every goddamned second.'

'But—'

'No,' I snap, and as sweat collects across my hairline, I wonder if she feels that too. 'If it is that useful, the bosses would have it too, not just us. You know, all those weeks you've been at WIT, just going along with whatever shit the Baxters demand, if you'd actually been on our side then, instead of just sucking up, maybe it wouldn't have gotten this far.'

'You want me there to work, to earn a paycheck and do all the boring stuff so you don't have to.'

'We need to make a difference there, or else. . .or else—'

'Or else Katarina continues to go on the warpath, and we end up behind bars? That's what you want to say, isn't it?'

I bite my tongue. She's right of course, but at least Katarina is on the right side. She may go about things the wrong way, but her priorities are where they should be.

Katarina's memories come to me in flashbacks and nightmares. Harry's panicked and bloodied face at the barred window, his scream and thumping the wall. The sight of the body bags being zipped up and wheeled away. His best friend. His colleagues.

They all deserved it, is what Katarina reminds me.

'It's not your fault,' Layla consoles.

She can tell when I'm spiralling, when my eyes can't focus on the here and now.

Whatever Layla says, my hands are tainted red. My lack of control did that. Harry's once handsome face is now twisted with scars. How can I not feel an ounce of guilt? All I can do is make things better going forward. All I can do is *be* better. And being better doesn't mean killing those who are worse. Being better doesn't mean kissing arse to my bosses. Being better means being my authentic self. Isobel.

'If you ever want to talk,' Layla says. 'About your past, any bad memories, I'm here for you.'

I scowl and shake my head. 'No. That's all locked away. I don't need to remember anything.'

'But it might help—'

'No!' I snap, and Layla bristles. 'I don't want to talk about this.'

I look down at my comfies, the pale pastel shades, the sort of drab stuff Layla would wear. She always thought talking was good too. I loved Layla once. Now she has invaded.

A news story comes on about the dead guy from the hotel, reports from those he'd harassed before the Clarity Directive came into force, the NDAs he had women sign, now apparently null and void after his death. He was worse than we even knew. This will only spur Katarina on.

Layla is right about the risks, but then, they both are. It's up to me to mediate this. An idea flashes in front of me.

'I think I know how to stop IMAtech working,' I say. Softer this time, and Layla's posture relaxes.

'Stopping IMAtech isn't enough to appease Katarina,' she says. 'You'd have to have the Clarity Directive repealed as well. She's not going to stop until she's had revenge on every wealthy man who wanted that Directive.'

'I know. I know. But with IMAtech out the way, maybe there's something else we can do.' I force some hope into my tone, sip my wine, and tell myself I can fix things, that I can somehow stop IMAtech and temper Katarina.

My lips twitch, the smile isn't mine. It's Katarina, and she's laughing at me.

Chapter Nine

Katarina

I can't help but laugh. Isobel and Layla, with their big ideas of diplomacy and fairness. They haven't learned such methods get nothing done. Literally nothing.

Layla disappears, cringing and squirming as she does, shrivelling away back to her mind space that's all brown-nosing and organising.

Isobel scowls at me, her arms folded in a half-angry, half-sulking way. 'Stop laughing at me.'

'I can't help it.'

'Why?'

'Because you're ridiculous.' I stand and take up the floor, putting my hands on my hips as I laugh again. 'You think you can fix things so easily? Things have been broken forever.'

She looks away and I swear I detect a sigh, like she's defeated already.

'What's our closest living relative?' I ask.

She pulls her chin in and knits her brows. 'Dad?'

'Not who, *what.* Like, evolutionary.'

She rolls her eyes in that way she does whenever I'm trying to teach her something. 'Chimpanzees.'

'Ha!' I knew she'd say that. It's what everyone thinks. 'Wrong. That's what they want us to think because chimpanzees are patriarchal and violent towards outsiders. So those dickheads in charge can claim they behave the way they do because of some ancient ancestry. But really, we're more closely related to bonobos. Peaceful apes, who live in a matriarchal society and aren't violent towards outsiders. Imagine if the world understood that!'

Isobel yawns, and I tut. There's no point trying to teach her anything sometimes. Luckily, a glass and a half of wine is usually enough to let me take some control. So, I ensure there's always a bottle of wine in the flat, some gin and tonic. After a tough day at work, I know Isobel will find it impossible to resist. After another yawn, she retreats and I can only hope I've imparted a tiny bit of wisdom.

When I'm alone, I trawl the internet, looking up the names of all the other people who were at that party. Seeing that man die was the most arousing, exciting thing ever. His face is all over the financial news still, his company unravelling in the wake of his death.

I won't refer to my victim by name. He doesn't deserve it. Such evil isn't even human. I shouldn't even think of him as a victim because he's not. The women silenced are the victims. The underpaid staff, the hushed ex-wife and girlfriends. The environment he pillaged and the poor he suppressed.

Such men aren't victims or people. They're animals, gorging on the rest of humanity. And not some elegant animal like a wolf or lion. No, they're worse. Stinky, uselessly intelligent, fuelled by nothing but greed. Pigs. That's what they are. Fat little piggies revelling in their own shit.

The photos of that pig are polished, smiling, his cheeks a normal hue instead of the beetroot purple of asphyxiation I witnessed. I remember his attempt at a scream, his death rattle.

I reach between my legs. The softest touch there sends bolts of electricity through me as I lean back and recall the sight of his bulging eyes, red and exposed, the fear, and I put a finger inside.

Blowing up the bar was exciting, but I never got to watch their faces as they burned. With that piggy, I eyeballed him, smiling, my face inches from his as sheer panic filled his eyes and he realised I wasn't going to help. I took the pillow off just in time to see his soul abandon his body, and it was the most beautiful thing I've ever seen.

I lie, panting on the sofa, wipe my hand on my top, then check my IMAtech and laugh. If that's what it takes to make my hormone balance favourable, wanking over corpses could become a frequent pastime.

I start scrolling through the internet again, looking for more I still want to kill. And there are so many. Isobel and Layla might think I'm evil, but I'm a product of evolution. Hate breeds hate. Centuries of toxic masculinity and I am the antidote. Fighting fire with fire.

Remember when women were burned as witches, their only crime ever was being female and intelligent. Well, why did men never suffer such a fate? These corporate arseholes' egos are nothing if not the product of a curse.

Eradication is well overdue. It's time all wealthy and powerful men were burned at the stake.

I resort to gazing upon the faces who I'm putting at the top of my kill list and salivating at my plans to work through every single one of them.

Chapter Ten

Isobel

I meet Harry after work the next day. I've been mostly ignoring his texts, not wanting Katarina and Layla to have any more to moan about, and me spending time with him would only stoke the fire.

When the Clarity Directive came about, the next day on my commute to work I was groped three times. There is nothing less attractive than a man who thinks he has ownership of you, that he has some God-given right. I went off men completely after that. It was a few months later I met Layla, the real, original Layla, and just before Katarina appeared in my life.

I swore off men, yet there's something alluring about Harry Baxter. Perhaps it's my guilt. Perhaps it's the Katarina part of me that enjoyed fucking him. This body wants another taste.

'Peter would never have allowed this,' Harry says as he shows me articles about the hormone monitoring on his phone, the big companies' responses to WIT's press release, as if I don't already know.

I shouldn't feel guilty about Peter Ward's death. It wasn't me who killed him. It was Katarina. In any case, I think Harry idolised Peter Ward, not because he was some good guy, but because his own father is that much of a dick. Peter was some angel in comparison. I find it hard to believe Peter Ward wouldn't have loved the pharmaceutical influence on IMAtech. It has corporate greed written all over it.

I go to the bar to order drinks. On Harry's tab, as usual. He'd never dream of letting me pay.

The server looks at me with a face full of scrutiny, as if I'm underage and he's going to ask for ID. I definitely do not look even close to being underage.

'IMAtech app please,' he asks.

'Excuse me?'

'I need to check your levels. Policy. I can't serve you if your levels are off, and no disrespect, you look a little peaky.'

My nostrils flare as I reach for my phone, then open the app and show him.

'Sorry, miss. I can serve you soft drinks only. Alcohol is a depressant, you see. And your levels—'

'Yeah, I know. Thanks,' I say through gritted teeth as I take my phone back and stomp my way to Harry. I'm not happy enough to drink, but happy enough to piss off. Someone explain that logic to me. 'Fuck this place,' I say to Harry. 'Let's go for a walk.'

'Really?'

'Yeah. really.' I glower at the server. 'Exercise is good for endorphins, right?'

Harry stands, then grabs our coats, placing mine over my shoulders. 'Sure.'

We walk in silence for a while, letting London's din do the talking. I keep my pace slow, so Harry's limp doesn't bother him. I shrug my coat off, the evening air still warm, and I catch Harry watching me as my strap falls down my shoulder. His coat is slung over his arm, his T-shirt snug around his biceps.

I consider another bar, an off-licence, to go back to mine or maybe Harry's. Perhaps we could have a bottle of wine back at his place. I've not been there before. Katarina and Layla both have. I look over at Harry's profile, his left side, the unburned side facing me. I can see why they were attracted to him. It's impossible not to be.

'We have to stop them,' Harry says. 'I see that now. Really, I do. The hormone monitoring, the tailor-made supplements, forcing that on the staff, it's wrong. It's going to work them to death one way or another. I was going to tell you the other night, but it was her, not you.'

'Tell me what?'

He stops walking and faces me, both sides of his body in view. It's so tempting to stare at his scars. They're so much worse than mine.

'I planned a meeting with some CEOs,' he says. 'A secret meeting at my place in Surrey. I was going to talk them out of IMAtech, to turn them off the idea. But it doesn't matter. They never even showed up. I have zero influence. Look at me, for fuck's sake. With scars like this, no one's going to listen to me. I'm a freak.'

Surrey. My bank statement. Katarina. My brain grinds the facts slowly like some rusty bike sprocket, but it dawns on me after a moment. I don't say anything and hope my expression doesn't give anything away. What the hell has she been up to?

'Hey.' I reach for his hand, the burned one. I stroke his scars. 'You tried. And we'll keep on trying. How about something just a little more. . .drastic.'

'Like?'

I step closer, our torsos almost touching, and check over my shoulders for prying eyes. 'I had an idea. Mess with the medication they're dishing out. Nothing that will hurt people. Just make it have the opposite effect. Show their prescribing practices are wrong.'

His lips twitch up, almost a smile, but not quite. 'That could work. We'd need to get into the labs.'

'You have any friends there?'

A full smile now as a twinkle flashes in his eyes. 'Yes. One in particular. And better than that. I'm being assigned there. The unglamorous role of manager.'

'Reckon you can swap a few yellow pills for blue?'

'I reckon so.'

He turns his hands over and grasps mine instead, and I jolt with surprise as my stomach does backflips. Is that me getting excited by his touch? Katarina hates the guy and Layla is the gayest of all of us, so it's a fair bet it's me.

Screw this. There's only one way to find out.

'Well.' I swallow and edge even closer. 'If they want endorphins raised, there's one fun activity that causes that.' I blush at my boldness and bite my bottom lip. Life is too short to hold back, especially when this body's life is shared.

He doesn't jump at my invite like I thought he would, and I stiffen, foolishness making my heart race.

He looks down, dodging my gaze. 'I'm not what I was. I haven't, since. . .my scars—'

'Hey.' I tug on his hands, grinning with relief it's the old cliché of not me but him. He needn't feel that way, though it's hard to look him in the eye when it's this body that caused those scars. How can I possibly repent for such a thing?

The sadness in his face sends the butterflies in my stomach into flight and I pull his hands up to kiss. 'You survived. That's what those scars show. Mine too.'

Chapter Eleven

Katarina

It wasn't my intention to keep them here. After luring them here with a flash of thigh, I planned on finishing each of them with a quick throat slit and chucking them into the river. But the sight of them now in this barn, tied up by their wrists, naked, begging, it's just too perfect. I want to sit here forever and watch them dangle and squirm and listen to their pleas. All that wealth and power reduced to swinging from meat hooks. Oh, my fat little piggies, what a glorious sight you are!

The joy of having Hugo Baxter taking me under his wing is I can personally order whatever pills I want. 'Whatever helps you get through your ordeal, Isobel,' he said to me once. I have the drug stockist on my email contacts and let's just say, to get through the day, I need a ton of sedatives and stimulants. Enough to keep these piggies in whatever consciousness state I require. And they are just starting to wake up.

I remove their gags and give them each a sip of water, taking down their blindfolds. It doesn't matter if they see me. They're never getting out of here.

'Please,' one begs, pulling his weight against the ropes that tie his hands together and are attached to the joist above. They've cut into his wrists, the wounds angry and red, a little blood trickling down his arm. 'How much? I can send you as much money as you want.'

Another one mumbles. His body is arched forward like he has no strength left at all, his tippy toes only grazing the floor. He's the smallest of them. I had to tie the rope extra tight against his skinny wrists. 'I own an island,' he says. 'It's yours.'

Oh, blah blah blah. It's so funny. I skip around the room in front of them. Barefoot, having left my heels by the door. It's warm in here. The minimal breeze through the gaps in the slatted walls isn't all that refreshing. The piggies, though, they look cold, their nipples shrivelled, grey skin pimpled with goosebumps.

The heat that fills me is a comforting warmth that comes from a sense of achievement. I mean, just look at them! My rough guess is there's two hundred billion in net worth tied up in front of me, each responsible for reducing women to objects for that damned Clarity Directive, and for propagating the idea women should *#behave*. And I have them strung up like they're in a slaughterhouse. This dark and dank barn in the middle of nowhere is my abattoir, and they are ready to butcher.

'Anything you want. Name your price,' another says with a squeal.

I haven't explained to them yet that I want nothing except their deaths. Maybe also the collapse of their companies, for their legacy to tank so badly their obituaries will slate every business decision they ever made, that they'll get the blame for the market crash years ago instead of the women and staff quotas like they claimed. For so many to sue their companies, even their poor, wronged surviving families will be destitute. I want to undo all the damage the Clarity Directive caused, to erase every man who ever supported it.

I want the bell tower and every hint of the patriarchy to crumble.

And he offers me money. The dick.

I want IMAtech and its associated hormones to be given only to the rich men, and for those prescriptions to cause impotence and kill off their sperm count, for them to grow obese and be dissed in glossy magazines for having love handles and three hairs out of place.

I want every rich prick to be as ugly as he sees ordinary women.

So, no. I don't want your fucking island. Thanks to the richest pumping out carbon emissions, that island will be under the sea soon anyway.

Fucking idiots.

Funny thing is, if they had IMAtech, if they were hooked up to the same invasive software that monitors all the WIT minions from the inside out, their current state of panic would be known. There would probably be more action in finding them instead of the current assumption that they are on some rich git work retreat.

Oh, I do love a bit of irony.

I like the glimmer of hope they still harbour. The way they plead with their whole faces like a puppy begging for a treat. I want to savour the moment that goes out. The last flicker of a candle before all they have ever known goes dark.

I slap them all around the face and scream. 'This is the abolition of the patriarchy, motherfuckers!'

There's an orchestra of groans, pathetic little pleading bleats, lost lambs trying to find their mummies.

'It's already happened. You don't need to do this,' one piggy says.

I walk to him, holding my face so close to his, the details in his irises are crystal clear. 'Excuse me?'

'The p-p-patriarchy. It's over, was a while ago.'

'And why do you think that, since the Clarity Directive is still in place? Remember that? You helped start it with that damned hashtag.'

'That's just a p-p-protection thing. Men need protecting. It doesn't mean anything. We're not even allowed to have board meetings at strip clubs now. We can't even go on our lunch breaks. Company policy.'

'Company policy!' I cackle.

'And. . .and we have quotas again now.'

My laughter dies as it's clear he actually believes what he's saying is a good thing. Like there has been progress. 'Quotas?' I scoff. 'For top jobs for women. And you think that makes the last few millennia okay?'

'It helps.'

'Quotas you yourself spoke against.'

His eyes widen and his bottom lip trembles. 'I didn't! I was all for it. It was the other John who was against.'

The other John. More men called John at executive level in big companies than women, according to the stats.

I walk to the adjacent piggy as the colour drains from his face. He has a gut that looks so squishy, I reckon I could stab it ten times and still have room for more. 'So, Other John. What do you have to say for yourself?'

Squinting eyes, barely focussed, find me in the gloom. 'I know who you are. I'll have you killed for this.'

From the back of my jeans, I take out a bread knife. It's thick and dirty, grime smudging the serrated edge. I run it through my fingers, the bluntness of it is more exciting than if it was razor-sharp.

'My family will come for you,' he says, a raspy voice, desiccated and weak. 'My company will come for you. I have clients who will hunt you d—'

His last word hangs on a breath before a splutter of blood spills down his lips. I twist the knife, driving it deeper into his plentiful gut. There's a tangly softness, like plunging into a noodle stew. My nose is an inch from his and I smile, unable to contain my joy.

'What was that?' I ask.

There's a gurgle from his throat, the blood now foaming with air and spittle. I wrench the knife up until I hit his ribcage, then angle it up to pierce his lungs before I yank it out, pulling some of his insides with it. I gaze into those beady eyes as they glaze over with death.

An exhale shudders from my lungs, and I give an excited leap and scream. 'Yes! That's what it's all about! You see that?' I skip over to the man tied up next. 'You see how fucking beautiful that was? Look at that!' I point at the puddle of blood and entrails on the floor. 'That is what we're all made of. How powerful he thought he was and look at him now!'

He sobs. 'Please. I don't think like he does. Please, let me go.'

I take a step back when I notice the puddle of other bodily fluids beneath him, then I reattach his gag.

God, I wish Isobel was here now. I have to concentrate to keep her away, only coming here when she's too tired to resist me. She's not ready to see this yet, but she'll love it though. Since I'm the darkest part of her, I'm sure she'll be as turned on as me.

I walk the perimeter of the barn. The nearest main road is a distant hum, the lack of streetlights allowing the starry night to sparkle. Sheep graze a few fields over, but besides that, the land is just deserted fields for miles. No one will be stepping foot in here for a while.

I need a plan. But it's hard to focus on one goal: to entice more here, or to finish these off? I'm having too much fun right now to stop.

I'll probably have to kill them and dispose of them separately, away from here. Four is a big number to deal with at the moment. The fifth, well, he didn't last long. He got weak quickly.

Spoilt all his life, five minutes of not getting what he wanted was enough to finish him off. I wonder if I'd sat on his face at the end, how much pleasure his death rattle would have given me.

That's probably what the piggies would do, but I'm better than them. This is not about pleasuring me. This is about fixing this broken world.

I know I'm getting worse. I know I'm taking things much further than Isobel would like. But what better way to end the Clarity Directive, to abolish the patriarchy, to address the imbalance, than to take out all the heavyweights? This isn't wrong. It's efficient.

IMAtech will make the imbalance worse. It exhausts the poorest slaves, exposes them, while the richest feed off their misery. So let Isobel go along with whatever little plan she has to try to stop IMAtech. My plans are bigger than that. I remember the IMAtech video, stating this is an opportunity the corporate world has never had before. Well, that's exactly what my plan is too.

When all the top brass are worm food, imagine how much better the world will be. No rich men imposing the Clarity Directive, no big companies imposing IMAtech. There are only benefits to my plan.

It's like the more time Isobel and Layla inhabit this skin, the more they push me to the fringes, forcing me to do the unthinkable. They're both too square, too boring. I'm the excitement we need.

Back in the barn, I take a knife and press the tip to another piggy's belly. He whimpers. It's a gorgeous sight: a man so rich and powerful reduced to tears and soiling himself. His sedatives still linger in his system, and as I carve symbols into his belly, he probably barely feels it. I look into his eyes. Such pretty blue eyes. I smile, and his whimper turns into a snotty sob. *Yuck.*

Chapter Twelve

Isobel

I walk to work light, gliding on air as my mind still swirls with the memory of my evening with Harry. His strong torso pressed against mine, his breath on my neck, his hands everywhere. Him inside me was like turning off a stress switch, and my usually frazzled brain is now calm, like he chased the mind fog away.

I have an hour free before Hugo Baxter arrives in the office, and I spend it asking all of my colleagues individually if they're okay today, if they're coping. I was hoping for some varied answers, for a few to claim they're stressed beyond reason. But no one dares. Some simply ignore me and the rest just give a wishy-washy response to say they're fine. Their protruding temporal veins and pale complexions tell the real story. Their hormone data no doubt does too.

After I have spent the rest of the morning in a meeting in the glass office, taking notes on my colleagues' hormones, the public reaction to the news, listening to some social media guy drone on about the latest trending hashtags and another one quoting stock interest, I'm about ready to start handing out hugs to the team, tissues and bottles of wine. Anything to make them happy.

It's so dull and depressing, it's no wonder I normally outsource this part of my day to Layla. I'll bet she sits up, paying attention and hangs off their every word without an ounce of sympathy for the staff. My mental state in that office bounces from bored to tears and borderline tearful. At times, it's so dull, I almost fall asleep. How can somewhere with so much air con be so stuffy?

What I find dull, Hugo finds exhilarating. His animated gestures and pitching voice is like a slap in the face whenever I find myself nodding off.

'I knew it! I knew the public would be onside!'

'Well,' Greasy Guy says. I still don't know his name and it now feels weird to ask. 'It's mixed responses.'

'Yes, but the *right* people are on our side. Big names, big money! That's all that's important. And everyone else, the new game should sort that out.'

The new video game spec hasn't gone public yet, not even the name. There's the WIT logo on billboards that fades out and says, *Coming soon!* The excitement in gaming news is palpable and WIT's share price is inching up by the day.

The previous WardZone game was such a hit, and the new game is going to be even bigger, so the projections say. A fully interactive and adaptive gaming experience and accommodating the new rules restricting violence in video games.

Weapons of choice: negative emotions: tiredness, sadness, anger, impotence (for the 18+ game).

How the goodies win: collecting the pill packets and necking their daily doses to gain life, strength, to power up, get it up.

If computer games made my generation violent, the next will be whatever Baxter Pharmaceuticals wants them to be. Profitable minions.

The world it is set in? Ours. This bog standard, everyday hell hole. Totally immersive where you can act out real life before actually partaking in real life. A dress rehearsal. And if it doesn't go to plan, Baxter Pharma has a pill for all of it. The characters spring to life on a rainbow of endorphins as soon as they recharge on the meds, and your avatar can simply try again.

And, of course, it will all be connected to IMAtech. The avatar feels the player's real emotions.

I have to hand it to them, it's marketing genius. It's not only working age who are going to be queuing up for their IMAtech chips and Baxter meds, but also the kids. And it'll be ready in just a couple of months.

When I'm excused from the office, I race down the stairs and out onto the street, the onslaught of London life hitting every sense, but it's a welcome relief to Hugo Baxter's voice, Malorie's silence, and the tapping of keyboards.

'Hey, Isobel.'

I snap around, and Joel stands next to me, stretching out his back and taking in lungfuls of London smog.

'Joel! So good to see you. I mean, sorry, it sucks up there. I thought down here was bad, but jeez. It's good to be out. How are you?' I feel bad as soon as I've asked. He looks like he hasn't slept in weeks. Whatever benefit he used to have from Texi seems way past him now.

'Okay, I guess.' He shrugs and scuffs the tarmac with his shoe. A cyclist whizzes past and is nearly taken out by a car pulling out of the junction. We both wince as he swerves and keeps going unscathed. Joel looks my way. 'You all recovered and everything?'

'Don't. I don't want to talk about me or the fire or anything. Tell me about you. What have you been up to? How are you?'

He leans back against the wall, looking up at the grey sky. I'm surprised he can spare the seconds on IMAtech. As office manager, I should probably ask. I bet Layla would.

'Well, tailored work-boost prescriptions are about to become compulsory. If hormones aren't where they should be, we risk the sack. So, I guess I'll pick up my first batch in a moment. You know they're actually going to be delivered to our desks. The app pings some drug waiter and they bring it over.'

I can't tell his emotion from his tone. It's a mixture of pleased and dismayed. 'Your levels not okay enough on their own?'

He snorts a laugh. 'Yeah, right. I've been laying off it all, since Antonia. . .' he then pauses a moment as we remember our colleague. I wonder if Joel believes it was an accidental Texi overdose? It's only me and Harry who know for sure that Adam Ward had her killed. 'I take some Texi sometimes,' he continues.

'That keeps me working, but apparently my stress hormone cortisol is prohibitively high. Anyway, what have I got to lose? I can't be any more miserable here.'

I put my hands in my pockets and join him in leaning against the wall. A couple of pigeons peck around my feet. 'Yeah. I know the feeling.'

'Hey, I became an uncle!' he says in a lighter tone.

'Aw, that's lovely.'

'Yeah. It's great.' His smile doesn't reach his eyes. He wears a look of wistful regret. 'He's a cutie. I always thought I'd settle down with someone and have kids before my sister, since I'm four years older, but I guess she beat me to it. Seeing her in a minute. I can't really spare the time, but she just messaged to say she's close by.'

'That's nice. And all in good time, your own family, that is. No rush for these things.'

He stands upright and lifts his hand to wave. 'Casey, hi!'

A woman walks over, pushing a pram. If Joel looks like he hasn't seen daylight in a month, this woman looks more like it's been a year. 'This is my colleague, Isobel.'

She smiles at me and gives Joel a peck on the cheek. From the pram there's a little grizzle, and I peer in. The baby is just waking up.

'Precious,' I say. 'How old?'

She strokes the baby's cheek and puts his dummy back in his mouth. 'Two weeks. And quite the handful already.' When the dummy fails to soothe the baby, she lifts him up and holds him to her chest. He's still all scrunched up like brand new babies are, his fist in his eye protesting the light.

'Here.' Joel holds his hands out. 'Can I?'

'Sure. Oh, wait.' Casey steps back. 'Hang on. You're on IMAtech, right?'

Joel nods.

'Can I see it, the app?'

He gets out his phone and shows her the app.

Casey takes another step back, putting the still grizzling baby back in his pram. 'Oh. No, sorry. Look, your cortisol is a little high and endorphins are low. I don't think you should hold the baby.'

My jaw drops, and Joel's hands fall limply to his sides.

'But holding the baby might make my endorphins better,' he says.

'He's a baby, not a science experiment,' she says. 'Sorry, Joel. You can look at him, maybe take a step back. There, from there I think it should be okay. I don't know if dodgy hormones are contagious.'

I scoff. 'I doubt it.'

'It's wonderful they can monitor such things better now, don't you think?' she says. 'It's really putting safety first. *Parent Net* is full of tips on how to use IMAtech to its full potential. It's not just about desk jobs. There's a woman on there who uses it to track how many minutes parenting she does, so her husband does his fair share. And another discovered her partner was cheating. Such a change in his hormone levels, he couldn't deny it. I'm just sad it's not licensed for babies yet. Wouldn't it be lovely to know exactly how happy your baby is?'

From his much farther away position, Joel raises his voice to speak. 'Erm, yeah. I guess so.'

'But I hear everyone will be on the tailor-made hormone supplements soon?'

'Today actually,' Joel says.

'Isn't that fantastic.' She's pushing the pram now, shouting at Joel from over her shoulder. 'You never know, Joel, next time I see you, you might even be able to hold the baby.'

She's eating up the pavement as if she's Road Runner escaping Coyote. I look his way and note his glazed eyes and reddening cheeks.

'Shit,' I say. 'Sorry, Joel.'

'So,' he says, a slight quiver in his voice. 'I better get back to my desk. That drug waiter will be around any minute.'

He turns on his heel and walks back inside, leaving me in the glaring sun of the day. A chilling doubt creeps over me, and my shoulders curl forward, a headache splitting me in two.

Harry is going to be swapping the pills around any day. A harmless move, we thought. A prank really.

Or maybe not.

If we mess with the meds too much, could we cause harm? Layla is clawing at my insides, telling me, yes, we'll make things worse. Don't trust Harry, she says, again and again.

To be fair, Katarina says the same on that last point.

I push a thought into my mind, across the fence I share with Layla, forcing her to acknowledge it too.

I will not do as much harm as Katarina.

Chapter Thirteen

Isobel

There's some more commotion across the street, a pedestrian hit by a car. Just clipped him, I think. I take a step along the street to get a closer look. He seems okay from the accident, the fight that ensues afterwards though, maybe not. My IMAtech buzzes to remind me my break was over a minute ago, but I keep watching. That is, until the nag is intensified by her presence.

'You need to go back,' Layla says, all flustered and panicked over a couple of minutes.

'Those people might need some help. I'll just watch for a moment.'

She huffs, folds her arms, and taps her foot. That's my foot, my arms folded, my lungs. It's only weird when I think about it. Otherwise, it seems normal. She's there, I'm here.

'I'm going in,' she says.

'No! Stop! Okay, okay. I'll go.' I try to sound breezier at the end. If Layla gets a whiff of my concern at her presence, I'm not sure if I can stop her steamrolling in. There's shouting behind, and the blare of a siren. The police have shown up for the incident. I mustn't look. I need to concentrate on work, on being here and present, on being Isobel.

They're about to deliver the medication to everyone's desk and no doubt Layla will take hers as instructed. She'll dose this body up with whatever Hugo Baxter thinks will keep her in line. I can resist though. I'm still sure they won't sack me. I need to keep her away, and to focus.

Loading up my phone, I check out my IMAtech and my—our—levels are particularly off. I'm surprised Hugo hasn't spiked my drink with Baxter Pharma's tailored pills already. I don't want it. I'll lie and fight it all I can. My emotions might not be great, but at least they're mine. If I'm dosed up on their meds, I might not be able to stand up to him. IMAtech will continue to roll out without me even trying to protest. I need to be lucid in case Harry's switching fails. I need to be in control.

Layla fades away as I turn to walk back in. I guess the goody-two-shoes portion of our mind is satisfied enough I'm going to work. As I step through the doors, my phone buzzes, but not with IMAtech this time. It's my dad calling.

I glance up at the glass office. There's no one watching, so I answer.

'Hey honey,' he says, all slur. It's been years since his stroke, and I guess this is as articulate as he'll ever be. 'Just thought I'd check on you.'

'Hi, Dad. I'm fine. Just tired. That's all.'

'I was wondering if you'd be a little low today, given the anniversary.'

I check the date and palm my forehead. I'd forgotten. How could I have forgotten again?

'Fifteen years ago today she passed.'

Has it really been that long? I count the years off in my head and yep, he's right. Fifteen years since my dragon of a mother died. I always forget because I don't miss her, not one bit. She adored my brother but hated me, always wanted me to be someone else. She'd prefer the Layla-version of me. I was always too distracted, didn't apply myself enough, wasn't ambitious enough. She was jealous of my dad's fondness for me, as if paternal love is something for a wife to envy. He loved her though, and I probably did too on some level.

'How are you, Dad?'

'Oh, you know me. Muddling on.'

I should visit again. I spent so much time there after the explosion while I was recovering. Dad couldn't help much, given his disability, but his neighbour, Scott, was attentive and it was nice to have some familiar company. Scott and Dad have been neighbours and best friends forever. Scott's an intimidating sight, twice the mass of my wasted-away father, who does little more than sit on his reclining chair. Scott is softly spoken, can cook, and took me to my specialist appointments. I wondered before if he and my dad are more than friends, but I'm not one to pry. Whatever makes him happy.

'Your brother sent a text.'

Great. Now even my dickhead of a brother is being more considerate than me.

'Perhaps you both could come over one weekend,' he says. 'We could have a family take-away.'

The last time I saw my brother was a couple of years ago, a few days before the Clarity Directive was voted in, although a few years seems like a lifetime when so much has changed. There was a time when consent had to be sought first, as strange as that seems now. Papers were rife with stories of men who forgot that small obligation. It was distracting, they decided. Better to take any ambiguity away.

I was at my dad's and Dylan was there, touting the benefits of the Clarity Directive.

'Men need protecting,' he said so many times, his chin in the air, a vibe of superiority about him. 'It's impossible for men, especially in the workplace with the law as it is currently. We never know where the line is. It's grey and changes from woman to woman. The Clarity Directive does exactly as it says. It makes it clear. Men or anyone—this isn't just about men—are free to do what they want. The other person simply has to say no.'

I hated him anyway, but actively avoiding someone takes a bit more effort. It's energy well spent.

I make my excuses and say my goodbyes to my dad, pass on my condolences, then hang up. Putting my phone away doesn't remove the guilt that's thumping me in the chest. I shouldn't have forgotten. At least for Dad's sake. I should try to remember.

My phone buzzes again and I read the message as I silence it. It's Harry: *all done. XX*

That's all it says. He's done it. Our little plan to make things better. My lungs inflate, and I bite back a smile. It'll be too late to taint the first batch. That went out too soon. But the next batch, or maybe the batch after. A little delay doesn't matter. Soon it'll all change. Mission not quite accomplished, but I hold my phone to my chest as I know now at least the ball is rolling.

A man walks ahead of me into the office, dressed sharply in the kind of suit only a certain wage can justify, and Hugo races down the stairs to greet him.

'Christopher Morely.' Hugo holds out his hand and shakes the man's so enthusiastically I hear his shoulder click. 'Hi. Thanks for coming.'

Christopher Morely glances around the office and I pause in my walk, searching my memory banks for the recollection. His face, so familiar yet it's been years. Good looks like that don't show up often, and age has only added some maturity without the blemish of hardship. He lived near me when we were kids. He didn't go to my school but the expensive private one down the road. He was a sleaze then, and looking at the way he prances around the office floor, he hasn't changed. He always went by Christopher, never Chris, stating that three syllables are the least he deserves.

That's who Hugo's big meeting is today, and I realise it's his company that's behind the AI functionality of the new game. There's no chance he'll recognise me from all those years ago. I was as easily dismissed then as I am now.

Hugo's laugh makes me grind my teeth. He's so damned haughty. My hand grasps my chair before I sit and I imagine throwing it at him, the rigid seat hitting him squarely in the nose. Christopher Morely is walking alongside Hugo, and he turns to leer at the office. There's some bad memory associated with Christopher Morely, something I've locked away from years ago. I can't recall it, can't picture it, but the feeling leaks out of the memory safe, the emotion slipping through the gaps and filling me with white-hot rage. My eyes glow like daggers. Anger fizzes like a shaken-up cola bottle, forcing its way out, and I have little strength to resist her.

Chapter Fourteen

Katarina

Christopher Morely. Of course I remember him. He was at the party the other day, but I couldn't place him then. Hearing his name now, it all comes back. His dad was some billionaire married to an actress. He was the rich little shit who went to the private school down the road and thought he owned everyone and could take whatever he wanted with his wandering hands. He had an aversion to being told no. There's no way he's mellowed into a respectable, considerate man now. Once a pervert, always a pervert.

He was a kid then, maybe sixteen or seventeen years old, the last time I remember seeing him. He had facial hair tufts over his chin that were soft like rabbit fluff, his late-developing voice still had the squeak of pre-adolescence.

Now he's all grown up. And he grew up hotter.

He's all defined features and close-cut stubble. His voice greets Hugo with a depth that makes my toes curl.

His family's money has clearly been kind to him, greeted at the doors of WIT with so much excitement, I'm surprised they haven't rolled out a red carpet.

Isobel chose a particularly dowdy outfit to wear for work today. Some pastel coloured trouser suit that leaves everything to the imagination yet would fail to rouse any kind of desire for such imagery. And thanks to her time outside, my face is red from the heat and my armpits sticky. I look like a prude librarian, and there's not much I can do about it now.

I skulk in the back of the office, lapping up the air con and hiding behind busying employees and office furniture. The first time Christopher Morely lays eyes on this body again, it will not be in this setting. There's another fancy function coming up. Isobel hates those things, so no doubt I'll be in control. He'll be there, and I can wow the pants off him. Literally. In the meantime, I can research, do my homework on this man, and try to dredge up the memories Isobel has locked away.

Then, what to do with such a prime target as he?

I should take him to the barn. String him up with the others. But what a waste of prime meat that would be.

I lick my lips. I want to play with my toy first.

Chapter Fifteen

Layla

I'm up early for work, too early. Nightmares, flashes of fire and gore expunge me from sleep. It's still dark outside, so I go to the bathroom and wash the sweat from my face, make a coffee, then turn on the TV. There's a fox outside, a noisy one. That probably added to my bad dream. Some idiot neighbour left food outside and attracted it. As if we need more vermin in London.

There's little on this time of day besides the news. With my laptop close by, I try to prepare for work, but the headlines draw all my attention instead.

Men missing. Rich, powerful men.

My stomach drops, and a chill tingles across the back of my neck. It's her, I know it is. The news stories of missing men have Katarina's mark all over them. All wealthy, influential in the world of business. Each have old reports of scandals: supporters of the Clarity Directive, underpaying staff, misogyny, coverups, all stories that were in the press for five minutes then forgotten.

All stories that are resurfacing now they're missing. I have to hand it to Katarina—she's done her homework.

I scroll through various news sites on my phone, my free hand alternating between rubbing my forehead and my temples. It's the revenge of scorned women, the media says. Some gathering of them, a cult, so one even expresses as their theory. *A cult of crones!* says one headline adjacent to a photograph of a woman allowing herself to grey naturally. She was one of the men's first wives, and his divorce lawyer saw to it she was left penniless besides minimal childcare payments.

An old employee on the rampage is another theory. *If only they put this much effort into their day job. . .*the article begins before I click it away. If the articles are meant to harbour sympathy for the missing men, they fail. The fear mongering about stock prices taking a hit and dividends being downgraded does nothing but make me root for Katarina. She's more distant from me these days. I'm not influenced by her like I used to be. The overlap in our personalities is now usually completely divided, Isobel as the buffer between, but sometimes she seeps through, one wound bleeding into another.

One of the men was accused of sending dick pics to a teenage intern, briefly, before some payment to silence her was made and his company's rising share price took over in eye-grabbing headline news. They hail him as a saviour, doing his bit to haul the stock market out of the gutter of the crash a couple of years back. What a hero. I almost start to wish it is Katarina who's taken these men. I hope she's castrated the lot of them.

But sensible me takes over. I stopped fantasising about harming people as soon as I had front-row seats to the live show. I've come to accept I'm Layla Daley, and my role in this body is my continuous voice of reason and caution. The one who obeys the rules.

Katarina is not a wronged ex nor victim nor disgruntled employee. She is a woman with a vendetta, and she's going to get us all locked up.

My studies on dissociative identity disorder and its associated amnesia have continued, and I'm now convinced it's linked to childhood trauma. If I can confront Isobel's childhood trauma, to unlock it from her mind, perhaps Katarina will go away. But accessing the memories from before my time is impossible. Isobel has doctor-approved methods and keeps them locked up tight. I always thought keeping that safe shut was sensible, now confronting Isobel's past seems less dangerous than Katarina.

Isobel gives Katarina too much time, gives in to her demands too readily. It's easy to see why. Katarina is persuasive, to put it mildly. Those two have chemistry. They've a bond I can't touch. Katarina is all fun and compliments, finding it easy to lead anyone astray. Someone like me can never be influential. Even Isobel, with her image of individuality and carefreeness, is too easily influenced, like her backbone is made of rubber. She only wants a friend, and no one chooses sensible over exciting. Well, almost no one.

A new headline flashes across the TV, one that makes my stomach cave in and my hands go to my mouth. A body has been found. A wealthy board member of Grande Pharma. Married, though the death is being linked to a hookup on a dating site. Chem-sex, they're saying. Common with these covert booty calls, the reporter says. Drug overdose with asphyxiation, a sex game gone wrong.

Katarina might as well have signed her name on his butt cheeks.

The naked man. A plush hotel. Narcotics. My gut churns and the room spins as I recall last time. It looks just the same. Even his grinning headshot shows the same glib smile, his mourning wife ushering their children away from the cameras and into their ridiculously huge London home. It's déjà vu. How can Katarina think she'll get away with it time and time again?

I look at my hands, shaking and weak. They're our hands, still painted with her trademark nail polish. She's going for a brighter red these days, a glitter sheen. Adding some sparkle into her misdeeds. I rummage for the acetone and remove it.

She's trying to oust me, I know it. There's not enough time for all three of us. Even when Isobel was lost in limbo, she was trying to get her back, never happy with it being me. Two is easier to maintain and Katarina has chosen me to evict. Isobel needs to see she's the dangerous choice.

The acetone removes the polish but still my nails aren't clean. Under the tips, a reddish stain remains. A dark crusting coats the underside. My stomach lurches and I swallow back bile, knowing it must be blood. How like Katarina to do a poor clean-up job. A shower of blood is just how Katarina likes it. She doesn't spare a thought to our shared fingerprints, our DNA.

I ram the heel of my hands into the side of my head where the splitting ache begins. I shouldn't be worried about me, us, this body. I should be filled with remorse for the life lost, his family, his employees, the stock market hit that'll affect pensions and whatever else it does. I'll have a pension one day, probably, or Isobel will. We should be concerned.

As I ground my thoughts in such sensible, compassionate tracks, my headache eases. Just slightly. I force it away.

Armed with a nail brush, I jump in the shower and scrub, working the soapy lather all over my hands, my hair, then everywhere. I scratch at my scalp with my fingertips, working the nails around each hair, and then the nail brush once again. Still with the water running scalding hot, I take the nail clippers and cut my nails down as low as I can, rinsing the cuttings down the plug hole. Then, I wash again.

I can't picture the murder, can't visualise at all what Katarina has been up to. She's too good at walling up her memories. That's probably a plus. What she gets up to will make me throw up.

I dress, then take the nail brush and walk down the street until I find a skip. After I dump it under the hardcore and rubble, I walk back to my apartment and wash my hands again.

I'm sure Katarina is delighted to have someone else to do her cleaning up for her. However, there's only so much dirt I can rinse away.

Chapter Sixteen

Katarina

I didn't kill that guy. I'm enjoying the news story though. I'm enjoying it even more knowing they think it was me. A little suspected blood on our hands should freak Layla out nicely. The missing men haven't gone unnoticed either. I giggle like a little girl every time I think of Layla stressing, scrubbing her hands, and sweating through her nightmares. If she's scared enough, maybe she'll give up and go away for good.

I check the time. This body can cope with being awake for an hour, so I can revel in the news. I get up to make popcorn, ready to watch the news all over again on another channel. It's better than the cinema, better than any shitty soap opera. Rest in peace, some writing says on the screen. What a stupid saying. Why don't we say live in peace, since we all die fighting in the end?

My limbs buzz with desire and energy to do more, so much so, I almost throw the bowl of popcorn across the living room. I'm light, like a bird ready to swoop into action. The missing men have made London's wealth jittery. When they're interviewed on the news, they stumble over their words, their snobby voices lacking the usual harshness of authority. I want to reach into their armpits and feel their sweat, to sniff their body odour, to sit next to them as their legs shake.

The hardest thing is observing men's fear from such a distance, it's like having the sweetest dessert just out of reach.

I lick salt and sugar from my bottom lip as I flick channels and find my news story again, the faces of my piggies adorning the screen. They look so plump and healthy in those pictures. Crudely so. They even show that fucking island one of them owns, like it's meant to drum up more sympathy. Oh, the poor island. Lonely and orphaned. Ha! I shove a handful of popcorn in my mouth, letting crumbs spill on the sofa.

It's delicious, watching sheer terror consume a piggy so intensely. I want to smell the terror on every wealthy man, to see his temporal vein pulse and watch as their hands develop a tremor and panic seizes their lungs. A little fear is just what men across the country deserve. Let them feel the essence of their own mortality, to acknowledge their flesh can be cut as easily as everyone else's. They're all the sort of men that think women should be banished to the kitchen, forgetting that's where the knives are.

There's a story about the dead man. Some chem-sex booty call gone wrong for the prick who snuffed it. He deserved what he got as much as my piggies do. The best thing, the thing that makes me want to sing and air-punch, is other people are linking the killing to the missing men. News sites and social media are assuming it's all the same person or people, that there's a gang of us seeking revenge on the wealthy. And not everyone is angry. Not everyone is saying we should *#behave*.

I scroll through my phone, reading the comments on the news sites, my grin widening by the second.

Good riddance! Hope his company tanks! His wife must be relieved! Men like him need to go down!

Whoever is doing this, I'll shake their hand. And I thought the Wards snuffing it was good—this is even better!

They blamed us for the market crash and have treated us like objects since. This retaliation is well overdue.

Fuck them. Fuck the Clarity Directive!

I told Layla once I was just tipping over the first stones. She thought blowing up the pub was the landslide, but it's yet to come. It's gravity now, unstoppable. The momentum is gaining.

I need something to wash the popcorn down with. Some wine will do, but Isobel has been ploughing through the lot. I find a bottle of gin and a fresh bottle of tonic, pouring myself a double. Days like these need celebrating.

It's an effort to keep the memories mine, but I have to for now. Soon enough, I'll reveal everything to Isobel. She'll see the glory then and revel in what I've achieved. We'll crack open a bottle of fizz together, the two of us, instead of just me celebrating on my own.

I stare into my empty glass. How have I drunk it all already? I pour another, cutting a fresh slice of lime for a garnish. The serrated blade is sharp. A blunt blade is more exciting in the barn. The effort it takes to cut is a glorious feeling. My fingers tingle as I carve up the lime, cutting more slices than I need just to keep cutting.

I put the leftover slices in the fridge, being tidy around the flat for once. Perhaps one of the others will enjoy them and wonder which one of us put them there.

I have to put up so many mental blocks, but that safe Isobel constructed with her whack-job doctor years ago has a twin. Mine has no key they will find. Isobel is so careless with her recent memories. That's because her memory safe is full to bursting. Once she opens it, a whole lifetime of shit is going to spill out. Layla, well, she has no memories she even tries to hide. What is she going to barricade away? Working on a spreadsheet or having an early night?

It's amazing we share the same cells, the same blood, the same neurons. I guess when the brain divvied up our personalities, I commandeered the fun and motivated quarters. The section that gets stuff done instead of being distracted by shiny objects or obeying every order from the top brass.

Simple tasks are all they're capable of, with Isobel's lack of ambition and Layla's desire to play along with the dickheads in charge. Screwing up IMAtech is easy. I can think of a million ways to do it. With the knife still in my hand, I imagine so many joyous ways to bring down a company. I sip my gin, stronger this time, sharp and burning.

Stopping IMAtech may not be enough to fix this broken country, but it's all chipping away at the patriarchy. They're removing a few bricks, but that bell tower of dickheads needs more drastic action, and I'm the bulldozer.

Chapter Seventeen

Isobel

When I wake in the morning, Layla is here. By the state of her and how I feel, this body hasn't had much sleep.

'Morning,' I say, my voice croaky with sleep, the taste of alcohol on my breath. I remember waking next to Layla in this bed before, the real Layla. She was always unrested when she stayed over, not a good sleeper at the best of times. Of all the traits for my imaginary Layla to inherit, insomnia is a bitch of one. 'You okay?'

She shrugs and I reach for her, stroking her arm. She is soft, so real to touch. But I know she's not my Layla. She hangs her head differently, gets annoyed more quickly. Why can't I manifest a more accurate copy?

'Bad dream?' I ask.

'The usual. Tortured men, blood. All the stuff Katarina is probably up to. I feel like it's always me who has to deal with the nightmares. Katarina causes them and you just send the fear my way.'

The hurt in her voice permeates my heart. I get up to put coffee on and she follows me. The kitchen is clean, the carpets freshly vacuumed, and I know it can't be Katarina who did that.

'Thanks for tidying the flat,' I say. She's done a good job.

'I couldn't get back to sleep. Just kept waking up, so I might as well be useful.'

I sit at the kitchen table, and she takes the other chair. No one else ever comes around. I've no other friends. I could manage with just the one chair fine, since they don't really need one, it just seems like they should have one.

'There's that wicker box there.' I gesture to the counter. 'You notice that?'

Layla looks at the corner and nods.

'There's nothing in it. Never is. It was a hamper set I got years ago, and I've never thrown it out. I've moved three times and still take that thing with me.'

'Want me to throw it out?'

'No. I mean, that's not the point. The point is, I carry it around with me, like nothing ever changes. On my own, I can't even manage to change a useless basket for something else or get rid of it. Without people like Katarina, everything just stays the same.'

'You sound like Katarina giving one of her speeches.'

'Well, she often makes good points.'

Layla huffs and folds her arms. 'How am I meant to compete with that, with Katarina? The seductive woman who's a catalyst for change? You know with the three of us it's hard, and I know

I'm never going to be good enough. I'll never be enough for you.'

I shake my head in what I hope is reassuring, but her scowl tells me otherwise.

'We need to talk, Isobel. Properly. If you don't confront your past, we'll never be rid of Katarina.'

I fumble for words, but they don't come quickly enough.

'You don't want to be rid of her, do you?' Layla asks. Her voice is strained, like she's forcing herself to sound stern.

'I don't want her getting us in trouble. I don't want her killing people.'

'Too late.'

She goes then, disappears as if her own anger drove her out, and I'm left alone in my empty kitchen. Layla's worries of never being enough ring true in my own thoughts.

My mother always made me feel that way, so did the kids at school who taunted me for being different. My throat tightens as I realise Layla's insecurities mirror mine.

I leave the coffee, my stomach too knotted to want it, and get ready for work instead.

***

The walk from the tube station to work is the same as it's been for years. I could probably take a decent stab at guessing the exact number of paces. I know which tube carriage to stand in to have the shortest walk out of the station, and by the familiar group of people in that carriage, I'm not the only one who has adopted this mild life hack. It's always the same.

Today, though, I stall in my final approach to the WIT building, as it's so different.

Outside the doors, instead of the usual barging crowd to get in, the race to get seated, to crack on and not waste a second, there is no bundle. There's the tail-end of a line instead, patient and organised. I join the back of it, walking in step with those entering the building. A silent and steady march that seems so regimented, I wonder if Hugo Baxter is at the front cracking a whip. It's all of my colleagues in front of me, whose faces I recognise but whose expressions I do not. Because they wear none. Blankness where expressions should be, as if every muscle in their faces has ceased to function.

I walk in behind them all, through the office, the line curling around the walkway, then delivering each colleague to their desk, me included.

I sit and watch the line disperse bit by bit as staff take their seats. Some bizarre silent dance anyone would assume it is choreographed and rehearsed.

Joel snakes through the aisle to his seat, and I hiss over to him. 'Joel, hey!'

He looks my way, his eyes keeping the same trajectory as if they can't move, only his head turns. When directing his gaze at me, he pauses for a second, then, as if someone has flicked a 'smile now' button, he smiles. Just with his mouth, the rest of his expression is as before.

'Isobel. Hi. Great to see you. Isn't this a great day to be at work?'

'Yeah. Erm. . . I guess so. Hey, why is everyone so weird?'

'Everyone is super happy to be at work and to work so super efficiently. Please excuse me. I am beyond excited to get started with my day.'

For all the joy in his words, his voice implies none of it. He speaks without intonation, as if he's saying numbers rather than words. His face turns back in the same manner, only in reverse, and as soon as he sits, his fingers start flying over the keys.

'Okay. . .' I turn away.

I glance over my shoulders around the office and note everyone is exactly the same, all engrossed in their work to such a degree it makes Texi look like nothing more than a vitamin. Every now and then, they all smile the same, robotic smile, and the only words I hear are along the lines of 'Gosh, I am so pleased to be working today.'

What the fuck?

'Isobel.' Hugo's voice resonates like a sledgehammer against a wall.

I jump up out of my chair. 'Hi, Mr Baxter. Can I get you a coffee?'

'What? No, don't worry about that. I just want to stand here a moment and revel in this atmosphere. Isn't it perfect?'

It's only then I notice Malorie Baxter beside him. Among the office zombies, she blends in too well. 'Atmosphere, sir?'

'And check out the levels.' He points at the graph on the wall. The hormone marker is right in the middle of the green. 'Not an ounce of adrenaline or cortisol in the entire office. Everyone is working efficiently and is moderately delighted to do so. This—' he opens his arms to gesture around the room, '—this is what IMAtech means to the working world. Look at the IMAtech seconds. On track for the first time ever. Even the women. Hormones all in balance. No drama, no faffing. Just work.'

My wide eyes take in the room as my stomach tightens, and I have to force myself to breathe. 'It's something to behold, sir.'

Chapter Eighteen

Katarina

I'm on my way to visit my fat little piggies tonight. I've grown quite attached to them. But I know the fun of playing with them can't last.

Oh my, though! The feel of the knife plunging into the piggy's gut. The warmth of the blood. The squishing noise and his final gurgling breath. That's better than sex. Sex is all done when it's done. That sound, that texture, will arouse me for years. Especially since I'm about to hear it again.

When I arrive, I take their gags and masks off and look at them all. It's like being in an art gallery, such is the beauty of it. They're wasting away, their cheeks all hollowed out like they're rotting corpses already, and their eyes are sunken into dark caves. I give them all a squirt of liquid stimulant to wake them and even when they stir, they're all too weak to plead.

The knife is on the side next to where I gouged out the last piggy's guts, still coated with his innards. It smells like a butcher shop in here, and it makes my stomach rumble. It'd be even worse if the dead piggies were still hanging around, but they're all wrapped up and waiting to be disposed of. Through the plastic sheeting their faces are visible, their noses squashed, their mouths open in their final attempt of a scream, the blood they spit up smudged over half their faces. I keep the wrapped corpses lying on their backs in front of the living piggies, just so they can see what awaits them. There's no denial in their faces anymore, just the lovely pallid complexions of acceptance.

I slap the knife in my hand and pace between them, pausing for a second in front of each one. They wriggle a bit, and there's a little groan from one and a pathetic cough from another. How many billions in net worth is still alive? A hundred, maybe. Too much. That much money could go around the country twice over.

I lick my lips and pace closer, the blunt side of the knife brushing past them as I walk. 'This little piggy went to market, this little piggy stayed at home, this little piggy had roast beef, and this little piggy had none. And this little piggy—' his breath wheezes when I push the knife in, '— squeals all the way home.'

It's like cutting a cake, the jam oozing out, such sweetness, I lick my lips. Time is so still for those seconds, it's like slow motion. My lungs freeze, my heart skips a beat. My nose is pressed into his, his final breath coating my face. His pupils dilate first, then constrict. Being so close to him, I catch every twitch of his facial muscles, noting the exact moment death takes him.

It's simply beautiful. I tip my head back and close my eyes, inhaling the last of his body's heat. I imagine his soul floating above me, and I'm flying with it on a cloud of sheer joy.

Tears of happiness wet my cheeks, and I open my eyes to look again at the glory I've created. His final expression is frozen in terror. And pain, I hope. The fact his end was agonising and terrifying makes my chest expand and electricity fizzle through me.

My stomach muscles push that breath from me, my knees weaken, and the world regains its pace, the room whizzing back into focus.

'Woohoo!' I scream. 'What a rush!'

The others' heads are turned this way and when I'm done staring at the corpse, watching the last dribbles of blood splutter out, I look at them. They both have tears tracing down their cheeks, though not of joy like mine. Snot protrudes from their noses, piss and shit collecting under their bodies. Purple bruising tracks up their arms, their shoulder sockets no longer aligned after hanging from the ropes for so long. The weight of their heads is too much, and they roll backwards and forward in some lolloping motion.

Look how much their billions don't matter. Flesh and bone. They're just flesh and bone. Ego counts for nothing when met with rope and a knife. Ego cuts like soft butter. Testosterone is made in the bollocks. And bollocks hurt the most when kicked.

I step up to the next piggy, then kick him squarely in the nuts. He whimpers and yellow foamy bile spills from his mouth.

'What are we trying to achieve here?' I whisper. 'Tell me.'

He mumbles a response. Inaudible little grunts.

'Louder, you piece of shit!' I shout so forcefully he jumps.

'The abolition of the patriarchy.' His words come out with choking breaths.

I run the bloodied knife over his torso, smearing it on his curly chest hairs. 'That's right. Good little piggy. And why is that?'

'B. . .t. . .toc. . .'

'Spit it out!'

'To make it fairer. Because it is all unfair.' He sobs.

'Well done. You get to live another day.'

There is no relief in his face. He sways on his ropes like he's near enough death already. Plucking out a nose hair will probably finish him off. He's broken now, obedient, a slave for the cause.

Perhaps I should release him, let him flee into the wild and back to the mud bath of his corporate world. If he truly has learned, maybe he'll help the cause. Maybe he'll destroy the patriarchy for me.

I pace the room a moment more, rubbing my hands together as I glance once again at my fresh kill. I'll wrap him up later. He can hang there a while, curing in the heat. Let the others see what the patriarchy has caused.

No, I won't let that piggy go. This is the abolition of the patriarchy, and there can be no survivors.

Chapter Nineteen

Isobel

His hand strokes my face, eyes boring into mine.

'Hey.' Harry kisses me firmly on the mouth. It's only our second time in bed together, but it's like he knows my body inside and out. To be fair, he knew it when it was Katarina in control. I wonder if she takes pleasure from the same things I do. We've had our moments together, Katarina and me sharing one body and all its sensations. It was, how can I describe it. . .efficient? With Harry, with another person, there's an unfamiliarity, a desire to explore.

'Where's your head?' he asks.

I tilt my head down and nuzzle into his neck. 'The news.'

'That's just what every guy wants to hear after sex.'

I look up at him now and smile, wondering if Katarina ever saw him the way I do right now. I hadn't realised how lonely I was before, missing skin-on-skin contact. Real skin, not imaginary. Since Layla—the real Layla—died, I've had no one. My fingers trace the welts and scars across his chest, pink and overly smooth, and I hope my touch lets him know how sorry I am.

How sorry I am sure this body is for the wounds it has caused him.

'I know it was her,' he says. 'You're the good one.'

I know that's true. I know Katarina has all the bad cells, all the reckless and indulgent and impulsive neurons on her side of this mind. But they were all part of me once, right? Before they were sectioned off. That's something I'm having to come to terms with. That Katarina is, or was, always part of me.

'Everyone has badness in them,' he says, his sweet breath warming my ear and making my entire body tingle. 'Just most people tuck the badness away and squash it under all the good stuff. Don't feel bad. Katarina isn't you. She is the absence of you.'

A little part of me melts as he says this, and I kiss him. It's still like kissing someone new. The pressure of his mouth, the touch of his tongue, all of it feels like the first time. Is it the same for him? Can he tell it's me and not her? I pull away and hold his face in my hand, cupping his chin like my hand was made to do so. Not my hand, our hand.

'Sometimes she just takes over,' I say. 'I can't stop her.'

He holds me tighter now, his body pressing against mine. I take the weight of him and wrap my legs around him.

'You need to try though. You need to be more careful,' he says between kisses. 'I know she isn't you, but this body—' he kisses my collarbone, '—I want it for myself.'

I breathe him in before replying. 'I'm not sure I can stop her.'

He rolls on his side away from me. 'I'm in the public eye. People are going to figure out we're together soon. I mean, we are, right?'

'Of course.'

'So, if she's seen with other men, that could get difficult. Not to mention, if she gets caught on her vendetta.'

'I know. Shit, I know. I worry about that all the time.' Just thinking about Katarina getting us caught is enough to make my heart race and my chest tighten. My breath shortens as I imagine it. How could I ever explain it? My dad, and the disappointment on his face, would break me. Not Katarina though. She wouldn't give a toss if he was distraught. He's been so pleased with me since Layla has been around, since my work ethic improved with her taking so much control there, since the promotion. He doesn't care or even acknowledge it was a bribe. He's just proud. Keeping the big man happy, so he always says.

Harry strokes my cheek. It feels hot under his cool touch. 'I can't lose you because of some crazy shit she's done.'

'She means well.'

'She's dangerous.'

I nod and twine my fingers with his. He's right. I know he's right. 'The only way to stop her is to stop IMAtech. You did a good thing, swapping the pills.'

'I hope it works. I hope my parents go ape-shit crazy when they realise it's all fucked. Well, my dad anyway.'

'Yeah, he's. . .erm. . .strict.'

'He's an arsehole. Always has been.'

I run my fingers through his hair, mussing it up a little. 'Must be hard being an only child. I mean, I'm an only child, but my dad is a ray of sunshine compared to yours.'

'I'm not an only child.'

I pull my chin back. 'Really?'

'I have a sister. Well, half sister. Different mums. She just doesn't have much to do with our dad. Can't say I really blame her.'

Of all the press I've read about the Baxters, I've never heard about Hugo having a daughter. Harry has always been the one they paraded in front of the cameras and touted his abilities in business. Which always seemed daft, as he's not really that bright.

'You two aren't close?' I ask.

'I see her sometimes. She's been there for me during some tough times, but it's not like we grew up together. She was with her mum. Dad just wanted a son. It seems easier being a woman. No one expects anything of you.'

I bite my tongue and remind myself of how hard his dad is on him. He's not a chauvinist. He just doesn't understand.

'I hope he has a total fucking breakdown when IMAtech fails,' he says. 'Either that, or I hope he's next on Katarina's list.'

'Shh. Don't give her ideas.'

He looks around, then back at me. 'Is she here?'

'No. Just me.'

'Thought so. Are you sure if IMAtech tanks, she'll stop?'

I smile. 'It's our best shot.'

How do I tell him no, that taking such a huge risk may be a good thing in stopping IMAtech, but Katarina wants more than that? She wants the Clarity Directive rescinded, the wealth gap narrowed, the end of all powerful men?

I know this because my blood boils with her anger, my muscles tense with her determination whenever I'm in the presence of what she wishes to destroy.

Stopping IMAtech is the most achievable goal. The rest of Katarina's to-do list is something I plan to tackle later.

Chapter Twenty

Layla

When I'm awake, it's often only me. Alone. Extradited. There's no room for me with the two of them around. I am not persuasive enough, too dull to tag along. But now Isobel is with me. She didn't answer any call from me, she just appeared.

Her forehead is wrinkled with her brows drawn in. She fidgets, her knees bouncing up and down. Her negative emotions are catching, and I find myself rubbing my temples, my neck stiffening. I bite at the skin around my thumbnail and wonder why she wants to spend time with me. Especially since she's even more distracted than usual. She doesn't need to open her mind space to tell me. I can smell him on me. This body has had him all over it. I should know. I've been there before.

She doesn't wall up her time like Katarina does, and she does a shitty job of covering her tracks. She could have at least washed after being with him and spared me gagging from his scent. That aftershave brings to mind memories that aren't mine. It hits the back of my throat like some potent solvent. The touch of his hands, his stubble on our neck. I cringe and wipe my hand over that area, scratching him away like his lingering essence is an insect.

She flaunts her recent activities, carelessly, as if somehow I will approve.

I do not.

She can't actually like him. This is her sweet nature, her guilt for what Katarina did. It's a fuck of contrition, that's all. Trying to boost his ego again.

She's sitting across from me on the sofa, messy hair matching the untamed look she has in her eyes. 'We should spend more time together,' she says. 'I feel like the only time you're around is when I'm not.'

'Well, that's not my fault.'

'I know. I'm sorry. I've been a bit distracted lately.'

'No shit.' My tone is too coarse. I want this time with her, yet I snap and push her away. I can't help it. His scent is still on our body, our hair is still knotted up from his hands and the bed. 'What do you want? I'm not stupid. And it seems all three of us have slept with Harry Baxter now. How marvellous.'

She smiles, not in the least bit taken aback by my quip. 'Come on. He's a nice guy.'

'He's a Baxter.'

'He's not his dad.'

'So? He's just as bad.' I huff and fold my arms, looking away from her and her smugness. 'You can't just fuck your guilt away, you know,' I say, softer now. From the edge of my vision, I watch her comb her hair with her fingers.

'It's not just a guilt shag.' If she is meant to sound convincing, she fails. 'I like him. And we were talking. He's worried, and he makes some good points.'

Is she just here to brag? She has a boyfriend, and I'm all alone and she wants to rub it in my face. 'What ideas has he put in your head?'

She shifts closer, leaning in as if Katarina is eavesdropping. 'Just that we need to stop Katarina being so. . .Katarina.'

'Fucking who she wants, killing who she wants?'

'Yeah. Exactly.' She nods with such enthusiasm like this is a new idea, but I've been screaming this for months. It's only now Harry has said so she thinks it seems like a good idea. I bite the skin around my nail until it stings. I hope she feels that sting too.

'We can make a difference at WIT, I know it,' she says. 'We are making a difference. We have a plan there to stop IMAtech. Harry and me, we're—'

'So you two are a *we*? Not you and me. It's you and him.' My tone smacks of jealousy. I can't help it. It should be me teaming up with Isobel, not him. The Baxters may be my bosses, but I still hate them. They're still pedalling IMAtech, still drugging the staff. Their son is still an entitled arse. Thinking about Isobel with him makes me want to take a bat to all the Baxters' faces, to smash their teeth in. It's Katarina bleeding into me, whispering the bad ideas whenever I get angry. It's Katarina trying to convince us to do things her way, and Isobel fucking that arsewipe Harry Baxter is only giving her room to grow.

'Come on,' she says, pleading now. 'You're my best friend. Just be happy for me. I know you've been trying to warn me about Kat, and I want you to know that I hear you. Kat is too extreme, and she's making our levels way off. You must have noticed IMAtech.'

'How could I not? And is that really all you care about? IMAtech levels?' Who's she trying to kid? She never cares about our levels.

'Oh, come on. You're more concerned about our job and getting in trouble than about any bad things she's actually doing.'

My cheeks flush and I fiddle with the cushion on my lap. It would be good if all those rich pricks were dead, if she manages to make a difference on the Clarity Directive, but that doesn't mean I don't care about my job.

'Whatever our reasons, she's going too far. I think we can both agree on that,' she says.

'Of course.'

'Okay. Well, I'm going to try to talk to her. I think it would be easier if it were me and her. The three of us together is. . .tricky.'

Then just get rid of her, is what I want to say. Isobel should be able to keep her at bay. If she would only learn to bloody focus, to keep her head out of the clouds, Katarina would stay away. I'll still be around to help with work, so Isobel can still have her fun.

Katarina doesn't need telling. She needs forcing. A little chat and suggestion will do nothing. Isobel's posture sags, her eyes vacant, like she's already defeated. She certainly doesn't appear ready for the fight Katarina will put up. There's no point in me telling her and any anger only makes Katarina stronger. Isobel wants to do things diplomatically, as always.

I choose my next words carefully, not wanting another row. 'I've been reading about our. . .problems. If, maybe, you think about what happened years ago, remember some trauma and confront that, maybe you'll have more control.'

'I said no. I'm not doing that.' She angles her body away, her gaze out the window. 'The past is the past. The future is what matters. Our future.'

I expected as much and I try to reason that, maybe, it is for the best.

Isobel disappears, and I am left alone, wishing I could help, wishing I could at least be there to see Katarina get told to calm down.

And more than that, wishing I had the power to oust her myself.

Chapter Twenty-One

Isobel

The zombie march into the office is the same, the atmosphere like some graveyard Hugo Baxter is so proud of.

I don't know why I still bother walking around the office in the morning, asking the staff if they're doing okay. I don't even get grunts in response anymore. It'd be worse if I stopped though, too uncaring. If there's even the slightest chance one member of staff might appreciate me asking, I tell myself it's worth it.

IMAtech apps ping, the dispensary staff hand out pills. That's the most commotion the office sees.

A few minutes after the second pill delivery of the day, the sound of scraping chair legs along the floor cuts through the quiet office. No one ever leaves their desk, not even to pee, so I jolt back in my chair and jump to stand. There's choking, then a thud as a person hits the floor.

I dart away from my desk and search the office. A couple of rows back is a woman, Ellen. She's fitting on the floor, her hands at her throat, eyes bulging, body jerking back and forth.

I run to her, then crouch beside her, her face pale, lips turning blue except for the foaming spittle in the corners.

'Ellen!' I shout at her as she continues to convulse, my shaking hands holding on to her shoulders. No one else moves. The rest of the staff don't even notice. 'Ellen! Hang in there. I'll call an ambulance.'

As I dial, the next row of desks along, a man stands, his body shaking, his breaths spluttering until he falls to the floor, hitting his head on the way down.

'Oli!' I drop the phone, then sprint to Oliver now, taking my jacket off and holding it to his head wound as his body fits and chokes.

The row behind, another one falls to the floor, exactly the same way.

Shit. My breath shudders until I'm almost hyperventilating. 'Oh, my God.'

I grab the phone again and dial, shouting over at the dispensary desk to help.

The operator takes forever to answer, each second stretching out like a year as I squeeze my eyes shut and hold my hand to my chest, trying to slow my racing heart. I'm sitting next to Oliver when his jerking stops, though his breathing remains erratic. By the time the operator answers, three more colleagues have started fitting. I run from one to the next as I talk on the phone, lie them on their sides, telling them they're going to be fine as I hope the tremor in my voice doesn't give away my uncertainty.

The dispensary has one member of staff today. There's only two of us tending to five sick people, dreading another.

Chills inch over my extremities, dread lodges heavy in my chest. Harry switched the meds. I shiver and sweat as I think of it.

Oh my God. Is this what we've done?

I glance around at the rest of the office. Everyone else seems okay, for now. I dart from one sick colleague to another, keeping them on their sides, away from table legs and anything else they might hurt themselves on, the dispensary staff keeping pressure on Oliver's head wound. The sight of his blood on the floor makes me dizzy.

Ambulances arrive to take them away, the wailing sirens and flashing lights like some nightmare.

There are no bosses in today. No one else to help, to reassure. The dispensary guy, Matteo, I learn his name is, looks as pale as the patients.

As the ambulances all speed away, I walk the office, peer at my colleagues' faces, looking for signs of anything wrong. I collapse into my own chair, weak and exhausted, when I'm sure everyone else seems fine.

When my hands are steadier, I call Harry. He doesn't answer, so I leave voicemail after voicemail. 'Harry, I need you to call me! Please!'

It's not until lunchtime that he calls back. His tone is breezy, but it would be. He wasn't here. He didn't see how awful it was.

I'm still wiping sweat from my forehead, still trying to breathe through my nausea.

'Relax,' he says after I've cried down the phone at him for five minutes. I'm pacing outside the office and other pedestrians give me a wide berth, like my hysteria is contagious. 'That reaction couldn't have happened. The drug switch I did wouldn't have even taken effect yet.'

'How do you know?'

'Because there were thousands of pills made and no way would the first ones be dished out yet. Relax.'

Relax. I almost laugh at this word. Like it's that easy. 'How can I relax? You didn't see it. It was horrible.'

Layla is with me, wriggling her way in with that disapproving head shake of hers, telling me I can't trust him. A zillion I told you sos hitting me across the conscious plane.

I lean against the building, the coolness of the concrete contrasting with my clammy back. I say goodbye to Harry and just stay there a while, looking up at the sky, too bright, too blue, and dread how much worse things could get.

Chapter Twenty-Two

Layla

Well, how can she trust a Baxter?

I take over to do the afternoon's work. She can't face it any-more. I want to bail then and go investigate, to see if Harry is telling the truth, but someone has to keep an eye on the staff still, just in case. Someone has to get the work done.

Harry could have made the pills a whole lot worse. That would explain today's dramas. He's no stranger to narcotics, I know that much. He could have tainted a batch with anything bad, and I doubt he has the conscience to care. Isobel does though. Her worries hammer at my chest, make my eyes well, and a lump form in my throat.

I need to investigate. I need to help Isobel somehow, since I'm the only trustworthy one out of everyone she knows. As soon as the office has emptied out, I take a bus to Baxter Pharmaceuti-cals.

The lab is on the edge of Zone 4, a huge concrete thing constructed of soulless straight lines and not an ounce of charm. It's even less inviting than the WIT building. Baxter Pharmaceuticals is in big blue letters on the side. Underneath is a smaller sign saying authorised personnel only.

I buzz the front door and security lets me inside, but I realise how unprepared I am for an interrogation. I rifle through my handbag for my ID when a woman at the desk recognises me. She's wearing a white coat and her hair is pinned back so tightly it drags her eyebrows with it. I have no idea who she is, but there must have been some interactions between this body and some of their staff over the past weeks.

'Isobel Harrison, isn't it? How can we help?'

I shift my weight and feign a smile. 'I. . .I was told I could have a tour at some point.'

She nods and steps around the desk. 'Oh. Oh, yes. Of course. Come this way.'

Lying, trespassing, snooping. Following her down the corridor, I bite my lips, jumping at every sound. As if this body isn't on edge enough after what Katarina has been up to, now I'm adding to the soup of nerves.

I follow her through a corridor past a research lab. My footsteps echo down the hall, doubling their sound, like one of the others is with me. They're not, but I glance over my shoulder often, and wipe my clammy palms on my trousers.

There's no sign of Harry. I doubt he spends much time at work. He's probably more interested in sleeping and partying.

Or at hospital appointments for his burn treatments, I remember with less guilt than I deserve. Isobel feels the most guilt about that and she was in limbo then. It may have been Katarina who set up the explosion, but it was me who didn't save them. I shake that thought away. There's too much else on my mind at the moment.

I nose around a few labs, mostly shut up for the evening. Polished stainless steel surfaces and shelves of glassware are as exciting as it gets. Then we make our way to the production lines.

Another woman in a white coat almost walks into me as she hurries down the corridor the other way. My breath catches when I see her, her face so soft and symmetrical. Her close pass leaves a scent of vanilla lingering in the air. She looks at me and apologises and my face heats, my whole body sweating as I fumble over my words. 'That's. . .don't worry. . .that's fine.'

I turn around to watch after her as she walks hurriedly away, the corridor lights glowing around her.

'Ms Harrison, did you want to continue the tour?'

'Huh?' I snap my head around. My tour guide's eyebrows are raised in an expectant way, and it takes me a second to remember what I was just doing. 'Oh, yes, thanks. Where are the pills made and packaged? Can I see in there?'

'Sure,' she says, elongating the word like she's considering each letter. 'This way.'

'It's okay. I can just explore myself and save you the trouble.'

'It's no trouble. And it's company policy.'

I nod. 'Of course.'

She's glued to my side throughout, though I get no sense of suspicion, just enthusiasm and doing her best to be a good host.

I want to swipe a pill, to test somehow, but there's no chance of that.

I glance at labels, packaging, ask questions that make me sound stupid just to give me some more time to inspect everything. I look for any colour change in some batches, staring at the dusty residue on the conveyor belt. I must look as crazy as I feel. After a couple of hours of making approving noises and squinting my eyes at every corner, I leave, none the wiser and more frustrated than when I arrived.

Chapter Twenty-Three

Isobel

The function is set to be like all the rest: wealthy men being propped up by bored-looking women who reach for the champagne under scrutinising gazes. Those men belly-laughing at inside jokes only understood if you have at least six zeroes on the end of your bank balance and went to a school that cost as much as a mortgage.

It's local this time, so at least I don't need a hotel. I get ready at home. Still in my dressing gown, I check the time, twenty minutes until the car collects me. I've applied a moderate amount of makeup, raiding Katarina's supplies in a bid to hide some of my tiredness. I shouldn't bother. I should go looking like shit just so they can know what it really is like working for WIT.

'It's a very important one,' Hugo said to me earlier as he rubbed his greedy hands together. 'Big investors, big customers. Big money! The entire tech world has its eyes on WIT.'

As if that was supposed to excite me. I swallowed back a yawn as he droned on about who would be there and I stared out of the glass doors, watching the pigeons peck at the crumbs I left out there earlier. My lethargy all afternoon is a testament to how much I give a shit.

The sun is setting and a sliver of light beams through the window, the thinnest of rays escaping the shadow of the buildings outside. It bounces off the mirror and creates a rainbow on the wall. I smile and remember when I used to colour my hair pink, when I used to wear more colours. At some point, I stopped enjoying the sunshine.

I pull on my dress. It's so not me. Too fitted, too revealing, too much red. I doubt Hugo will be pawning me off on men again tonight, not after last time, but he still wants me for the PR, to show what nurturing he can do, what WIT's attention to employee detail can deliver. That even someone as traumatised as I'm meant to be can be useful at work again with the right help from IMAtech.

I'm his fucking show pony.

The dress digs in more than I like at the waist, and I have to concentrate on breathing through the top of my chest. My tits balloon out as I do and Katarina nods, half her mouth curled up in that malicious grin of hers.

'That's better,' she says.

'Not for me.'

I fan myself, beading sweat around my hairline already threatening to frizz my hair and smudge my makeup. It's too hot to be annoyed. I need to find some tranquillity and relax. The two double espressos I had half an hour ago aren't allowing such calmness, and where ambivalence was, anxiety is taking over.

My heart races and my fidgeting hands reach for something else to use as a fan.

Katarina steps closer and rests her hand on my forearm. 'I've got this.'

'No,' I snap, my temperature spiking further. I'd rather be tired than this buzzed.

Katarina narrows her eyes at me and doesn't back away.

'I need to know what you're going to do,' I say.

'I thought that tasty treat Christopher Morely might be fun to play with.' She licks her deep red, plump bottom lip. 'Don't worry. I'm not going to drug him. I just need a release.'

'Sleeping with the enemy?'

'You're one to talk.'

I step away from her and fold my arms, which makes the dress feel too tight across my back. 'I like Harry. I'm not whoring myself out to some prick.'

'Whoring!' she scoffs. 'That's supposed to be an insult?' Her nostrils flare and she glares at me. 'What exactly is wrong with being a whore?' She holds her hand up and I lean away, readying myself for one of her life lessons. 'Don't answer that. I'll tell you. A whore is a term dating back yonks, and is used to insult entrepreneurial women, using what they have to survive and exist independently of a husband. It's a way for men to belittle women who are not under their control. What's wrong with fucking who you want? Only generations of egotistical men being intimidated by it. Those men who want to own women for themselves instead of rent them as the woman sees fit. Fuck you with your man-approved insults. I'll use my body to whatever advantage I damn well want.'

Except it's not her body. It's our body. Mine, really. Her rage courses through me, taking over, heating our veins.

She leans in closer to me now, her dark eyes piercing straight through me. 'The Clarity Directive gives men free rein to put their hands where they want, but if we accept, we're branded as sluts. Let that sink in. How fucking backwards that is.'

I open my mouth to speak, to protest, but I lose my words before they've formed. My arms unfold and hang at my sides. She's right, I know she's right. But she's going about things the wrong way.

As if sensing my argument, she reaches for me, her hands pressing down on my shoulders. 'Every man who's groped you, plus all the other men who have done the same thing to other women. You struggle to make rent, while they buy a new Rolex a week. The way they put their hand on the small of your back as if they own you, every man who got a promotion over a woman just because he's a man. . .'

She doesn't need to continue, but in a voice laced with venom, enunciating every syllable, she does.

'. . .You think we're small, short, powerless. But look at that.' She holds her middle finger up in a vulgar gesture into the final ray of light. It casts a long shadow that snakes all the way to the wall. 'Even something as small as that can cast big shadows. You just have to wait for your time in the sun.'

I stare at the shadow, my arms curled around myself as her other hand still presses on my shoulder. Where she touches burns, hot and angry. If it's the caffeine or nerves, I can't tell. My heart hammers in my throat, and my breath shudders. The heat from that sunbeam is stifling, nothing a makeshift fan will touch.

The pressure of her takeover is like fingers digging in everywhere, pushing my skin away, hers slipping over and tightening. I can't stop her. The room dims around me and the physicality of the room, the hardness of the floor, the air pressure, all of it dissolves until I am floating nowhere.

Bodiless, without control.

Chapter Twenty-Four

Katarina

I always think of Layla as the ambitious one career-wise. She always wants to climb that ladder, to be noticed at work. Now, as I walk into the function decorated with enough crystal and velvet to make it look like the perfect place to whore myself out, I swish my hips, roll my shoulders back, and lift my chin high, aware our ambition is all mine. I smile, flutter my eyelashes, and pout my lips in such a way all Harry Baxter's InstaFriends would think I'm one of them.

My ambition dwarfs Layla's and Isobel's combined.

My entrance causes several heads to turn my way. From the men, I'm met with exploring gazes, puffed-out chests, and parted mouths. From the women, scrunched noses and eye-rolling.

I make my way to the drinks and lick the droplets from the rim of the glass, keeping my chin high, my lips kinked into a smirk.

Women's attitudes towards women rile me, make me want to bare my teeth at the females who look at our positions with such belittlement. Like every other woman's tits are worth less than theirs. I'll get branded as some woman who sleeps her way to the top. But who cares? That's another man-originated insult, the kind Isobel would throw about without a thought as to the mentality behind her words. It's time society flipped such views around the right way. Women don't sleep their way to the top. Men hold back promotions until they get sexual favours.

It's the twenty-first century, and we're still digging around in the ditch of nineteenth century misogyny. That dirt should have been cleaned away years ago. I'm here to do just that. The filth of men is long overdue a visit from a scouring pad. The abrasive kind. The one that gets off the baked-on grime. So coarse, it draws blood.

The Clarity Directive is on show all through the room. Men jostling for hand space around women's waists, their eyes angled down to view chests rather than faces. There's the odd arse slap and pinch as women, tight-lipped and rigid with discomfort, flinch but say nothing. No one wants to create a scene, not here, not in front of such intimidating wealth.

Christopher Morely is already here, standing in the centre of the room in a loose circle with other sharply-dressed dickheads. I've been doing my research on him in the late hours when Isobel sleeps. He's big in artificial intelligence these days, having used some of daddy's money to buy his way into Japanese companies developing the cutting edge of artificial conversations. That chatbot that you speak to instead of a person? That's his company. When the online doctor diagnoses you, that's him. And now he's getting his claws into gaming. The new WIT game, where Baxter Pharma can pedal their drugs and where everyone's levels are monitored. Imagine the metadata. Imagine what that's worth.

He's an aesthetically pleasing specimen, which is going to take some undoing. Taking a knife to his nose, perhaps, or cutting off his lips, his chin, maybe even gouging holes into his cheek dimples. Though it seems a waste to string him up straight away. My own pleasure demands other forms of satisfaction. A flood of heat envelops me as I imagine straddling him, digging my nails in, biting his still-living flesh. I might as well make the most of him before he's in the barn. Although, I reckon he'd look just as good all unwashed and strung up for days.

Hugo Baxter nods to me and I walk over, keeping my gaze low, obedient and demure as he thinks I am, though the movement of my hips keeps pulling eyes towards me.

'You look lovely, Isobel.' His hand is on the small of my back. I should rub something foul smelling on there, the sort of stuff that goes on the furniture to stop puppies biting table legs. 'Tonight is particularly important for the new video game. Lots of these men work in AI. They're ready to be wowed. Can you help wow them for me, Isobel?'

So he's planning on passing me around like some prize. I look at him as he takes in the room. He might as well be dribbling. Such a function like this isn't even necessary. Schmoozing these corporate arses isn't to sell product, it's to show off. It's some tax-deductible boys' club and an excuse for Hugo Baxter's ego to inflate even bigger.

I need to take a pin to that ego. Burst it like a balloon.

He introduces me to someone dull, someone who would only elicit any excitement if I held a blade to their neck. He'll be on my list for later, but is way down on the pecking order. Tonight, I have more pressing matters. I need a release. All these fleshy necks on show have me fantasising about tearing them apart with my teeth.

As dull-as-shit guy drones on about some tech issue, my focus flits to Christopher Morely. He sips his champagne between laughter, his voice as loud and obnoxious as all of them. He has the sort of definition to his face Harry once had, only he wears it better, stands taller, is more confident without the help of cocaine that always saw Harry through any social function. However handsome and confident he seems, he's still a man, which means he's pumped full of testosterone, the most pre-dictable hormone going.

I count down from ten in my head.

Ten, nine: glance up from me.

Eight, seven: lock eye contact.

Six: look away for a second.

Five, four: lock eye contact again.

Three: a quick smile from me.

Two, one: he's walking this way, heavy footsteps announcing his arrival.

Piece of piss. I could laugh at how simple men are. Primal creatures. Their minds unevolved since before they were apes.

'Christopher, hi,' Hugo says. 'Let me introduce Isobel Harrison.'

His dark eyes lock on mine as we shake hands. 'Pleasure to meet you, Isobel.'

A jolt of electricity shoots up my spine. 'Likewise,' I say.

The three men engage in conversation as I stand by, not counting the seconds now, but instead counting down the hours before I get his clothes off. Not hours, minutes, the extra seconds needed to have him inside me, and how many times we'll fuck tonight.

I take a glass of champagne from a waiter, then drink, batting my eyelashes while smiling my sweetest smile, and I know from the hunger in his expression that mirrors my own, my projected time is an overestimate.

Chapter Twenty-Five

Isobel

I can smell him on me when I wake at home, the musky scent overriding the perfume I used. I groan, my tongue pasty in my dry mouth. The light coming in through the curtains is an assault on my eyes and I squeeze them shut as I roll over, then open them and groan more. The dress I wore last night is in a crumpled heap on the floor, little care given to how much it cost or how delicate it is. As I reach to inspect it, the room spins. The zip is broken, a tiny tear along the seam as if it were taken off in haste. My desiccated mouth becomes drier still as I wonder, was that haste here, as Katarina got into bed, or somewhere else?

My underwear also litters the floor. She didn't bother to put them in the laundry basket or even wash his scent from our body. I'm invaded, my body pimped out to do Katarina's bidding. Layla isn't fully here, but her presence is. There's her disapproving ambience that gets under my skin and makes me want to shed.

I lie on my back, massaging my temples and search our mind, trying to access Katarina's memories, but they're walled up so strong I've got no hope.

My alarm sounds with a harsh beep, robbing the last of my fatigue as I grab my phone to shut it up.

I rub my eyes, then open them just a crack, enough to look at the alerts on the screen. Tiredness takes over again as I note the text alerts. Six unread messages from Harry that make me want to crawl back into bed and hide under the duvet for eternity.

It was her, not you. I know that. But please, do something.

I palm my forehead. *Shit.*

My snooze alarm buzzes, and I silence that too as the tinny noise threatens to make my head explode. Katarina had too much to drink last night. She should have the decency to stick around and put up with the hangover she caused. Outside, a starling makes a similar noise to my alarm, nature not allowing me to go back to bed any more than the tech. The onslaught of rush hour is building on the streets. Beeps and revving and the never-ending march of time continues, but I've no motivation to leave the bed. My head pounds with every movement and my muscles ache all over. Katarina has worn this body out, and now I have to walk to work, maybe go to a meeting with people who know more about what I was apparently up to than I do.

I pick up my pillow, then squash it into my face as I whimper. Harry's right. Layla's right. I need to stop her. Somehow.

I should hand the reins to Layla, but I can't trust her to do right at work, and I can't lose any more hours of my life. I don't even know what day it is. I also can't deal with her *I told you so* face this morning, her upturned mouth and the slow shake of her head like I'm some delinquent child.

Once the room has stopped its vortex, I drag my heavy body to the bathroom, dry heave into the toilet, then shower until the hot water runs out. I swear I can still smell him on me.

Wrapped in a towel, I sit on my bed and search my phone for clues. There's nothing that hints at what she was up to. I call to her in my mind, but there's no response. My stomach roils again and the back of my throat burns with bile. I can't face work, I just can't. Hugo will be there, knowing whatever she did, and I know it was nothing good. My extremities tingle and my chest is weighed down with dread and self-hatred. Not just mine, but hers too. Regret transcends the mind barrier between us.

Katarina, answer me!

There's nothing from her. She doesn't want to face what she's done. Oh, what a luxury! To get up to all sorts of mischief and not have to deal with the consequences. Perhaps the ground would be kind enough to swallow me up.

I dress in a trouser suit that accentuates nothing, pale grey to blend in with the furniture at work. Perhaps it'll act as camouflage, and no one will see me. I pair it with a high-necked shirt that hides all the skin I can. A balaclava would do nicely if I had one.

As I walk to work, more of a shuffle on legs like deadweights, I know the only way to stop Katarina is to achieve her goals myself. I'm going to take photos at work, videos maybe. I'll tell the world what the game is meant to do, to get kids hooked on meds, to collect all manner of data on us. Every person in the country will know soon anyway, but if WIT release the info about the game, they control the narrative. If I get word out sooner, they'll have to go on the defence.

It's a shitty, lame plan, but it's all I've got.

Even with a plan of action, my back arches forward, squashed down under the mass of my worries. I've blistered feet and my headache isn't abating despite the paracetamol I took. The sun is shining, too bright and too hot. Sweat pools between my shoulder blades and in my armpits, but I don't want to take my jacket off. I need as many layers as possible, a shield, keeping my skin under wraps.

***

There's no sign of Christopher Morely at work, not that I know if he's due in today. Has she done something bad to him? God, I've no idea, and now it's too late to wake her up and ask as here, I don't know if I can keep her under control.

I can't keep her under control anywhere.

It doesn't matter anyway. She's here. I can sense her here. There's that prickly sensation of being observed, scrutinised, like a parent busting a kid.

My skin tingles with desire to do something bad. She's fizzing, sharing my vision, making grey splotches appear. I've blind spots and shadows where she's elbowing her way in. Anger broils in my stomach and muscles at the sight of all the staff like medicated zombies doing their work without even blinking, without drinking, impossible to distract in any way.

I'm mad, too, but I'm pragmatic mad. I want to call it out, write to unions and cite the human rights act. Katarina wants to throw something, to smash things, to cut those in charge. I reach for my hot coffee, spilling it as if I have the jitters, but it's all I can do to stop Katarina from chucking it at someone. Better it's over the desk than over a person.

I stand to get a paper towel just as Hugo Baxter walks in, toothy smile and chin high like he's some God. His hand goes to the small of my back, and then sneaks a few inches lower down as he leans in close, too close, and says, 'My office, Isobel.'

Where his hand was burns hot in contrast to the rest of me that is so cold I tighten my blazer. My breath catches and the room spins once again as I dread even more what she did last night. Hugo Baxter was being too familiar, even for him. He's usually more subtle in his contact, at least more private. To be so openly a leech is a big step.

Did she fuck Hugo too?

I don't move. I can't. If I move, I'm going to throttle him. And I can't be in a room alone with him. My entire body trembles as I fight to contain my rage—her rage. It's ours. It's in our blood.

Maybe I should give in to it. To let anger overwhelm me in the hope she'll be here to take charge. At least I won't have to deal with it. At least I won't have to feel Hugo Baxter's hand on my skin.

His hand would have still been on my skin though. Whether it's me that feels it or her.

She knows about me and Harry, so is this her way of making that stop? I'm sure there's no way Harry would be with me still if his dad has had this body.

I swallow, my throat thick like sludge. The tension in my legs gives way to weakness and I kneel to the floor, my knees slamming into the tiles like a thump to the guts. All the air is ejected from my lungs and I scream. My hands go to my hair and I pull, yanking it from the sides, and I scream some more. Screaming out the bad, screaming out the uncertainty and ambiguity and fear and dread. My vision clouds over, more and more grey splotches replacing the garish light until all the air from my lungs is gone.

The IMAtech zombies don't look my way. Malorie Baxter is standing at the edge of the office, her wide eyes fixated on me, her face a picture of nothing.

My face is on the floor, its coldness sharp against my clammy forehead, and in this hunched foetal position, my screams are muffled and my tears soak the floor.

Hugo is standing next to me, his overbearing presence inciting nausea like some bad smell. He doesn't help me up but takes my handbag and removes my phone, grasping my thumb to unlock it and loads up my IMAtech app.

'Your levels are off,' he says. 'You've not been taking your prescription.'

My breath shudders, my mouth too parched to speak.

'Silly girl. This is why we have IMAtech, you see? Set an example. Now, go clean yourself up. Christopher Morely will be here in a moment, and we can't have you looking like that. Your pills will be on your desk in a moment.'

In his hands, my phone buzzes. IMAtech disapproves of my meltdown.

'Chop, chop,' he says, as casually as that. 'You're on the clock.'

Chapter Twenty-Six

Isobel

I sit on the toilet, gazing into the space around me, willing Layla to come, but she's nowhere. I need her support, a friend, some empathy and kindness. There was a day months ago when work was all getting too much and Layla—the real Layla—came to the staff room and just hugged me. It was all I needed to get through the afternoon. She gave me strength. I suspect I'll get none of that from this mind's impression of her, but at least she'd understand. At least I'd have someone.

I cry into a tissue, squeeze my eyes shut and try again to conjure her here. How can such a vacuous body be so heavy? With just me here, it's like it's only a third full, yet I slump against the cubicle wall, weak and exhausted. She's deserted me.

Katarina is now absent too, as if she doesn't want to take ownership of my outburst. My limbs are heavy, though my entire body is filled with nothing.

Standing, holding onto the wall, I exit the cubicle and step over to the sinks. From the mirror, my reflection peers back at me, ghostly grey, smudged makeup, hair that would look better on a scarecrow. I look just like the crazy woman I am.

I'll call in sick, that's what I'll do. Say I need a mental health break, trauma from the explosion, whatever.

I can't face Christopher Morely without knowing what happened. I can't face Hugo again either. My skin crawls with some memory of touch, like insects live in my clothes. Every tiny hair stands on end. Their breath on my skin, their hands on me, and the thought of that makes me shiver and heave.

Whatever Katarina did last night, she's hidden deep in her mind space. That and the blackout effect of the booze means I've no hope of finding out. Everyone knows what my body has done except me. There's some interrogation light on me, a spotlight putting me on show, yet I am too dazzled to see.

My hands shake so much it's hard to hold my phone, but I manage, and I call my dad. I just want some company, some reassurance, to hear from someone who loves me. He answers after one ring and I use my other hand to cover my mouth, stifling any sobs.

'Hey, darling. You okay?'

The sound of his voice brings fresh tears. 'Yeah, Dad. Just wanted to say hello.'

'You sound upset.'

'Just work pressure, you know.'

There's a pause but I don't speak anymore. I want to hear his voice, for him to tell me everything will be okay, that the bad times will be over before I know it.

'Hey, now,' he says when a sniff escapes me. 'Don't let them put too much pressure on you, but you're tougher than you know. Keep your head down and be my good girl.'

A pit forms in my stomach. I'm letting him down. This version of me is not what he always wanted. Meltdown Isobel. Too-stressed Isobel. Failure Isobel.

I'm supposed to be better than this. I'm supposed to be a hard worker and make him proud.

When I hang up, I sit back in the cubicle for a while, trying to will myself into action, to find some sense of purpose in this shithole. It's a therapy technique, to picture what I need to do, and so the body follows, to kid yourself into muscle memory. Every time I envision myself going up into that office, it ends with me screaming or scratching Hugo Baxter's eyeballs out.

The only thing I can imagine doing safely is getting the hell away. Back to bed. Back to some quiet place where I'm alone, away from Baxters and IMAtech zombies and everything that's wrong in my life.

Without another word to anyone, I walk out of the office. I can't be in a room with everyone knowing my body's actions more than me, squirming under my boss's gaze.

On my way home, I scroll the news, and my back hunches as I catch the headlines. Despite my head nagging at me not to look, I'm unable to tear myself away. Katarina's antics are captivating in their debauchery. My eyes sting from lack of blinking as I stare, entranced by the images, by the words of concern from the family, by the ripples of fear across the big companies.

It's wrong, what she's doing. I know it's wrong.

And yet. . .

It's all fuel for the most cynical part of me, from the part that delights in the terror. The concealed part that remembers what this body has done. The comments on the news story fill me with a juxtaposition of emotions, torn somewhere between pride and shame, my conscience lost in some limbo of moral purgatory. A splitting pain shoots down my forehead and I squint at the screen, reading the comments.

Whoever has done away with these dicks is a hero.

I could name a few more rich pricks that they could do away with.

I hope they're six feet under.

This will teach them a lesson for the Clarity Directive. Fuck 'em.

The concern and sympathy are drowning under the praise and admiration. Anonymous comments from people who hate the patriarchy and the Directive as much as Katarina, as much as all of us, yet most are so conditioned to put up and shut up, we ignore it. They're happier under the guise of ignorance than the garish reality of the perversion.

My shame outweighs pride right now, I'm sure it does. My cheeks flush with it, coming out in body tremors that try to force me to curl into a ball and allow the world to pass me by.

It's wrong. What she is doing is wrong.

It's better than doing fuck all.

I don't see her, but her voice rings loud in my ears, a licking whisper that gives me goosebumps. At least she's with me now. The company I craved has turned up.

I send thoughts back her way and hope she hears me: *I am doing something, or at least, I will. I intend to. My methods just take more time.*

There's nothing about Christopher Morely on the news. God knows what she's done with him, if anything. His scent has gone from my skin now. My lungs fill with London soot instead, and I wish it were colder, windier, to blow my fears away.

My heart aches when I think of Harry. I'm so lucky to have found such an understanding person, yet even his high bar of acceptance isn't going to be enough. This body has betrayed him, even if it wasn't me.

I message Harry, finally replying to his texts, apologising. What else is there to say? He says we can get together later, and my arms cramp with emptiness as I long for him to fill them. Tears spill over onto my cheeks, and I wipe my eyes with my cuff.

Katarina would scoff and tut that I need the embrace of a man. I know it shouldn't be that way, yet it is.

My phone pings with a message from my dad, reminding me how proud he is, and suggesting I go see Doctor Cottrell. A session with a therapist doesn't sound like the worst idea, but locking away memories isn't what I need to do. I need to release them from wherever Katarina has hidden them.

I can't risk accessing my mind safe. As Katarina said, that safe is full to bursting.

Chapter Twenty-Seven

Isobel

An evening with Harry isn't enough to make me feel safe. I doubt any arms could ever be strong enough, could ever envelop me enough. He says he's not mad, though he says this with a pinched mouth, his jawline more defined than ever.

'I'm not sharing you,' he says. 'She can't be with other men.'

I doubt Katarina even understands the concept of monogamy.

We make love and his hands trace every contour of me, him on top, pinning me down, taking me entirely for himself.

'You're mine,' he says when he's finished. 'This body is mine.'

I nod and snuggle in closer.

'And I'm yours,' he says as my caresses reach his scars. 'No one else will want me now after what she did.'

I snap my hand back and lower my gaze, dodging any chance of eye contact. He's just had bandages removed from his latest graft at his waist, the skin there particularly pink. However much my cheeks burn with shame, however much I try to right wrongs, I'll never be able to 'fuck the guilt away,' so Layla said.

Only a few minutes later, and he's lying on his back snoring. His leg interlocks with mine, his hand palm-down on my hip. As exhausted as I am, I lie awake, staring up at the blackness. Every inch of my skin itches with the sensation of strangers on me, faceless men with greedy hands. In the darkness, it's Katarina's images I see. Not full memories, just single frames, bits she wants me to see. To tempt me or to rile me, I'm not sure.

I walk through to the living room. The hardwood hallway floor is heated and warm on my bare feet. Not stuffy warm, the climate control sees to that. It's just right. I sit with the company of a lamp. It's dim enough that shadows still lurk in the corners, the tricks they play on my vision making every hair stand on end.

I stare into the lamp's glow, willing her to come.

She has the same meticulously styled hair she always has. Her smooth skin fitted snugly into that lacy black and red outfit, no bulging or sagging hemlines. She looks just how I remember her from school. I didn't hate her then, despite her hating me, the real Katarina, because she did exist. She was Miss Popular, with all the other kids hanging off her every word, and those words were often insults hurled my way. It didn't matter how much they upset me or hated me, I still wanted to be her or, at the very least, be friends with her. She was happiness and fun personified. How could anyone not want to be her?

I just wanted to be anyone else but me.

Girls like Katarina are never riddled with self-doubt and fear. They're going places and everyone can see their future of endless glamour with streets designed to suit their every whim. People like Katarina can laugh out loud without hating the sound of their own voice, can smile without cringing at their own face.

The rest of us are just faking it, pretending to fit in. Katarina is like some invasive species: she doesn't need to adjust to her environment. She makes the world adapt to her.

'Nice to see you,' she says with a sly grin, licking her bottom lip. There's desire there. A glint of yearning in her dark eyes.

I glance at the hallway to confirm it's empty, and listen out for Harry's next snore. When I hear it, I turn back to her. 'We need to talk.'

'Layla been telling you boring stories about me?'

I shake my head. 'It's not that. I need to know what you've been up to. I need to know what I've apparently done. We're worried, about you, about us.'

She leans back, brushes a strand of hair from her forehead. 'I'm careful. Don't concern yourself with the practicalities.'

Her tone is so breezy it makes my biceps tense, though I swallow back my frustration. It won't do to let on, for her to think I'm concerned. She plays a game and I need to play it better.

She cracks her knuckles. Is that me seeing an image of her doing that, or is she cracking our knuckles?

'That gives you arthritis,' I say and look at her hands. 'Although, that's probably just an old wives' tale.'

She stops cracking then, and balls her fists instead. 'Don't say that.'

'What?'

'Old wives' tale,' she says through her teeth. 'You know what that means? It's used to make anything sound like nonsense. It's used to describe nonsense, and they credit that nonsense only to women. Why old? Because women past their aesthetic peak don't say anything worthwhile? What about old husbands' tale? Why isn't that a phrase?'

I sigh, then peek at Harry's watch on the coffee table. 'It's a bit late for a life lesson, Kat.'

'Just makes you see though. Women have never been allowed to have a voice. They're silly little girls or old wives. As long as we continue that trend, we'll never be treated properly.'

'What's the endgame here, Kat? Change some age-old sayings, or murder every man on the planet?'

'Only the oppressive rich pricks,' she says, that glint in her eye now sparkling. She looks around the room, raises her eyebrows and nods at the luxury. High ceilings, dark wood furnishings, antiques. Then I remember, she's been here before. 'Nice one fucking Harry Baxter. He knows what he's doing, doesn't he? I might fancy another go myself.'

'Don't,' I snap. 'Leave him alone. He can tell when it's you anyway.'

'I reckon I can convince him.'

My eyes bulge and my chest tightens, yet her voice is unwavering in its certainty. 'Seriously, Kat. You're out of control. Stop whatever it is you're doing and leave Harry alone. I'll block you. I'll keep you out—'

'You reckon you're the one in control here?' She laughs, throwing her head back. 'I'm protecting you. You want to be the one that had to endure last night? You want to see what happened?' There's the slightest quiver in her voice when she says this. Her head dips a little lower, that sparkle in her eyes extinguished. 'I am your shield, Isobel. You want to see all the bad things? Be my guest.'

I shake my head and cover my eyes. 'No. No, I don't.' Part of me does, the part that panics over the blank spaces, the part riddled with human curiosity. But it'll be worse. I'm sure of that now. A lost memory is better than a bad one. That's why I used to see Doctor Cottrell years ago. Locking away the bad memories helped me move on. That's what Katarina is now. My mind safe.

'You send me away, and all the shit you locked up comes spilling out,' she says. 'If you knew what I know, you'd be congratulating me, not trying to control me.'

I bristle and stare into her dark eyes, wide with sincerity.

'That's why I'm here,' she says. 'Haven't you figured that out by now? I keep you from all the terrible things. If I deal with them, you don't have to. You can just be carefree Isobel going about your feckless life. I'm the bad bitch so you don't have to be.'

I lean in and whisper as loudly as I can. 'But you're creating more bad memories.'

'I'm seeking justice.'

'That doesn't mean you have to kill people. That doesn't mean you have to get us thrown in prison.'

She shrugs. 'What's wrong with prison? There'd be no men there at least.'

Sweat breaks out across my brow and my heart hammers in my chest. 'Please. Kat, I'm begging you. Thank you for all you do for us. But please, this has to stop.'

She rubs my knee, her hand like ice and I try to recoil, but she grips so hard, I can't get away. 'Sweet, Isobel. I'm just getting started.'

Chapter Twenty-Eight

Isobel

Katarina thinks I don't know what makes her take over, but she's wrong. I'm not stupid. I know a cheeky glass of wine in the evening and she can more easily elbow her way in. That's why she keeps the cupboards stocked.

There's one bottle of wine left and half a bottle of gin. I pour the lot down the sink, then replace it with water and Ribena. She'll think she's poised to take over, but I'll stay in control. I'll see what she's been up to.

The next night, I pour myself a fake drink, try to ignore the disappointment, and I wait.

At eight-thirty, there's a buzz, a vibration in the sofa. A phone, only not my phone. I rummage through the cushions, and underneath, there's a cheap burner phone with a message from a number I don't know.

Come meet me, gorgeous. XX

The address of a restaurant follows.

My breath shudders, and I rub the back of my neck. Katarina has a date. She really was expecting to be here.

I push my glasses up and stare at the phone for a while, as if the text is written in code and I have to decipher it. I go to reply, thinking I should cancel, telling them I'm sick or busy or something. But then, what would Katarina do? She'd go, spy, and take the fun for herself. Fun isn't what I'm after. I need to see what she's been up to.

Maybe I can break up with whoever they are and make Harry happy.

I sit a little straighter, then roll my shoulders back. Okay, I can do this. I can pass for Katarina.

In the bedroom, I rifle through her end of the wardrobe and take out the sort of clothes I would never wear. Too short, too low cut, too tight. Fabrics that cling and colours that alert attention, like warning stripes on a wasp. It takes me an age to put her contacts in, and trying to get my makeup to look like hers is a challenge, so unaccustomed am I to applying so much eyeliner. Getting that smoky effect is harder than it looks.

After spilling some of her makeup powder stuff—I don't even know what it's for, it leaves a dusty sheen over the mirror—I check the time. None to spare to clean up now, so I grab her hair tongs and plug them in the hallway instead. The chord just about reaches the bathroom mirror. How does she get her waves to look so effortless? Whatever I try, they look like they've been starched in and then exposed to relentless humidity.

I squeeze myself into a little skirt and top combo. But in the mirror, I don't see Katarina. I see myself doing an impression of her. Some faker. I practise some poses and postures, feigning confidence as doubt niggles all over.

I shake the doubt away. Her level of self-assuredness isn't something that can be falsified. But she was part of me once, so surely, I remember what it was like to hold my chin high and own a room.

I can do this. I can be her.

After a few practice walks in her heels, I head to the address.

It's a restaurant in SoHo, understated and easily missed among the neon signs of other establishments. A steamy window covers the front wall, the smell of Asian spices mingling with London air.

I stall as I approach, realising I don't even know who I'm meant to be meeting, just hoping it's obvious when I arrive. My feet already hurt in the heels, my skirt riding up so much, I constantly have to pull it down. Being mentally comfortable is a challenge enough, being physically comfortable is even more impossible. How does anyone live like this? There's a reason Doc Martens and Converse are so popular.

There's a bar opposite, and I stare longingly at the cocktails, nerves drying my mouth. A bit of Dutch courage would do nicely. But then I may let my guard down and Katarina in. I need to keep a clear head, so after a steadying breath, wobbling in her shoes, I go in.

He's waiting at a table by the window. Christopher Morely.

Any relief that comes when I release this means Katarina hasn't killed him is ushered from my head by asphyxiating anxiety. I still have no idea what happened between them, but the smile he bestows on me, warm and sultry, gives me enough of a clue. He smiles at me in the way someone does when they've seen you naked, like his eyes are remembering what they saw last time.

'Isobel.' He stands, then leans in to kiss me. I instinctively offer my cheek, unsure if he was aiming for my mouth. 'I've ordered for us. The seafood here is amazing.'

Isn't Katarina vegetarian like me? God, I'm actually going to have to eat fish.

'I thought this place would be perfect,' he says as we sit. He's wearing jeans and a T-shirt, a stark contrast from the suits I'm more used to seeing him in. 'Hugo would never come here.'

'It smells great,' I say, forcing some enthusiasm into my voice. It mostly smells like fish. Horrible.

'You looked stunning the other night. Did I tell you that already? I wanted to rip that dress off you as soon as I saw you.' His eyes take me in up and down, and I struggle not to squirm under his gaze.

'Yeah,' I say, my voice scratchy and dry. 'I felt the same.'

'I was pleased to hear about the success at WIT, with the IMAtech hack. It's certainly useful to have someone like you on the inside.'

I smile, hoping my flinch isn't obvious, and take a sip from a glass of water before replying. 'My pleasure.'

'A few more cases like that and it'll prove IMAtech has no place in the workplace.'

I freeze a moment, not even moving as the food arrives, the waiter having to angle around me. His words repeat over and over in my head. I keep my eyes diverted from him, as if making eye contact will mean he can see through my skin. I'm not sure if it's the sight of dead animals in front of me or Christopher Morely's words making me want to gag.

He reaches for a prawn, then peels its shell off. It squelches, his fingers shining with grease. 'Making IMAtech fuck up was a genius idea. Don't you agree? Soon WIT will see that an entire AI workforce will be required.' He puts the prawn in his mouth and sucks the oil from his fingers.

My ears are ringing, all the background noise muffled, my stomach so twisted there's no way I can eat anything.

An entire AI workforce will be required. That sentence repeats itself on a loop. I take another gulp of water, but the bitter taste in my mouth remains. I close my eyes, and all I see is the fitting and choking staff at work.

Katarina was meant to be on the right side. Going about things the wrong way, but she's helping this arsehole.

I look up at Christopher Morley now, his face proud and expectant with bouncing eyebrows and a poster-boy grin, and I can't contain my anguish any longer. I run to the bathroom to throw up.

Chapter Twenty-Nine

Layla

I've been at work all afternoon, heaving this tired body around the office and blinking these tired eyes while I stare at my screen, trying to organise the mess of notes Isobel left me. My feet ache from impractical shoes, my mouth dry from too much salty food. I've brought lunch with me today. Fruit, a sandwich, a bottle of water. Sensible. I'm intent on caring for this body we share, even though it's clear the other two punish it.

After I've tidied the desk drawer and caught up on a hundred emails Isobel had been ignoring, I fidget and tap my foot. Why don't I ever get to have any fun? I get the exhausted aftermath, but none of the action. They rely on me to do all the boring stuff, and it's making me a boring person. Sensible and productive does not have to mean boring.

I can't get that woman from Baxter Pharmaceuticals out of my head. We bumped into each other for seconds, but it's like cupid's lightning bolt struck me. My whole body tingles with desire, and every time I'm in control, all I can think about is her.

It was like that the first time I saw Isobel, I'm sure. It certainly was the first time Isobel saw Layla.

I'm not a stalker, definitely not, but the need to see her again is intoxicating. Perhaps it's lack of excitement or my loneliness. Isobel so rarely wants me around, and I know she won't come if I call her. I certainly don't want to talk to Katarina. No one at work talks to me. Human beings aren't meant to be so isolated, so alone.

I've been in control all day and as soon as I'm done in the office, I race to Baxter Pharmaceuticals. It's a slim chance and totally spontaneous, so out-of-character for me. I should be checking to see if some last-minute emails came in, should be checking the staff are all up-to-date with their work, but instead, here I am, waiting outside Baxter Pharmaceuticals, hoping she's about to leave.

I hold my breath as I lean against a tree and gaze over the carpark. Some staff get into their vehicles, but none are her. Pressing my hands into my chest, I lean in closer, the door ahead now empty. But there are cars still parked. One could be hers.

This was a stupid idea. Reckless and a waste of time. Then, after a minute, I spot her, my body tingling just as it did the first time. Not in her lab coat anymore, now in a plain fitted T-shirt and chinos, walking towards her car. Her hair is pulled back in a French twist, some loose strands blowing about her face. For a moment, I'm frozen, glued to the spot as I realise I hadn't thought this far. I'd yearned to see her but hadn't considered the practicalities.

She has her key in her hand and as she presses the button to beep open her car, instincts taking control, I jog over, frantic not to miss her.

My footsteps on the tarmac draw her attention and she looks up. 'Oh, hi,' she says as I approach.

I'm sure my face must be the colour of a beetroot, way more out of breath than I should be for such a minor exertion, but my heart skips several beats

'Hi,' I say, and inwardly kick myself for sounding so stupid. She's looking at me now as I stand like some mute idiot. 'I. . .' *Come on brain, think of something!* '. . .I think I bumped into you the other day.'

'Oh, that's right,' she says. She smiles and sounds the polar opposite of me, relaxed and serene instead of a wobbly mess. 'Except, I'm fairly sure it was the other way around and I bumped into you.'

I laugh, hoping it comes across as breezy instead of insane. 'I guess the lab is closed now?'

'The night shift is on. Is there someone you wanted to see?'

I jam my hands into my pockets and lift my shoulders, rocking on the balls of my feet. 'You know what, it's not important. I'll call tomorrow.' I turn to leave, kicking myself for not being more prepared, sure this exchange is awkward enough.

'I'm Amy, by the way,' she calls after me.

I take a slow step back towards her. 'Isobel.'

She smiles. 'I know.'

I try to laugh it off, but my face is too rigid to do anything but stare.

'Well, I think you've been really brave,' she says. 'The fire. That must have been horrible.'

I lift my left shoulder up a little more, an instinctive attempt to hide my scars. 'To be honest, I don't remember much. Though my bosses like to stick me in front of the camera like some show pony.' *Shut up, Layla!* I chastise myself. She probably knows the Baxters. I shouldn't be saying such things in front of her.

She nods. 'That sounds about right.' Her face is all sympathetic knitted brows and upturned mouth as I bite my lip for being so outspoken.

She steps a little closer. 'I don't suppose you want to get a drink?'

My stomach drops five storeys, and I attempt to swallow in my parched mouth. 'Yeah. Yeah, that would be great.'

'Now? If you're not busy. There's a place just down the road.'

If it were possible for my stomach to drop further, it would. Instead, my knees bend a little and my mouth moves like a goldfish before I manage to reply. 'Sure. No plans. Sure. Yes.' *Stupid!*

We walk to a bar just around the corner from Baxter Pharmaceuticals. Luckily, the streets are rammed for the walk, noisy traffic adding to the racket so there's no awkward silence. At the bar, there's no such luck. It's fairly quiet, with only a few tables occupied and no music playing. We'll have to keep conversation going, the thought makes my hands clammy. So clammy that when I take my drink from the bar staff, it squeaks in my grip.

We find a table and the chair makes an obnoxious creaking sound when I sit on it, and we both giggle. Her laugh is like raindrops on a cottage roof. A bird announcing the morning. The butterflies in my stomach fly in a whirlwind. I take a long sip of my coke, hoping for the ice to cool my flaming cheeks. I know Katarina would want alcohol, but I'll be damned if she's going to spoil this for me.

'So, how is working at Baxter Pharma?' I ask.

'Probably better than being at WIT.' She points towards the IMAtech chip on my collarbone.

I rub the red bump there. 'Ah. Yeah, it sucks to be honest. Not so bad for me as they're going easy on me right now. But for all the staff.'

'When we started rolling out Atexamine, I never knew this is how it would end up. I'm sorry. I really am.'

The way she says Atexamine rather than its shorter street name, Texi, makes her sound so smart.

I stare at her in awe a moment before I reply. 'Why apologise? It's not your fault.'

'It kind of is. I work for the lab that makes it, right? And all the hormone stuff now. We're not supposed to talk about it, but I suppose you aren't either, so together we're okay.'

Together. That sounds nice.

'Doses just can't be that precise,' she says. 'The bosses won't listen though. It just doesn't sit right. But they've funded the research, so they'll get the results they want.'

Her lips are pale pink, like candyfloss, and her voice is as sweet. I'm acutely aware of how thick I must seem next to her, and ugly, with my plain face and scars. I should have made an effort before I came, at least changed clothes. She's got this classic girl-next-door vibe. I can't imagine she's ever felt insecure in her life.

'It must be tough at WIT,' she says. 'Are the staff suffering?'

And she's caring too. She's perfect. I clear my throat, then regret it as I sound like I'm harbouring phlegm. 'I mean, they're not great at all. And then there were the ones who went to hospital—'

'Hospital!' Her jaw drops. I guess no one informed the lab.

'Yeah. The app didn't sync with their IMAtech and they got the wrong dose.'

She shakes her head, her hand going to her cheeks. 'This just isn't right. I've been saying it from the start.' She leans in, and her hand brushes my knee, an inferno now going on in my cheeks. She must see I'm probably the colour of a tomato by now. Her face is close, those candyfloss lips just inches away.

I need to kiss her. Just one taste. . .

I lean in and kiss her lips for the briefest second, then jerk away.

My eyes widen and I sit upright, adrenalin screaming at me to run. Why did I do that? Surprise is plastered all over her face, her lovely eyebrows arched, her eyes even wider than mine.

Even Katarina wouldn't be so stupid. It was totally inappropriate. I jolt back, sweat collecting in my hairline as I spend an excruciating second or two willing the ground to swallow me up. When it doesn't oblige, I apologise and make for the door.

Chapter Thirty

Katarina

She's been snooping, and she thinks I won't realise. I sit at the kitchen table in the apartment, sipping on some grape juice meant to be wine, then chew the inside of my cheek.

Isobel is crap at sectioning off her memories. She saw my date and threw up. At least that stopped him wanting to kiss her.

This body is tired. If even I can tell, then it must be exhausted. I lean back, some vertebrae crack and I stretch out my arms. I wouldn't mind sleeping now, but I fear I'm missing out on too much.

The TV blaring from the living room snags my attention, and I curse I've only grape juice to drink. Such news stories require champagne.

Another murder features on the news. Not one of my piggies. This dead guy has just a pound sign carved into his gut, and what a scrawny guy it must have been looking at his photos. Even the photos on the news, the ones that are supposed to be their best portraits, that smile looks like a sneer. You'd think for that many billions in the bank he'd have gotten his teeth fixed.

By the sounds of it, he didn't go in for much personal grooming. His credit card was the lure he used rather than a nice smile. The story broke less than an hour ago and already three women have come forward, declaring their NDAs null and void and revealing him to be deserving of his fate.

I hope it hurt. I hope they carved him up slowly, bit by bit. I hope he choked on his own blood.

I push that thought to the back of my mind. It's not for me to decide how piggies are served their hand. These are women fighting for their freedom, and that's a beautiful thing. The man wasn't just hacked up and killed; he was carved by a sculptor, made into her vision. Whoever she is, she's an artist and her creation is hers alone.

Although, I still hope it hurt.

I sip on my grape juice and lick the sweetness from my lips as I flick between channels, wanting the BBC, Sky News, and Channel 4's takes on it. The difference in their tone is subtle, with the slightest inclination of bias shifting. They'll all come around eventually. No one wants to stay on the losing side.

We have always been seen as the weaker sex, expected to roll over and take our punishments. There's strength in numbers and right now my cause is gaining volume. We are a pack, stronger than the sum of our parts.

Despite the late hour, I need to visit my piggies. Starving to death is far too boring. They'd suffer, sure, but I want to witness the pain, their last essences of hope dissolving into fear. I want to hear them plead with their pathetic squeals.

Dressed in black, I make for the station. Even in my flats, my feet hurt. I need to make sure this body gets more time to rest.

When I get to the station, I slump and curse. No trains tonight. They really might die without me there to watch. No, that can't happen.

I take my phone from my back, slouching more when I'm reminded of the late hour, then shake some motivation into my limbs. I can't let my piggies down. If that means summoning another enemy, then so be it.

I dial his number. He's a piggy, but I know he'll help. Dissatisfaction gnaws at me as I wonder if I turn all those on my list to the pigsty, it still won't be enough. The other women too, the artisans of freedom, their work is needed in addition to mine.

He answers the phone and I smile, sure that such an expression comes through in my voice. I compliment him, then lure him in. Make him think he's satisfied. It'll make ripping him apart all the better.

Chapter Thirty-One

Isobel

My levels are bonkers, swinging from one end of the scale to the other like some emotional boomerang. Between Layla stressing about work, Katarina taking delight in whatever crazy shit she's up to, and me worrying about the staff and my job and all the evil of the world, levels being bonkers seems about right. They're a constant seesaw.

In the office, the collective graph shows, as a whole, the staff are in the green. But those fluctuations that flicker throughout the day, they're me. I'm sure of it. I'm threatening Hugo's paradisiacal emotional void, and it's all I can do to stop him looking at my phone, then ramming pills down my throat. At least he's not turned up at the office today. My desk is tidy and work all caught up—I'll thank Layla later.

Mentally listing the small wins slightly quells my anxieties, according to my IMAtech, but then a rock of dread hits me square in the gut when I wonder if these are my levels or the result of some hack. I didn't want to take the pills before, but now I have an inkling what Katarina and Christopher Morely are up to, and I *really* don't want to take them.

That hard rock in my gut softens a bit when I think that maybe this means Katarina is merely messing around with the tech, not killing people. The missing and dead rich guys could be some other reason, some other vendetta.

Yeah, right.

The sight of my poor colleagues fitting and choking haunts me every day. The staff still take their supplements, to them, it's like nothing happened. Many didn't even notice. The ones who did are likely too worried about their job not to take them. Or too trusting. I mean, it's tech, right? What's not to trust?

The morning, at least, passes without consequence. Though cool beads of perspiration trickle down my spine constantly as I am on high alert. My afternoon off the other day saw no drama, so maybe the worst is over. Maybe everyone will be okay.

I meet Harry on my lunch break at a cafe. I'd prefer a glass of wine but indulging at lunchtime would be noted on IMAtech, and in any case, with my cortisol levels as they are, there's no point in me trying to get served in a bar again. Probably for the best. I can't let my guard down at the moment. Katarina may only be messing with the tech, but she's still using this body in ways I don't want. In ways that upset Harry.

I hug him when we meet, holding him longer than I usually would. Despite his injuries and surgeries, he's still so strong, so sturdy. With all the chaos around me, it's nice to have him to cling on to.

I order a decaf coffee and he orders the same, though as tired as I feel, he looks more so. I reach for his hand across the table. 'You okay?'

His thumb strokes mine. 'Yeah. Just work, family, the usual. You?'

'Same. Listen—' Our coffees arrive, and I sit back while the server places them on the table, waiting for her to leave before I lean in and speak again. His hands are on his lap now. Out of reach. 'I heard something. I'm fairly sure IMAtech is being hacked to mess up the meds. With that and them being swapped, I'm worried. Can you unswap them?'

He knits his brows. 'Hacked? Who would do that?'

'It's just a hunch, really. But I'm sure.'

'Lemmie guess. Kat.'

I give him a pained look, and he picks his coffee up to sip. The frothy milk leaves residue on his top lip that he licks off. 'I can't. They're all sent out now.'

I lean back in my chair and look up at the ceiling, releasing a long breath, closing my eyes a moment. 'We're screwed then. Swapped meds, IMAtech hacked.' I tilt my chin down and wipe my eye on my sleeve. 'We could do real harm here.'

Harry gives a half-hearted shrug. 'You wanted IMAtech stopping, right? Seems like in this instance, the crazy one has done you a favour.'

I wipe my other eye now. 'I don't want to hurt people.'

'All those staff are recovering fine, right? They felt a bit iffy for a while, that's all.'

His nonchalance riles me and I press my hands into the seat, pushing forward a little. 'A bit iffy! You didn't see them! It was horrible.'

He leans in and rubs my arm. 'It'll be all right, Isobel. You'll see.'

I swear his *there-there* voice is the same as his dad's and my shoulders shoot up. I wriggle away from his touch and shuffle back, holding my coffee now rather than his hands. No one cares. Literally no one cares.

I swallow the last of my coffee and leave the cafe, walking out into the crowded streets that blur into a fog of faces and traffic noise. Some way behind, Harry calls after me, but I don't turn around to check. I should go back to work, to check on the staff and get through the jobs list forever building on my computer, but I can't. How can I go back and risk seeing people ill from a stupid idea I had?

I blink away tears and load up my emails from my phone, then email HR to say I need another mental health break, explaining I need another afternoon off.

I arrive at my flat to see someone has taken the fox's food away. The poor thing will be hungry. When I get up to my flat, I put some more cheese and ham on a plate, then put it outside again. Someone has to look after the other creatures.

I take a packet of biscuits from the cupboard, a crappy lunch, but it'll do, then sit on the sofa, hugging my knees, my head hanging low and tears falling onto my legs.

No one cares. No one cares.

Chapter Thirty-Two

Layla

As soon as I wake, I relive the embarrassment of kissing her. I curl into a ball on the sofa and squish a cushion into my face as my cheeks burn, even my ears are hot. Why did I do that? It was too forward, totally inappropriate.

I need to get her out of my head. I'll never see her again, so it's an easy fix.

There was a second though, a fraction of a second really, where it was wonderful. My heart was in my throat as I breathed her in. It was Katarina, her bleeding into me that pushed me forward those extra few inches. Her impulses, her persuasion, her influence that pressed my lips into Amy's. For that fraction of a second, the rest of the world melted away.

But I'll never see her again.

I uncurl from the foetal position and remove the cushion from my face, brushing away the crumbs it left on my face. The sofa is covered again and needs a vacuum. Is that why Isobel isn't here and I am? She makes the mess and I clean it up. Same for both of them.

I grit my teeth and stand to fetch the vacuum.

I can't dwell on Amy and let that fraction of a second distract me. It doesn't matter how amazing that fraction of a second was, how my body turns to jelly whenever I think of it. I'm the one that needs to focus on the important things. Practical things.

I grab the vacuum and press the start button. Nothing happens. It wasn't plugged in and the battery is flat. As I look at the plug, it's clear why. Hair tongs are plugged in instead. I pull out their plug with enough force to rip the entire wall off and curse, then walk through to the bedroom where the tongs should be plugged in, cursing again.

The tongs weren't used in the bedroom because the mirror is grubby. Why not just clean the bloody mirror rather than use a different plug? I groan, then grab a cloth and start wiping.

Isobel doesn't even care if our levels are off, about how that will look to our employers, or of what that means to our career and our paycheck. She doesn't care about the state of the flat. She doesn't care about anything except for screwing Harry Baxter. Although, the messages popping up on our phone from him tell me they've had some barmy.

I'm sorry. Call me.

Don't be like this. You know I mean well.

I don't want to search her memory banks to see what that's about. With any luck, they'll be finished and I won't have to smell his aftershave again.

I know she had a meltdown at work the other day, and I can guess why. No doubt it was something to do with Katarina and the chaos she leaves in her wake. Whatever Katarina is up to isn't going to stop the rollout of the tech. Her methods are evil, but you can't fight fire with fire. And, as much as Isobel berates me for not taking action, she's borderline useless, too interested in making sure the staff are okay to actually get anything done.

With the mirror clean and the vacuum charging, I sit again among the crumbs and turn on the TV. The news is blasting out reports. Two more bodies have now turned up around London. Both wealthy company leaders, propagators for *#behave* and the Clarity Directive. Each having a scandal in their past that involved some poor woman who was silenced. Both filthy rich with their companies paying meagre wages to the lowest employees, if indeed, they haven't sacked them all in favour of AI. Though both are hailed as heroes for helping the stock market recover from the crash. Pioneers of the country, one report says. The backbone of the economy. The sort of people who make Katarina's eyes darken and her inner fire rage.

I hope it's not her. I really do.

I inspect my hands. My nails are clean, well, blood-free at least. They're now mucky from cleaning the mirror and covered in little dents from the crumbs. Biscuit, by the looks of it. I like biscuits, but I never have the appetite to eat. The other two do all the eating, leaving me with a full stomach and no chance for even that enjoyment.

I should allow myself some reckless pleasures, and my mind goes to Amy again. Then the news article expels her from my thoughts, the volume of the TV snapping me back to the here and now. There's a piece about the excitement around IMAtech, how wonderful it will be to know everyone's hormone data always, they say.

I pick up the cushion again and groan into it.

I turn the TV off, then open my laptop instead, scrolling through social media. It's filled with praise for the killings rather than praise for what the dead guys did. No doubt Katarina's endorphins will go through the roof when she sees the following these killings are generating: the praise, the awe, the camaraderie. It's like some cult of toxic feminism. There are anonymous posts promising to carry on the good work, hailing the original perpetrator as an icon. The comments on social media have grown exponentially. There's more love than hate for these actions. More and more hate than love for the victims.

We are the real victims!

This action is long overdue.

Fuck the Clarity Directive! Fuck the patriarchy!

I hear Katarina's voice say it all. It has to be her. I feel it in my bones, my muscles. There's an ache that is the aftermath of what these hands have done. She's started a movement I'm not sure can be quelled.

My IMAtech buzzes and it's then I notice the time. One-thirty Tuesday afternoon. I should definitely be at work now. The levels are far off what Hugo Baxter would like. Perhaps the supplements would be a good thing, might calm her down a bit, might keep any rage at bay and Katarina contained. Will the medications subdue one of us or all of us? Probably all of us since we have the same blood system, but since certain emotions seem to rouse us, it's hard to know if the effect will be disproportionate. Pills in our situation are a lot riskier. All we need to do is find some inner harmony, and we can't do that with Katarina causing havoc. No amount of fucking Harry Baxter can undo the stress levels from the aftermath of Katarina's antics.

Antics is a mild word for her actions.

I close the laptop and hold my head in my hands. My arms ache, my hands, and I can't turn my head as far one way as I can the other. Is this all from too much time at a desk, or is it from hauling corpses and whatever else she did?

I need to find a way to shut Katarina down before she can do any more damage. I'm not going to rot in some prison for the rest of my life just because she has anger issues. Isobel shouldn't have to either.

Katarina is part of our collective mind, the part that's all impulse and urges. I know why Isobel sectioned off part of that mind to me. She admired me for being organised, for being a good worker. It's hard to imagine what she took on Katarina's personality for. She knew her from school, that's all I know. If I can figure out why she's here, perhaps I can erase her.

All the scientific literature blames childhood trauma for our condition. There's something locked away in Isobel's mind safe, something so deep I can't access it. I need to trespass into her old memories, and to do that, I need to learn her techniques for locking them away.

I pick up my phone and call Doctor Cottrell.

Chapter Thirty-Three

Layla

Doctor Cottrell says he can see me straight away, but it's two hours door-to-door if I'm lucky, and I need to keep the other two away. Isobel is easy enough. She'll want some down time after whatever was said between her and Harry. Katarina, well, it takes a lot to keep her away. I need to stay calm, focussed, and repress any anger.

I grab my coat, then walk to the train station slowly, keeping my heart rate steady, telling myself it's just a normal trip, nothing that should ring any mental alarm bells.

By some miracle, that makes me think this is the universe telling me this is meant to be. There's a train, on schedule, departing in ten minutes. I order my ticket at the machine rather than speak to a cashier, then opt to stand in the vestibule rather than bother looking for a seat. All such actions create a predictable environment, allowing my emotions to flatline and not create any sort of spike. For the entire journey I stare out of the window, the graffiti-painted concrete whizzing past, giving way to suburbia and countryside.

The salty air and sound of seagulls greet me when I alight. The late afternoon sun is still warm, although mercifully cooler than the stagnant London smog. I continue at a slow pace to Doctor Cottrell's, crossing the street to avoid gangs of youths and taking my time at traffic lights. I know the way there. Isobel didn't think to hide that memory. But what goes on in that room is a mystery I'm about to unlock.

I arrive at the doctor's sweat and adrenalin free. When I knock, I grin, my shoulders back and chest inflating. So far, I've outsmarted them. So far, my plan is working.

Doctor Cottrell opens the door and smiles in such a way it dwarfs my smugness. His face is plastered with notes of aged vanity. Such self-appreciation is hard to justify from a man so unkempt, who looks like he hasn't been outside since adolescence and last washed his clothes at about the same time. The nicotine stench is intense, the air hazy with smoke. I guess a last-minute appointment didn't give him much time to aerate the place, and I make an effort not to show my distaste.

'Take a seat, Isobel,' he says as I walk into his office. 'I was surprised to hear from you so soon. Are you having any troubling moments? Any flashbacks?'

'No, no. Not at all.'

'Is there is a new memory you'd like to lock away to help you move on?'

I swallow, then take a moment to find my words, cursing myself for once again being so unprepared. 'No. no. Well, yes. Nothing major. Just a work thing.'

'Very well. Lie back and relax.'

I need to stay in control, but I also need to learn how to traverse our mind space, to reveal what Isobel has shut away. I lie back on the sofa and close my eyes, but relaxing is a long way off.

Doctor Cottrell's seat groans from the edge of the office, followed by a creaking of knees and a pen scratching on paper. He talks me through some breathing exercises for a few minutes, then says, 'Are you in your old bedroom?'

It takes me a while to think what he means. I am obviously not in my bedroom.

'Your safe space, remember?'

The penny drops, pink carpet and dusty shelving easily coming to my mind. 'Yes.'

He coughs, and the sound of him swallowing water is nauseating. I try to block it out, to stay in that bedroom, in Isobel's safe space.

'And there,' he continues, 'the safe should be there, all locked up as you left it.'

It's like eavesdropping, prying on a friend, or sneaking a peek at Christmas presents hidden in the back of the cupboard. My skin tingles as a swimming feeling loiters in my stomach. But it's there. The safe. Isobel's safe. I can picture it.

'You remember how to open the safe, Isobel?'

I do. Instinctively, this mind knows. I'm trespassing on her turf, and it's like there are signposts nudging me the right way, showing how to cross the boundary from my neurons to hers.

On the shelf, the only non-dusty thing is a key. I pick it up. The coolness of it, the weight of it in my hand is all so real. So familiar.

'Now,' he says, 'in your hand, do you have the memory you want to put in there?'

I look down at my free hand. It's empty. There's nothing going in the safe today. Locking a memory isn't what I'm here for. Opening the door to Isobel's memories is what I need to do. I want to see inside. 'Yes,' I say, and hope my lie doesn't show in a blush.

'When you're ready, open the safe and throw it in. Remember to shut that door quickly and keep all those bad memories inside.'

I take a deep breath, insert the key, then turn it. The safe has a heavy door requiring a tug, and my muscles tighten with strain.

In my mind, the safe grows, as big as me, or I shrink. Either way, the giant door is open and I walk through, deep in Isobel's mind space now where baubles of memories hang like decorations, bobbing around as I walk past, jingling like the crystals of the chandelier in that fancy hotel. There's an entire corridor of them, long and snaking back through time. The farther I walk, the corridor gets darker and the glow from the memories dimmer. I search earlier and earlier, each new step like flicking through the pages of Isobel's diary. Emotion leaks from the memories and it takes so much concentration not to absorb it, to witness the emotion from a distance instead of succumbing. There's so much pain she's shut away, so many anxieties.

I don't have time to look through everything, but somewhere ahead is a mixture of feelings: dread, sadness, insecurity, anger, and hatred. Goosebumps prick all over my skin as the safe grows colder. Somewhere deeper inside, there's a red glow seeping from the memories, and I make a beeline for those ones.

One glows brighter, dangles lower, this mind showing me exactly what I seek.

I reach up and take it, plucking an apple from a forbidden tree. Even in my imagination my hand shakes, so I take some steadying breaths, slowly exhaling, then I look inside.

I'm at school with Isobel, squinting in the sun's glare. We stand in the playground, alone. Isobel picks at a plant next to her, rolling the leaves in her hands, though she steals glances off to her right. Across the tarmac is Katarina, the real Katarina from her childhood, not the part she's conjured up. I can sense Isobel's emotions as if they are my own, a heavy stomach as she longs to be in whatever conversation Katarina's having, all the while loneliness makes her eyes sting. Isobel picks at the leaves of the plant, dropping them into a gust and they flitter away bit by bit.

Katarina's laugh carries across the playground, loud and brash, a squeal, she has her arm around another girl, with more friends surrounding her behind. Her school uniform is unbuttoned at the front and hitched up at the waist, revealing legs that go on forever.

I note the intricacies of Katarina's personality Isobel adopted as her own. The confidence, the hair flick, the never-ending grin.

When I watch Katarina, the insecurities melt into awe, and the distance between us stretches out farther. She's a world away, another life away. Out of reach.

Katarina has no such gripes. She's admired, popular, telling the boys to fuck off. Living life on her terms.

The memory blurs into the next, the final memory Isobel has of Katarina.

I watch the sunset, feel Isobel's excitement, then her isolation, the coldness that envelops her as day gives way to night. I blink away tears, my chest caving in and the memory spins around me in a dizzy mess. I want to scream at it, to shout no! But of course, I'm only observing, like a movie when your insides twist and muscles tense as if you can make the actors run away, your body telling you to change things, the image fooling you into thinking you have control.

The last time Isobel ever saw Katarina turns my bones to ice. I shut my eyes at the end and force myself awake.

I'm on the sofa in Doctor Cottrell's office, staring up at the nicotine-stained wood-chip ceiling. My throat is dry, and as much as I want to, I'm unable to unsee that memory.

I know now why Isobel took Katarina's personality. And I know I'll never be able to make her go away.

Chapter Thirty-Four

Isobel

I'm on my dad's sofa, suffocating in the fusty stench of his house, biscuit crumbs littering my front. There's a void in my mind, my journey here a black hole. The last thing I remember is being in my own flat, leaving some food out for the foxes. I'd just left Harry at the café and didn't go back to work.

Then, nothing.

I try, squeezing my eyes shut and rubbing my forehead as a headache threatens to split my skull in half. Still, nothing.

'You seem off, kiddo,' Dad says, taking his eyes off the game show on TV for a moment.

I wipe my eye on my sleeve. My clothes smell like cigarettes.

'It went okay—at Doctor Cottrell's?' he asks.

I went to my therapist? That makes sense after my episode at work. It also explains the cigarette smell. 'Erm, I think so.' I don't remember being in his office at all. My stomach churns. I could kid myself and say it's the smoke smell or the stuffy air at my dad's that's hitting me with fresh waves of nausea, but the pressure on my chest won't let me dismiss my anxieties so easily. My amnesia can be down to two reasons. Either, I locked away the memory of being there, which is wishful thinking but makes no sense. Or, the other, more worrying reason, the one that makes my blood freeze, I didn't go. One of the other two did.

Despite the stuffy air, I shiver. I bring my knees to my chest and grip, as if I fear being ripped in two.

Or three.

On the mantle is a picture of my mother, her portrait eye-balling me as if from beyond the grave, judging me, picking apart my flaws and behaviours, like she knows more about me than I do. My brother's picture is next to hers, set in a gold frame. She did that when she was alive. I remember her polishing the glass, smiling at his prideful face and selecting the best place to showcase him. My picture is farther along, in a cheap wooden frame, the glass missing, the picture faded.

'You'll be fine, dear,' Dad says, looking at the TV again now. 'Lock all those bad memories away and you'll be right as rain. Back to work in no time.'

I mumble in agreement. 'I know, I know. Don't anger the big man.'

His arching back straightens a little, and he looks my way. 'You remember that?'

'Sure. It's what you always say.'

He turns his head back to the TV. 'How strange to remember that.' He reaches for his bottle of juice and takes a sip. Swallowing is an effort for him and he takes his time. His hand has a tremor, and a splash traces the side of the glass. 'Just that saying of mine? That's all you remember?'

'You have loads of sayings, Dad. Keep your head down, the bad times will be over soon, be your good girl.'

He places the glass down, spilling even more, then coughs a little, wiping a little spit on a tissue. 'Well, let's see that we make another appointment with Doctor Cottrell. Just to make sure you're all okay. So you can move on.'

I let the game show take away the need for conversation. It's background noise, drowning out the voices in my head. Katarina's voice is rattling around in my mind, telling me to wake up. It's breathy, seductive, heating my ear, but I can't listen. I try to block her and shut her out of my mind. This is meant to be my safe space, away from those two, where it's just me.

'Scott may pop 'round later,' Dad says. 'He'd like to see you.'

My bedroom. That's my real safe space. There I'll be rid of her. I yawn and stretch out my arms. 'I think actually, Dad, I might just go to bed.'

He nods and I give him a peck on the cheek, then head upstairs. In my real bedroom, there's no mind safe on the shelf. Just old books and nicknacks, things I should get around to clearing out or at least cleaning, but never have the time for when I'm here. I sit on my bed and look at my phone. It's filled with messages from Harry, asking if I'm all right, where I am, to call him. I'm still so mad at him, but without him, I'm back to being lonely.

I can't think about him right now. I turn my phone off, then look up and jolt, pressing my back into the wall until the windowsill digs in.

She's standing there, here, in my safe space.

'You shouldn't be here,' I say. 'This is my space. My safe space.' But I know that if she's here, it's because I want her here.

Katarina's face wears a smirk. Her arms are folded like she's a club bouncer. 'Some snooping has been going on.'

I look at the door, instinct telling me to check no one is listening before I talk to myself. But of course, there's no one there. Dad can't hear me from downstairs. She must have figured out I met with Christopher Morely. Heat wells up from my chest to my face, and I swallow in my parched mouth. 'What do you mean?'

'Don't play dumb. Layla. She's been sticking her goody-two-shoes nose in where it doesn't belong. In your mind space.'

My tension dissolves slightly and I exhale. 'Well. . . I. . .'

She lifts one eyebrow and tilts her chin down. It's a pose that could be either stern or seductive, and as my breath catches, it's the latter option that excites me, sending bolts of electricity coursing through me.

'She's been messing around in your mind space. You need to get rid of her,' she says. 'She's not looking out for you. She's trying to destroy you.'

Katarina steps closer to me now, biting her bottom lip. My heart races. I smell that sweet musk of body spray from when we were at school, when I yearned for friendship but would have loved so much more. Those lips look inviting, and I could get lost in her eyes. I so wanted to be her friend years ago. The real Katarina. She's so much like her, this one that shares my body. I reach out and touch her cheek. She's hot, soft, alive.

'Everything I do is to make things better for you, us, all women,' she says, and angles her face so my hands now brush her lips.

I pant as she licks my thumb. 'I know.'

'And Layla, she's only out for herself, work, to brown nose those corporate shits. You know that.'

I sit straighter, breathing her in deeper. 'I do.' It doesn't matter I know she isn't real, that this is all my imagination, our condition, whatever. She's as real as anything, hyperreal, like gravity.

'So, we need to stop her from sticking her nose in.'

I reach my other arm out and caress her midriff. The rough lace of her top in contrast to the softness of her skin underneath. 'Of course. We do.' I pull her in close and nuzzle into her waist.

'You'll stop her then? It can be you and me, Isobel, if you learn to stop her.'

I'm lost with her, entangled, impossible to tell who is who. I've been here before with Katarina, overcome with desire, my mind adrift in its own impulses. She draws me to her, hurtling, absolutely inescapable.

'Whatever you want, Katarina.' I say. 'I'll do whatever you want.'

Chapter Thirty-Five

Isobel

After my night with Katarina, I know she's right. I need to embrace her boldness. She seems reckless, but she's a meticulous planner. Layla, well, she wants Katarina gone as she disapproves, but she always disapproves. Fuck knows what she dredged up at the doctor's, but it doesn't matter. She pretends to be the good one, the one with the moral compass, but she's a trespassing bitch.

I get the train from Portsmouth to London the next day, renewed with feistiness, though still with some deep-rooted lethargy. Such tension over the last couple of months doesn't just disappear.

There's a return train ticket in my purse. I know exactly where it's stored, even though it was Layla who put it there. She's so predictable. So mundane.

But Katarina. . .just mouthing her name brings back memories of last night. Together, the two of us, with our heat we can fight fire with fire. I am in control, but that doesn't mean I can't enjoy Katarina's influence. Katarina gets what she wants and if

I mesh her tactics with mine, we can really solve the IMAtech issue. More than that, the patriarchy.

I take my seat on the train, and rest my forehead against the window, my breath fogging the glass. In the mist, I trace the outline of my lips. Her lips.

I'm bored of Layla. To be honest, I can't believe I was ever in love with her. This Layla is so different from the real Layla. If she was real and alive, I would welcome her company, but this Layla sharing my headspace is a waste of time. I wish I could get rid of a personality as easily as conjure one. Although she is useful to keep around for work, to live out the dullness I can't be bothered with.

I scroll through my phone. Some other dead guy has been found, all cut up, some rich prick. What's the tally now? Oh, who cares? It's not enough since the companies are still afloat, since there's no sign of the Clarity Directive being repealed. Since IMAtech's launch is still full steam ahead.

Despite the sombre tone of the article, people are hailing the death, saying good riddance, and my chest swells. I don't know if Katarina did that, I'm sure she has killed, but this many seems unlikely. The good news is people are taking action. It's creating a dialogue about how screwed up everything is and how change is needed. That man was part of the problem, and we are the solution. That's what Katarina would say, and she's right. Her logic feeds my thoughts, her motivation fuelling me.

My lips recoil at the dead guy's photo, at his smile that oozes arrogance and his eyes that have definitely looked where they shouldn't. So typical. A pervert. These men, their money can't save them. As I read the comments, my skin prickles with electricity, linking me to other women who feel the same. There's too many of us, women, trampled and silenced for years and now we've had enough.

Katarina's voice licks at my ears, and a flush of warmth filters through me.

A weapon doesn't fire itself. Someone makes it fire. That's all I am, Isobel. A weapon. Those men, their arrogance makes me fire.

I take a bottle of water from my bag and sip, the coolness quelling some of my heat. Niggling fear returns and my stomach drops as I wring my hands out on my lap. I can't convince myself that her illicit meetings with Christopher Morely are all she's been up to. I sink into the chair, looking from one side to the other, sure someone's going to know it's me, this body, that's guilty. My skin itches everywhere. I scratch and fidget and squirm in skin that doesn't fit right.

We have to stop them all, she whispers. *You know we have to put an end to them.*

I thump my forehead a couple of times and nod. I know things need to be better. I know Katarina's doing what she thinks is right. She appears in front of me, just a glimmer for a few seconds, and I sit straighter, smiling back at her. 'I know,' I whisper into nothing. 'I know you only want what's right.'

***

I meet Harry in the morning instead of going straight to work. I need a release and sod work. They won't sack me, and I'm off sick anyway. I can take another morning off.

We fuck at my place, as unclean and messy as it is. We get to it before any conversation, like the world is about to end. It's fast and frantic and exactly what I need.

We lie catching our breaths afterwards and I roll onto my side, satisfied but wondering if he'll be up for another go in a minute.

He looks at me with narrowed eyes. 'I know it's you, but there's a blur today, like she's affecting you.'

'You mean I fuck like her.'

'Sometimes.'

I tut and start to dress, the desire for round two melting away rapidly as his tone is more nagging than teasing.

'It's you I want, Isobel. I'm not up for a threesome.'

I think about her when we fuck sometimes. Can he tell? I wonder as I take my trouser suit out of my wardrobe, my hand brushing over some of Katarina's clothes. My skin tingles as I touch the lace.

'And that means she shouldn't be fucking anyone else too, right?' he says in such an authoritative manner my back stiffens.

Does that include me? I wonder and wet my lip. I don't answer. Harry doesn't need to know about her antics with Christopher Morely, assuming it's more than just dinners and work trouble.

'I got questioned,' he says, and I turn to him. His face is twisted with emotions, I can't tell if he's scared, angry, or pleased.

His scars on one side make it hard to read him. The other side, smooth and perfect, isn't enough to tell. 'Since some of the missing men were on their way to mine for my IMAtech meeting. They searched my Surrey house, went through the CCTV.'

'And found nothing, I assume.'

'Right. But still.'

'And they're suspecting women with a vendetta. You don't fit the bill.'

He shuffles to the edge of the bed and strokes the back of my leg as I button up my top. 'I know I'm innocent. That's not the point. If they see you, or who they think is you, fucking some guy who then ends up dead, you'll be a suspect. I'm only worried about you.'

'And the fact that we're fucking makes them also suspect you.'

He takes his hand away and leans back. 'She just needs to be more careful.'

My jaw tightens, and I fold my arms. 'You don't care if she's hurting people?'

'All the guys that are dead and missing are arseholes, the lot of them.'

'You were going to talk them out of IMAtech.'

'Yeah, but there was a fat chance of it working. With a few of them out of the picture, we might as well see it as an opportunity. It levels the playing field a bit, helps out the little guys.'

I scoff. 'Little guys?'

'Yeah. Like me.'

My mouth hangs open a moment. 'You think of yourself as one of the little guys?'

'Sure. I don't run some massive company. All those guys have more money than me. Maybe not as much as my parents.'

I stand frozen, shock making me rigid, then I quickly grab the rest of my clothes and put them on, grasping the fabric with clenched fists and dragging them on so forcefully I almost rip the trousers.

'Oh, come on, Isobel. You must see things from my perspective. It's tough out there for guys like me. It was hard enough before, but now I look like this and it's even tougher. You get all the sympathy for your scars and what do I get? Nothing.'

I cover my face with my hands and my stomach tenses as I fight my need to scream.

'All I'm saying is, if all these men going missing causes a market crash, a few companies going under might not be a bad thing for WIT. And I'll be there to pick up the pieces. It's probably going to be a cyclical thing from now on. Women caused the last crash and they're doing it again. It's the world we live in. It's good to be prepared and ready to take advantage.'

I pull my hands down a bit and glare at him. 'You don't seriously believe that?'

'What? That women and quotas caused the crash? Sure I do. Peter did.'

I sit back on the bed, the farthest edge from Harry, keeping my back to him, my hands balled into fists at my sides. He's never stopped idolising that prick of a man, Peter Ward. Good riddance to Katarina killing him. He believed the market crash was caused by women in top jobs and the quotas to put them there. He was one of the original supporters of the Clarity Directive. I hope he's rotting in hell.

Harry takes a baggie out of his wallet, then taps some white powder onto his hand and sniffs it. I watch, recoiling my nose and turning away.

'It helps, okay?' he says. 'This is all so shit. I'm stressed like mad.'

'Your IMAtech—'

'Fuck that.' He sniffs another bump. 'IMAtech is for the staff. Mine isn't linked to the WIT database. My parents just want to keep an eye on me. IMAtech is not for the likes of me.'

I grit my teeth and sit still as he dresses, tucking in his shirt that costs as much as a month's rent, not giving a shit what his parents see, immune to the oppression of power when he is so rich, so male.

'The mixed-up pills should be hitting the workplace soon,' he says. 'So IMAtech won't matter much anyway. We fixed it. See? All sorted.'

'Right.' I still don't turn to face him.

'You just need to make sure she's more careful.' His arms wrap around me now, his head burrowing into my shoulder. 'I'm not sharing this body, Isobel. You're mine. Just you. See a shrink, take a pill, whatever it takes.'

In the corner of the room, Katarina's here again, folded arms, one side of her mouth curled up into a smirk. Her voice resounds in my head, louder than the noises from Harry kissing me, louder than his groans when I reach down and feel his renewed energy.

'Privilege is privilege,' Katarina says as she watches us. 'He's the same as all the rest.'

Chapter Thirty-Six

Katarina

I haven't visited the barn in a while since Isobel needed to go to her dad's. That put me behind schedule. Oh, how I've missed them! I walk, almost breaking into a run, across the field to the old barn, my body buzzing with excitement. The smell hits me instantly, though I don't cover my nose. I smile instead. It's the stench of my accomplishment. Nasty piggies in their sty make it smell like rot and shit.

There's one still lying where I left him, all nicely wrapped in plastic, like a little cocoon that no butterfly will emerge from. If Isobel or Layla could see this, they'd be delighted with how tidy I am. Just because I'm messy at home doesn't mean I'm messy at work. I'm the tidiest thing in this sty.

The last three are still strung up by their wrists, just their bare toes touching the floor. One still has some colour in his cheeks. That's a shame. I'll have to see what I can do about that. Another is ashen grey and stiff, his belly swollen like he's been dead a while. Dammit. I missed it. I so wanted to see his last moments of despair. There's shit all down his legs, the nasty, filthy piggy.

The last one, well, he's alive. Just. He's floppy all over, his shoulders dislocated and purple and black with bruising. I grin. I bet that hurts. His eyelids half open when I take his blindfold off, though his eyeballs roll back in protest. I squirt some dissolved stimulant into his mouth when I remove his gag. He tries to cough it up, but with a dose that strong, some will go in. When he's stopped spluttering like he's drowning, I offer him some water, which he gulps back like a greedy beast.

I want more fight than this. I didn't mean for them to get so weak. Preying on the weak is the coward's way. It's what pervert men do and their big companies. They dominate and destroy everything weaker than them.

I am not so evil. I only want to abolish what is strong.

I need better piggies. Fatter piggies.

The one most alive turns his head to face me, trying to rub his blindfold off on his arm. He won't get far with that. The masking tape keeps them in place nicely, but if he so wants to see, I should allow it. I take his gag off first and give him a stimulant dose as well, before taking off his blindfold and watching as his eyes adapt. It takes a while before he's coherent, before his eyes really focus on the horror.

'Good evening.'

He mumbles something I can't make out, and I squirt some cold water over his face. His body convulses with the chill. It's a cool evening, a gust fingering its way through the barn from the gaps in the wooden walls, and his nipples shrivel up like raisins, his balls too. I laugh at the sight of them.

'I said good evening. Where's your manners?'

'Who. . .who are you? What the fuck is this? Don't you know who I am? I'll sue you for everything you're worth.'

I'm close enough to bite his nose off if I wanted. It's tempting. 'I know exactly who you are. And luckily for me, I'm not worth anything.'

He tries to see around me and tugs on his ropes, lifting his feet up to pull even more. I watch and chuckle. They never learn, these stupid piggies. 'Oh,' he says as he tries to wriggle free. 'You're just some crazy tart with petty jealousy.'

His voice rasps, and I can tell from the contractions in his stomach he's straining to project it. Forcing his voice louder in his dehydrated throat, trying to sound all big and important. I smile, glancing down at his dick dangling between his legs. A tiny thing, so small even his shrivelled balls hang lower.

'Jealous? Me? Of you, with. . .that?' I laugh so hard my tummy cramps.

'So you're after money then. All right, crazy bitch, name your—'

The cold touch of my knife to his ballsack renders him speechless besides a little mouse-like yelp. It's funny, the amount of pleasure I can take from the smallest noise.

'Price? Is that what you were going to say?' I run the blade up his torso, allowing the serrated edge to graze. 'Thing is, money means nothing to me. Fairness, equality, women's rights, reducing the wealth gap, the abolition of the patriarchy, that's my price.'

'Fuck you, crazy bitch.' He attempts to spit, but it's just air. 'I'd rather be dead.'

I shrug. 'Okay.'

I lift the handle of the knife and trace the tip higher, his eyes so wide they might pop out as he looks down at it, watching as I jam it into his throat. It makes a neat hole as I push it all the way through that erupts with a geyser of blood. I keep my eyes on his, but they stay down. His last view is of the gushing claret coating his torso.

There's a fleeting moment of regret across his face, the way his mouth hangs open, the redness in his eyes. But if I'm being honest, the regret is more mine than his, and I take the knife back and exhale a heavy sigh. I didn't mean to hit an artery. As the blood continues to pour down his body, I pinch the bridge of my nose and stare down at his blood-soaked feet. The wound was too quick. I should have plunged it into his gut, from the back, maybe. I was hasty, not savouring the moment enough.

It's fine, I reassure myself. I have one piggy left. He's sobbing, snotty and dribbly, and I look at him, his face as pale as the dead ones. Fear has drained him of any colour. I squirt some more stimulant in his mouth, then clamp his lips together with my hand to make sure he takes it all in. He coughs as he swallows, and it makes me think drowning him slowly might be a fun way to end his life. But then I look at the blood and think, a death without blood would be such a shame.

I'll cut him slower, bit by bit, when his time comes. I'll enjoy it for longer this time, but until then he needs to stay awake to see the dead piggies, to observe what awaits him.

One more piggy isn't enough. My work is not yet complete.

I need more.

I look at the dead piggies and salivate. I know exactly which one I want next.

Chapter Thirty-Seven

Isobel

I walk into the office, then freeze on the spot as I take in the scene. I'm barely through the entrance to WIT but it's clear that the meds seem to have been cranked up, as any personality has been syphoned out. No one talks at all, no one smiles, not even those fake smiles. They don't even look sad. They're all zombies with the same deadpan face as Malorie Baxter.

I sit at my desk and glance over my shoulder for a moment before facing my computer again. It's too hard for me to look at my colleagues. When I try, my eyes sting and my chin dips low, my hair falling forward to shield my view. Leaning on my elbows, I rest my forehead in my hands, pressing against my head, as if that will squeeze all the badness away. I should have thought of them before I took time off. They're all suffering and I've been too absorbed in my personal dramas. I'm supposed to be there for them.

The ones who were ill at work are back, looking as well as zombies can. I ask them how they are as they take their seats and I get a 'Fine now. Thank you' response, lacking any sincerity or intonation. I suppose that's the best I could have hoped for. When the dispensary comes around, I give him a look, and he places the pills in front of them according to their IMAtech.

This is madness. They take their pills without hesitation, still trusting that damned bit of tech.

But then, like Harry said, they're all fine now.

Greasy Guy and Hugo are up in the glass office most of the morning. At least Hugo hasn't asked for me. The longer I can avoid him, the better.

On my way in this morning, I picked up some chocolates and cupcakes, handing them out now, expecting to at least get a thanks or a smile, but no one reacts. There's no animosity towards me. There's simply nothing at all. It's a slow task, the morning stretching on forever as I drag myself from desk to desk. By the time I am handing out the last chocolate, I'm wiping my eyes with a tissue.

I attempt some conversation, to drum up some morale, to have a bit of a gossip like we used to once. A wasp comes into the office and no one even blinks.

Ellen has a snotty nose and she just lets it run, yellowy sludge pooling across her top lip that she doesn't even wipe, she doesn't allow her hands even that much of a break. I grab a tissue and wipe it for her, in the way that a mother would a child as she continues to type. She's such a pretty thing. She has a lovely smile usually. Now her mouth is a straight line, her eyes fixated only on her screen.

Hugo checks my levels just before lunch, clicking his fingers to get the dispensary assistant to deliver pills to my desk. His hand is on my waist as he says, 'I'm only looking out for you, Isobel. I know what's best for you.'

He's still too familiar, too close, his hands making contact where they shouldn't. I swear, he's being like that just to try to make my stress hormones worse. Katarina never showed me what happened, and I don't want to know because the memory doesn't matter. What matters is the aftermath, and that's making me want to stab him with a hot poker.

The pills are placed on my desk and Hugo stands there, watching me, eyebrows raised in expectation. I step past him and sit, loading my computer up, mustering every ounce of patience I have. My levels aren't that bad, or they weren't until I got to work. If they were any worse, I think he may have pinned me down. I ignore the pills, and him, like he's Katarina or Layla, and I can steady my emotions and create a wall between us.

He does go away eventually. I suppose he has other work to do besides lording over me. His phone rings and my heavy sluggishness changes to weightless joy when he speaks. There's a quiver of worry in his voice. Fear, I'm sure. With the news still reporting on lost CEOs and the bodies, there's anxiety in wealthy men across the city.

'Yes, Charles, simply awful,' he says, and I rock back on my chair to listen. 'They'll catch whoever is doing this. I made a donation to the police last year. They're on our side. . . Spoken with the MP? Good on you. . . Yes. . .a donation should help. .

. Really? Well, you're welcome to follow me around and make use of my security if they're all booked up!' He laughs at his own words. 'Ah, yes. Ed has some contacts in Eastern Europe. Some proper thugs there. Brutes. Probably cheaper too. You know, that's not a bad call. . .'

The dark shadow of security at the glass doors pace the entrance constantly, batons and tasers hanging from their belts, earpieces worn, their eyes scanning every passerby with suspicion. The beefed-up security are meant to protect Hugo, though he doesn't know from whom. He has no idea he just touched the waist of the body responsible. Or at least partly responsible. I bite the inside of my cheek to try to hide my smile as his terror delights me. As I get to work on my computer. My usually hunched shoulders roll back, my lungs inflate, and I sit a little taller.

When Hugo is occupied elsewhere, I look up his social media and find old posts have been deleted, no evidence of his trail of support for the trending *#behave* when that was big a couple of years back. There's no mention of his support for the Clarity Directive. His social media profiles reek of cowardly ambivalence.

And he's following the actions of many other men across the country. Erasing their trail, denying their part in the campaign.

The internet is alive with support to shame them all, to maintain a trail of their misogyny. All the CEOs and wealthy men who campaigned for the Clarity Directive. However much they delete their old posts, there are ones they've forgotten, newspaper articles and screenshots. Opinions live forever these days. The past is ever-present.

Hugo looks over his shoulder often, jumping at the slightest noise. When he walks past, I scratch my chair along the floor just to see him flinch, then pretend to blow my nose to muffle my laughter.

My insides fizz, and I smirk. *Let him squirm.*

However much joy I take in Hugo Baxter's discomfort, it's only to cover up my own. My mental ping-pong ricochets from one thought to the next. Pride and delight in the wealthy mens' agony, then bouncing back to fear for myself and shame at how evil it is.

My headache returns, ripping my skull in half. It spreads to my neck and shoulders, as if she's bursting to get out of me.

Would she do that? Would Katarina take control and assign me to limbo forever? I'm not sure she could even do that, but this fresh dread comes and brings with it searing hot pain and nausea. All this time I've been trying to keep them both on side, refusing to shut one away forever as I couldn't do that to them, to us. It never occurred to me they might be planning the opposite. I'm the primary. I'm meant to be in charge. But I'm not even sure if that's relevant.

My blood runs cold as I wonder, if I don't appease Katarina in some way, could she oust me?

I pace, alone, marching the length of the office floor several times, fidgeting and uncomfortable however I sit or stand. Despite the harshness of the air con, I sweat through my blouse by the end of the day after reading news alert upon news alert so many times.

IMAtech on the news.

Dead men on the news.

Missing men on the news.

The staff all suffering.

I'm drowning.

But then, when I gasp for air, there's the odd bubble of lucid glee. I recall the hint of fear in Hugo, the support from women everywhere. There's an army of women coming for these men.

This could be the end. This could be real change.

No! I thump my forehead when my mind wanders to such thoughts. I can't think like that. Katarina is seductive in so many ways. She rams her views into my brain, her wickedness intoxicating. But it's wrong. I have to do things the right way.

With all the talk on the news about the men being targeted, the press need to know why, and how bad things are at WIT. My lame plan might actually generate some traction. I film work, secretly, then, when I've collected enough evidence, I'll post on social media about the state of workers.

Even the thought of that breaks me out in more sweat. Maybe it's a hormonal thing, women's problems. I should check my levels. . . *No!* That's what Layla wants. My levels don't matter. I am me and I have a right to my emotions.

I rub my temples, picture my room at my dad's, my safe space, trying to summon some contentment, a few breaths, to be his good girl.

Chapter Thirty-Eight

Isobel

Harry meets me after work, around the corner away from the office. The paparazzi don't bother with him these days since he's not the socialite pinup boy he used to be, but his parents still don't know about us, and we'd both prefer it stays that way.

It was his idea to meet, to spend time with me or to keep an eye on me—this body—I'm not sure. Maybe to repair the cracks that came between us yesterday. I watch his face for signs he's high, dilated pupils, chewing his cheek, but he appears sober. I can write off what he said to the drugs. Coke makes everyone egotistical, and Katarina stressing him makes him do coke. It's not his fault.

As we walk hand-in-hand on the way to my place, I'm at least glad of the company. I squeeze his hand tight, just wanting to feel something real. The difference between stroking his skin and Katarina's is subtle, a tingle, an unevenness to the temperature. When I squeeze his harder, I feel resistance.

Harry is silent as he walks beside me a while. The first time I brought him back to my flat, I was worried he'd turn his nose up. His bathroom is bigger than my entire apartment. But he didn't care. A bed is a bed, so he said.

We arrive outside my building, and I stop to find my key. It's buried in the bottom of my bag somewhere, underneath piles of chaos and the detritus of three people. Just as I find it, there's a thud, and a sparrow falls at my feet. He'd hit a window, the poor thing. He lays stunned, rolling around. In my surprise, I take a second to register, but Harry's reaction is quicker.

I gasp. My hands go to my mouth when his shoe cracks all the bones in the little guy's body. The squelching and snapping noises turn my stomach. My tear-smudged vision sees Harry's face, his top lip recoiling.

'Yuck,' he says. 'That's ruined this shoe.'

My hands fall to my side, my jaw hanging open as I gaze at the poor thing. 'Why the hell did you do that?'

He shrugs. 'Putting him out of his misery. Don't be sad. Come here.' He pulls me in for a hug. 'I assume you don't have a concierge? I'm sure a fox or something will clean up. You're so kind. Don't worry. It's the circle of life.'

The side of my head is squashed into his chest, his strong arms enveloping me, my tears soaking through his shirt.

'It's just a bird.' His grasp on me tightens for a moment. 'Come on. I know how to cheer you up.' He takes my hand, then leads me upstairs.

***

A little snore tells me he's still asleep. In the half light of the room, the outline of his features carve a line between light and shadow. His scars form craters and crevices, blotchy red and pale skin like bad render. I stroke the roughness. He snores a little more, and I snatch my hand back, but he doesn't wake. He rolls over instead, taking up more than his share of the bed, and I shuffle over.

I tried to talk to Layla and Katarina earlier at work. I crouched in the toilet cubicle and begged them to come, to hear my plan and help me through the day. I needed a friend, but neither would talk to me. They feel less like friends now and more like competitors. This body is a vase, three wilting flowers competing for light.

Harry is here when I need him. To be with me. Or maybe it's to keep an eye on Katarina. When we fucked, I was meek, quiet, sedate, proving it's me.

I am not like her.

I am not like her.

I am not like her.

He shifts over a little more, his body arching over, and I curl into a ball to fit next to him. A protective position, perhaps. Or selfish, owning it, to make me feel small?

Maybe Layla and Katarina are right. He is one of them.

But I have no one else.

Chapter Thirty-Nine

Layla

I know he's next to me before I open my eyes. The dip in the mattress, the snore, the scent of him. A male's presence is so much more intrusive than a woman's. Manspreading isn't just with their limbs, it isn't just a physical space. They invade everything.

I slide out from between the sheets, pull on my dressing gown, then tiptoe to the kitchen. Why did Isobel bring him back here? It would be much easier if I were at his place. I'd be confused for a minute when I first woke, but I could leave then. That's a much simpler task than getting him to go. What if he gets up and hugs me or kisses me? My skin crawls just thinking about it. That one night we spent together, I was so drunk, any memory of it is patchy and foggy, but it's enough. More than enough. I don't ever want those hands on me again.

After I put some coffee on, I open up the laptop, wondering how behind Isobel must be at work. I know she wanted to talk earlier, but I'm not ready to face her yet. Not after what I saw in her memories. She'll surely know and want to argue with me.

I'll make it up to her today and help at work. I can make her see I'm the useful one, for more than just tidying the flat.

I pull my dressing gown across tighter, stroking the soft, towelling material, and I scrunch my feet over the floor. The physicality of being in control is something I never appreciated once, before I knew. Now, I relish in it. It's funny what you take for granted. The simple feeling of touch. Isobel takes my friendship for granted. She appreciates none of what I do, no matter how hard I try.

I get the least time out of the three of us, I think, which means when I'm in control, I have more worries, more gaps, more life missed. It's not fair. Perhaps I should try to oust them both sometimes, to take a little control. I squeeze my eyes shut a moment, then apologise into the air, into the nothing, mouthing the words to say I'm sorry just in case she can hear my thoughts. I could never oust Isobel. She's made mistakes, but she's still Isobel. She's still the woman I love, even though she doesn't feel the same about me anymore.

Katarina, though, she's a different story. Isobel is the bridge between us. I just wish it was a drawbridge and I could pull it away, cutting her off.

I know why Isobel clings to her. I saw what happened. And freeing herself from the shackles of that memory isn't going to be easy. She may have locked that memory away, but the aftereffects linger, like a bad smell, a headache she'll never shift.

The news fills the laptop screen before I have a chance to check work. My breath catches when I read the headline, though I shouldn't be so riddled with surprise. More bodies have been found. Four, carved up, naked, dumped on the edge of the city somewhere. Pound signs carved across their bodies, dollar and euro signs too. It's the men that went missing a while ago. Wealthy men in charge of big companies. The exact sort of men Katarina hates.

The previous two bodies sickened me, but these four feel different, personal, my hands tingling with familiarity. Katarina did this. My bones know it.

I turn the coffee off as my stomach twists, and I sip some water instead, parched and needing the blandest solution possible. It's hard to hold the glass, my clammy hands are shaking so much. My hands. . .the hands that likely did that carving. My shoulders and back ache. Is that from hauling corpses around? There's an ache in my fingers, overworked and cramping, some bruising. I search for the nail brush to scrub them but remember I threw it away, so opt for a shower instead.

I let the water run scalding hot and step in. It's too hot but I cope, hoping to singe away whatever Katarina has done. I scratch at my skin, abrading off all the cells I can until I am red-raw and sore. With the bathroom thick with steam, I wrap myself in a towel. It smells old, a fustiness to it from being damp too long since I've been away a while and so no one's done the laundry. It should bother me, but right now, all I can do is sit on the edge of the tub and shut my eyes. Doctor Cottrell's technique of accessing memories comes back to me, and my mind wanders into Isobel's old bedroom, into that mind safe.

There is nothing of note recently. Because that's Isobel's method. Katarina walls up her memories like a fortress that I've no idea how to penetrate, and even trying is exhausting. Then, my morning breath turns sour and stale as some images flash through my mind. They're vivid, they have texture. Katarina is taunting me, releasing tidbits of gore and cruelty, just enough to let me know she's aware of my snooping and my disapproval. My heart races and crashes into my chest. I don't want to remember. I shouldn't have tried. My eyes don't want to open but I force them, then lunge forward and dry heave into the toilet, hoping to God Harry Baxter doesn't hear me and wake. The thought of having to interact with him makes me heave some more.

If she wanted a reaction, then pat on the back to her. She's got one.

I open the bathroom door to let out the steam and sit on the cold tile floor as I towel my hair. I won't use the dryer in case it wakes that stranger in my bed. My head spins when Katarina's memories keep playing on a loop, when I think of the news, when flashes of the horror flicker in her edge of my vision, my nose recalling the butcher-shop smell. I rub my hair harder, hoping for some sensation other than dizziness and nausea.

There's still snoring from the bedroom, and I grab what I need to dress by fumbling around in the dark, then get ready in the bathroom. I can do without hair styling and makeup. If I'm quick, hopefully I can leave for work before he wakes up. I'll be really early, but that's not a bad thing.

I text him as I walk down the street towards the tube, telling him I had to go and to please let himself out. A couple of kisses at the end because that seems to be what Isobel does. As if I need my stomach to churn more.

Despite the early hour, the morning is hot and London's pollution hangs like yellow lace across the city. The air should be less polluted by now, according to targets. Those targets are reevaluated and reset annually, with excuses lined up at the end of each cycle. Next year, they'll be achieved. Next year, there'll be the budget. Not now though. Never now. Now it's too expensive, too disruptive. The petrol companies need more time to make engines cleaner, and councils need more time to get the electric hookups installed. Too busy, too skint. The excuses roll through the streets thicker than the smog. They should have improved the bus links in this area by now, but there was no money for that. There was, however, plenty of cash to spare to restock Parliament's wine cellar, and Uncle Sam could afford to write off several hundred million in tax when massive companies, staffed mostly by AI, decided to haggle on their dues. It was cheaper to write it off than to sue them, apparently. Cheaper to pay out in pollution-induced health issue compensation than actually fix the pollution, so stated the freedom of information request. It's all about value for money, they said.

As I cough, I cover my mouth with my sleeve and it makes me wonder if my—*our*—situation, multiple personality disorder, schizophrenia, I don't know for sure what a psychiatrist would call it, our general mishmash of crazy, is worsened by the smoggy air. Pollutants, lack of oxygen, whatever. If I typed that into a search engine, it would definitely say so. But then, type anything into a search engine and someone, somewhere, agrees. Access to the internet does not mean access to facts these days.

Graffiti has sprung up around Greenwich that causes my walk to slow. I rubberneck past the first bit, but there's no need. It's painted again and again. There's always some street art and gang tags, but this is different, and it's all fresh. Red bold letters are smeared across buildings and bus stops shining through the smog. It all says the same:

Down with the patriarchy!

At least it's not painted in blood this time. I suppose for that I should be grateful. The letters don't look like Katarina's hand. There's a symbol too, staining every surface. A circle with a cross underneath. The symbol for women. And it's everywhere.

Some commuters stop to take photos, a few tuts and heads shaking. Whispers of vandals, of what a disgrace, of how they should know better.

Funny, no one ever gave a shit about the graffiti before.

The commuter traffic is lighter than it will be at peak time, and such stalling will cause bottlenecks later. I try to keep my gaze averted, sure my cheeks are ablaze already.

I grab a copy of the *London Daily* before I get on the tube. The front page headline reads: *Fear Across the City.*

I have to hand it to Katarina. She once again gets what she wants. Scared little rich boys are going into hiding across the city. Personal security firms are inundated with work, their prices quadrupling to help with demand.

And the public is revelling in their fear.

There are gangs now, according to the news. Like Katarina has disciples. Gangs of women who are combining their strengths, the many taking down the few. Katarina is rubbing off on some people. She always had leadership qualities, always had a way to inspire, though I wish she'd limit it to trending fashions and makeup.

Guilt creeps in even though I'm innocent. But this body isn't. The pinpricks of goosebumps that chill my arms are as if my skin cells know. I jump at every cough and siren. Guilt is a reflex, bypassing my part of the mind, rippling through our shared flesh.

This offers me some reassurance. If Katarina had more control over this body, there would be no guilt response, only pride.

Six major FTSE companies are now left without their CEOs, the news speculating on who will replace them. Some banker being interviewed says, no one. Not one man is willing to step up for fear of his own safety.

There is carnage on the streets. How have women become so out of control? he says. *There is no one up to the task.*

Perhaps a woman? asks one journalist in her interview.

The man replies, *As I said, no one is up to the task right now.*

I crumple the paper in my fist, then stuff it in my bag. If I get angry, I risk Katarina making an appearance, and if she's this destructive outside of work, God knows what damage she'll do at WIT. I don't fancy Hugo Baxter's chance. Penned in by security with Katarina the angry bull rampaging through the office. We'll get the sack for sure. Or worse.

I know what she'll say, what she'll be thinking. She'll be delighted, in awe of herself, gleeful with how much of a success her plan is. Companies losing their shit quicker than they cover up a scandal. The stock market has taken a hit as a result of uncertainty. Katarina will rub her manicured hands together, and her deep red lips will grin from ear to ear.

She won't listen to reason. She wouldn't have planned past her initial desire to rid the world of wealthy men.

There would be no point in me trying to ask her, what of the rest of us? If these companies fold, what of the staff? When the companies' money runs out, it's the little people who take the hit first. The rich at the top of the pyramid are hardly going to suck up the losses themselves.

She's planned the apocalypse, not the aftermath.

Katarina is like a tinnitus sometimes, buzzing in my ear. Right now, I know what she'd say. She whispers, trying to influence me with her seductive persuasion, trying to sway me to her side.

The press blame women, she says, though it's a gust of wind, a bird calling. *Why is that?*

I shake my head and resist the urge to swat her away like a bug.

Do you blame the damage on the fire itself, or the one who poured the petrol and lit the match?

I hold my phone to my ear. I may be crazy, but no one else needs to know that.

'This isn't a fire, Kat. It's a massacre.'

I can see her smile, a translucent image of her standing in front of me, her dark eyes locked on mine. *Cause and effect. The massacre is the effect. The generations that came first and all the patriarchal bullshit, that is the cause.*

I take my phone away and slow my pace to help steady my breath. The day is only getting hotter, but I rub chill from my arms. She's still talking to me, her voice bouncing around in my head, but I zone it out, focussing instead on the traffic, my breath, some ruckus between drivers ahead, the smell of morning bakeries. I need to keep her out of my head, to stop trying to oust me by making me blend with her. She's not going to stop. I know that now more than ever.

She's not going to stop until all of London is burning.

Chapter Forty

Katarina

There's an abandoned apartment block round the back of Camden Market. A metal fence surrounds it with danger signs pinned to the front. The cable-ties that keep the panels in place have been cut, and I squeeze through the gap. I look up at the building, the bricks still pale with newness, not blackened by the pollution yet. Apparently, there's some structural issue with the new build. Residents had to leave for fear of the entire place falling down, though the developers still got their money.

Seems like the ideal place for a meeting. Poignant.

I didn't choose the place, nor did I suggest the meet. I stumbled across it on some forum where they relish in panic among the men. One of many such forums where groups of women with a desire for justice talk freely. Not even justice, fairness. I read page after page, comment after comment, with wide eyes and a buzz surging through me. Some women are as ambitious as me. So many are calling for change. Though it shouldn't take ambition. It's something that seems so simple, so incredibly achievable. If there weren't wealthy men determined to stop it.

The evening is sticky; the humidity rising the last few days and not a breath of wind to offer any relief. Despite this, I wear joggers and a long-sleeved top, all in black. I can keep to the shadows that way, keep this shared body out of view.

London is never quiet, not really. This area in particular is rife with people jostling for territory in the endless street trades that end up in criminal records and violence. People from poverty, trying to make their way in a world pitted against them. Such people are branded as criminals because of the way they go about their business, but rich people buy as many drugs as the poor, they just do it in more socially acceptable places like swanky bars and hotels. It's the poor people with nowhere else to go that end up convicts. Poor people's crimes are acted upon, but rich people—people with plummy accents and Bentleys and titles and expensive lawyers—they can break all the laws they want.

What's the stat? I heard it somewhere on some news article. The top one per cent of the richest cause fifty per cent of greenhouse gases. They bury homes beneath water, cause old bacteria to wake up in the heat, cause millions to die in droughts and famines. Yet the weed dealers who get into the odd ruckus are the criminals.

A poor guy sexually assaults someone and he's locked up. A rich guy does it, and they change the law to suit them.

Here, on the streets of London, is where utopia meets dystopia. The underground creeps up those ivory towers.

After a final look over my shoulder, I nudge the wooden board out the way as the forum instructed, then crouch to get through the hole in the wall. Inside the abandoned building, the carpeted hallway—dusty as it is—still smells new. There's a resident's notice board advertising pilates classes and new mum brunches. A hairdresser that comes to the home, a chiropractor. The glass over the noticeboard is smashed, a gouge down the middle like a broken dream.

Still, the developers made their money. A particularly wealthy firm built this block.

The gathering is denser than I imagined. Thirty, no, more like fifty women, also dressed in black, are congregating in the communal living area. Plastic sheeting still covers the sofas. I wonder if they were ever sat on.

The women smile at me as I walk over, the flash of teeth catching the sparse light under the shadow of their hoodies. They're all tired faces, pale with wide, wary eyes. Some wear the bruises of matrimonial misery. There are mumbles of hello as more arrive after me, though there seems to be little to no familiarity among attendees. No friendship groups, no cliques. The threadbare clothing and bargain brand footwear says more about each of them than reciting their professions. Among the dusty brickwork of the building lingers the musty smell of thrift stores.

We don't introduce ourselves. Names aren't required. By standing among these women, we all know that we have a right to be here. We have our own stories to tell.

One woman with the saddest eyes I've ever seen speaks up. 'None of the press, no one is talking about those seven murders.'

'Five now, I think,' another woman says.

'No. Seven. From the week before.' She looks around at all of us, and is greeted by blank faces. 'See what I mean? Seven murders last week. Four in London and three in Southampton. I think the papers gave it a small slot on page ten. Four men and three women, all murdered, and no one even knows about it. Because they weren't wealthy. My daughter wasn't wealthy enough to make the headlines. Just another case of domestic violence. She wasn't pretty. Her picture wouldn't make an attractive front page. But she was beautiful to me. She was so beautiful.' The last words sound like she's been thumped in the gut and she doubles over.

A cry comes from some ungodly place within her, a haunting sound that makes a lump form in my throat. A woman next to her puts her arm around her and shakes her head.

Another woman steps towards the centre of the group. 'My son. Killed last year. A driver ran him over when he was cycling. He was a bike courier. The driver was on his phone, late for a meeting, he said. Extenuating circumstances. He didn't even lose his driving licence. No prison time. A slap on the wrist and my son is ash.' Her tremulous voice struggles with every word, biting back the tears she's likely shed non-stop. 'Only the rich deaths matter. The rest of us are expendable.' The last word is punched out through gritted teeth.

Another woman steps up. 'My daughter is doing community service for assault. She broke a guy's jaw. He felt her up, and she defended herself, but it's she who's the criminal due to the Clarity Directive.' She holds her head high as she speaks, so much pride in her tone.

My hands are in my pockets, but every story makes me clench my fists a little tighter. Their pain fills my blood, my bones. Each story stokes my fire.

'Six hundred thousand cases of domestic violence towards women last year, and nothing changes,' she says. She's got a voice of such clarity, I could imagine her in a senior job role, public speaking, someone important. 'Now there's a risk of men being harmed, and did you hear? They're doubling the budget. *Doubling.* There's never been any public funding for vulnerable women, but now there are funds available for men. The men in power protecting their own. Police are being called back from their holidays to protect the streets. But the streets are no more dangerous for the majority. Just those few.'

I step up now, using my voice before the urge to punch a wall becomes too great. 'Power is a club. And people go to clubs with the same sort of people as themselves. Big companies that control the economy are nothing more than gang culture. Ghettos of impenetrable posh pricks. Those with the most money have the power to tell the government what rules to make. They say we live in a democracy, but it's just a dick swinging contest.'

The women all nod with murmurs of agreement.

'And I say we have had enough,' I continue. All eyes are on me, lifting me up higher. I roll my shoulders back and project my voice farther. 'What's happening on the streets right now, it's showing that women across the city, across the country, have had enough. The scales have been tipped the wrong way for too long. Taking out the heavyweights is the only way we stand a chance. The only way we're going to matter is if we show them we're all the same. They think when they cut, they bleed gold, but I say we show them we're all the same. Flesh and blood.'

The women repeat after me. 'Flesh and blood!'

I am not the last to speak. There are more stories, more horrors of women being manhandled, ridiculed, passed over at work, beaten, and objectified. Of all genders being held back because they're not in the rich boys' club. I note the clenched fists, the tight jaws. Even in the half light of the room, the anger glows.

I am not the only one with blood on my hands, and from the rage among these women, I know there is going to be so much more.

Chapter Forty-One

Isobel

Some days, I feel as much of a zombie as all the rest of the staff appear. Tiredness makes my walk more like a shuffle, motivation sapped from me by the tedium of the office without a friendly face or even a hint of conversation. I lean against the wall for a while, ignoring the buzz of my IMAtech telling me I'm wasting time. I don't care about that.

I watch the staff like a hawk, waiting in dread for the next seizure.

Layla used to bring me in a bar of chocolate for lunch, the real Layla. We'd share a quick kiss while making a cup of tea, then make plans for a drink that evening. It wasn't much, just a few seconds of distraction that made coming in to work seem like less of a chore. Stealing glances at each other across the office were the highlight of my day. She kept me motivated. She was an inspiration.

Now I have no one to speak to except Hugo Baxter, and that's about as enjoyable as a toothache.

However bad the office is though, it makes my plan all the better.

This morning the Baxters aren't in yet, so it's easy to take photos and videos. The staff pay me no regard and I'm free to break every NDA I've ever signed. The sun glares through the front windows, and I angle my body to offer some shade as I walk around the room, concealing my phone partially behind my blazer. At my desk, I take photos of email threads, the notes Greasy Guy sent me, Hugo stating that hormone levels must be within a certain range, clearly showing his total disregard for any sort of discrimination laws. Where normally reading such things makes me flush with rage, today my pulse races for another reason. Excitement. I'm going to send all this away and show the world what WIT are doing.

'It's a perfect company,' Hugo says when he arrives this afternoon, flanked by security, some of which wait at the entrance, while two others patrol the office. Hugo rubs his hands together like he can smell the cash, licking his lips as he salivates over the boost to his billions. 'Perfectly efficient, a perfectly functioning workforce. No emotions, none of that woke bullshit we had before the financial crash. And all because of IMAtech and Baxter Pharma. It's the coalition this country has been calling for.'

Hugo has a tumbler of whiskey in his hand, and he downs the lot. I've never been able to stand the smell of the stuff, and even being close to his drink makes me detect notes of musty barrels and burned grass. His will be some fancy, single malt top shelf stuff too, but to me, it reeks the same as the bargain crap people might carry around in paper bags.

He shares his drink and celebration with no one, just parades around the office, the so-called Powerhouse of Productivity. He looks down his nose at his minions, revelling in his own glory. Malorie Baxter is, as always, a silent shadow. Buttoned up shirt, blank face, as zombified as the floor staff.

Every time someone takes a pill, I hold my breath, wait for some bad reaction. So far, today, all is well.

So many jobs are being handed over to AI, but here in the WIT office it's different. This isn't artificial intelligence, but artificial mobility. Limbs being controlled by medication. Like puppets on a string.

For now, at least, until Christopher Morely gets his way.

'What about the people who ended up in hospital?' I ask.

If eyes were daggers, Hugo's would slice through me right now. After a second, he steps closer, his hand around my waist and leans in close to my ear. 'Teething problems. Very normal in tech.'

There's a slight buzzing sound, only slightly louder than the whirr of computers, and the hormone chart flickers, the result swinging from one end of the scale to the other. I look over at Matteo and he hesitates in preparing any supplements.

'Dammit,' Hugo says, before marching up to the office. 'This is all I need today.'

My rigid body softens when he's no longer in contact with me, and I walk to the dispensary desk. 'Don't give them anything.'

He shakes his head and looks at the floor.

The chart continues to swing wildly from one end of the scale to the other. IMAtech apps ping every couple of seconds. The staff are all still too under the influence to notice, confirming it's not mixed up drugs that are causing it. This is either a genuine glitch or Christopher Morely's doing.

That devil arrives in the office, but I'm not in Katarina-mode. As he walks through, my jaw tightens as I attempt to return his smile, though squeezing such an expression out of rigid facial muscles is impossible. I'm sure it appears more like I have sucked some sour fruit than delighting in whatever Katarina sucked on. I must look like the Joker or someone totally insane.

Well, I guess if the slipper fits.

Christopher Morely's entourage of security waits outside the entrance, creating a blockade along with Hugo's men. If it's true and security firms are booked up and raising their rates, I would guess there's a few grand in hourly rate now flanking the doors of WIT.

I don't have even a grain of courage to face him at the moment, and I run to the toilet and lock the door.

Katarina would be pleased about this glitch. As long as it's not harming the employees, so am I. But for how long are they safe?

Layla would be worried about the glitching IMAtech and try to help with fixing the damned thing.

I can't trust either of them. They're either criminal or complicit. My stomach knots when I even consider summoning them to deal with this. My plan is the best way. I still need more footage to really concrete my evidence. It's a wonder that hasn't made the papers already, although less of a wonder when I imagine how much money Hugo Baxter pays to keep the press on his side.

I can't stay in the toilet forever. With a sluggish posture and head hanging low, I skulk back to my desk on tiptoes, then sit and hunker down below the partition wall, allowing my hair to fall forward to shield me.

Hugo Baxter and Christopher Morely are across the other side of the office, engaged in some animated conversation that they both seem to find hilarious. Their guffaw laughter cuts through my skin and irritates my bones. Still keeping my head as low as I can, I glance up at them, their close torsos, pats on the back. Are they laughing at me? My eyes dart from one to the other, my hands tapping the desk, my need to fidget relentless as paranoia squirms through me.

What happened that night? It's the first time I've seen them together since. Are they talking about it now?

Hugo is still being too familiar, too sleazy. I ground my emotions, keep any anger at bay, a headache pulsing down my forehead. My IMAtech app buzzes to note anxiety and suggests a pill. That feels too accurate to be a glitch. I calm myself, steady my breaths, then I wipe the sweat from my forehead.

Hugo shouts over at me, clapping his hands like I'm supposed to jump to attention. 'Isobel. Meeting. Now, now.'

I suppress a sigh and stand, following them both up the stairs, padding slowly, about to be in the room with two powerful men who know more about me than I do.

Chapter Forty-Two

Isobel

The journey to work was so uneventful, here I am, working unflustered instead of the usual summer stickiness. There were no dense crowds, no wandering hands, the sun shone, and the air pollution was non-existent. I even got a seat on the tube.

At work now, I'm the most comfortable I've been in a long time, perhaps ever. The light coming through the glass wall at the front of the office is dappled instead of glaring. Outside, birds sing.

My colleagues greet me, there are smiles and courtesy conversations. We gossip for a moment about the bar we went to the night before. I have a coffee in my hands. I don't remember making it, but its perfect leaf pattern crafted into the foam is before me.

I sit at my desk, the chair not creaking. The partition walls are gone and my colleagues on both sides smile, then greet me. My computer loads up without hesitation. I lean back in my chair, take a deep breath and my chest swells, content with an inner knowledge that today will be a good day.

Hugo is here, his voice less loud than usual, and he's talking next to me. No hand on my shoulder, no leery eyes. He's the picture of professionalism, and he mentions how pleased he is the staff are all happy and even asks about their welfare.

It is, to say the least, idyllic.

An alarm sounds and the room goes dark, red lines criss-crossing my vision to tell me the Virtual Reality session is over. I remove the VR headset, squinting in the bright light before my vision adapts and I am, once again, in the glass office with the Baxters and Christopher Morely looking at me with their expectant expressions and too-loud voices.

'So?' Hugo says as removes his own headset. 'How was that, then?'

It takes me a moment to find my voice as reality hits like a brick and disappointment makes my headache return. I look out of the glass wall down at the office below, where everyone works so silently, so different from the Virtual Reality. 'It was. . .good.'

Next to Hugo is Harry. When did he arrive? His unblinking eyes are staring at his own headset, his slack jaw in a half-smile.

Hugo nods and rubs his hands together in that greedy banker way he does. 'Excellent stuff, Christopher. The AI is simply brilliant.'

'All possible due to IMAtech, Hugo, and the data you provided.' Christopher Morely flashes me a wink at the end and my stomach rolls.

Harry's mouth moves like he's a goldfish for a moment before he says anything. 'It's simply brilliant. We're going to be market leaders with this for sure.'

I narrow my eyes at him for a split second before looking again at Hugo.

'See, Isobel,' Hugo says. 'See what we're achieving here? IMAtech makes the office perfectly productive, but by pairing it with gaming, it creates a real-life experience. With the data we're getting from IMAtech, the game knows and adapts to whatever makes you happy or sad, and provides you the environment you wish you were in. You can work, go to college, socialise, and it will always be perfect. Every time. The others around you behave exactly as they want to behave, but to you, it's exactly as *you* want.'

I rub my temples, sure the headset has left indents across my head. I still feel it on me, digging in and heavy.

'This gives everyone free rein to do what they want to whoever they want, without any repercussions as the other person, in the game, is completely unaware!' Hugo's grin is sinister, his eyes like lasers that can slice through clothes. 'You don't want to know what my avatar was just doing!' He laughs in a way that makes my skin itch, and Harry laughs with him, the same haughty laugh.

'Now, Hugo,' Christopher Morely says, 'that's not really the point. It's more so people with social anxieties can cope better in stressful environments. It's like a dress rehearsal. And it makes working from home much more like being in an actual office.'

'Exactly.' Hugo slams his hand down on the table, and I jump. 'So, if you want to feel someone up, ask them out, whatever, you can do that. The simulation plays out, and then when you do it for real, you know if you're going to crash and burn. That's worth knowing, right, Isobel?'

My cheeks are on fire. Is that what happened to Katarina? I swallow. 'Right.'

'In the VR world, you can be whoever you want to be. Confident, outgoing, quiet, studious. The game knows, based on your IMAtech data, and learns. This is exactly what the world has been waiting for. Everyone can live their—'

Hugo's voice fades away. I've zoned it out as just one phrase repeats over and over.

Be whoever you want to be.

Who do I want to be? That's what I'm always wondering these days. The game didn't show me that, only who I want everyone else to be. Happy, respectful. I was neither Layla nor Katarina in that simulation. I was me, and the world respected me.

Perhaps that's been the issue all along. The problem I have isn't me, it's everyone else.

Chapter Forty-Three

Isobel

Harry stays in the office upstairs all day. I shouldn't be so surprised. He's still a major shareholder in the company, he's just so rarely in the office these days, since the pub exploded.

I stay downstairs, out of sight, keeping him out of mine, then when the day finishes, I wait around the corner again to meet him.

His unmistakable black 4X4 pulls up, with his personalised reg: H4RRY. From the back seat, he rolls down the window. 'Get in.'

I do as I'm told, and he greets me with a kiss. 'Dad insisted on the car, with all the danger at the moment.'

'I'm very sure you aren't in danger.'

'I know that, but he doesn't.' He kisses me again, then air-punches like a kid who's just got a present. 'I'm just buzzing! That game is unreal, isn't it? This is going to be huge for the company!'

I give him the side-eye. 'Shame IMAtech failing will tank it all.'

He winces, then fidgets. 'I mean, that might hurt a bit. But the game will undo any damage to the company.'

I angle around to face him. His glee is ridiculous, like a bloody jester. I want to slap some sense into him. 'We need IMAtech to fail, and the game only works with IMAtech.'

'We need IMAtech to not be used for employees, right? That's the aim? There's no harm in using it for a more interactive gaming experience.'

I sit back and fold my arms. 'You sound like a fucking brochure.'

'Sorry, I'm just excited. My shares are going to be worth so much more when this game launches.' His voice is all squeaky, like he really is a kid.

'A game that used invasive, drugged-up slave labour to make.' I tut. 'You saw the staff today?'

'Not really from upstairs.' He waves his hand at my comment, dismissing my concern. 'But listen. I know the staff situation isn't ideal at the moment. But it's temporary. And, I've decided, after the game launches, I'm going to sell my shares in the company.'

I sit up and face him again. 'Really?'

'Yep. No longer a board member or majority shareholder. Imagine all the good I can do with that money. I can start my own company from scratch.'

The driver takes the route to Harry's, but I shout through to the cab and ask him to go to mine instead.

'I'm tired,' I say to Harry. 'I just want an evening in.'

'At yours? Might as well be in a nice place.'

I grit my teeth. 'I like my flat.'

When the car pulls up at mine, Harry goes to kiss me again but I offer him cheek, then get out and slam the door behind me.

When I get up to my flat, I press my back against the shut front door, a pain pressing on my chest, and I hold my hands to my mouth to muffle my cries.

Katarina had said: privilege is privilege. Have I been so blind?

I don't call them, but they both appear, grainy and rippled like I'm looking at their reflection in water. My knees slacken and I slide to the floor.

'No one will help me,' I say, pathetic and sobbing. Layla crouches beside me, bending yet still so rigid. 'He's a Baxter. Maybe not the worst Baxter, but you're better off without him.'

I look at her, her features identical to when she was alive, even though her demeanour is sometimes at odds with how she was. I miss Layla, and when those waves of grief hit, I choke, drowning in my loneliness. 'I'm going to end up some spinster. I've no one.'

Katarina, still standing, arms folded and wearing that relentless grin, scoffs at my outcry. 'And what's wrong with being a spinster? You know that was a word used to demean women who made a living from sewing? Ones who weren't rich or reliant on a man for money.'

'She's right,' Layla says, which almost makes me choke on my own tears. 'You're independent. That's so important. That's why it's important to keep your job, to earn your own money.'

'Oh, piss off,' Katarina says. 'This isn't some work meeting. Fuck that company and all the people who own it.'

'You know what?' I stand and make my way to the bedroom. 'I'm going to let you two argue this one out. I'm going to bed.'

Chapter Forty-Four

Katarina

There's something to be said about taking a few moments of joy in a task as simple as reading the newspaper. *London Daily* is free, so thrifty Layla can't even moan about me spending money. She didn't stick around after Isobel went for a nap. One look at me, and she scurried back to her mental hole.

It's a warm evening as I sit at the bus stop, not waiting for a bus, just enjoying some time out. I sit taller as I read the headlines, a grin spreading wider with every word I take in. It's all about the fear in the city, the graffiti springing up everywhere, the rise of women.

So many women in the city, and not rich people, live in fear every day, and it never makes headlines. Make rich the men quiver in their brogues and it dominates the papers. Fucking cowards.

Domestic violence is on the up, not because women are becoming violent, but because they're fighting back. We have weaponised inequality. It's about time.

In the middle pages of the paper there's an article about how to get that bikini body in two weeks. Another about fashion, hairstyles, then a gossip column berating some celebrity for being too fat, then commending another for being body confident despite her plus size.

All of us are either too loud, too quiet, too demure, or too confident. A nun on the street and a whore in the bedroom is what they want. Like women are made of Playdough and can be moulded to their every whim. A flash of cash is all it takes. Money talks, and it tells women how to behave. It doesn't matter, our shape or manner or appearance. As long as men hold so much power and the Clarity Directive stands, we will never be enough.

There's another meeting tonight. Almost every day, they're springing up in various locations. Some get found and broken up by the police, women told to go home when all they're doing is talking. They never cared about women talking before, not when it was disregarded as gossip and old wives' tales. We used to talk and talk just to cover up the fact there was nothing to say. Now things are different, and the rich men know dialogue can be more deadly than a knife.

It's not even just London now. All across the country, women are shouting.

And the men carry on their same old statement, telling the women to behave. Telling them: you are not enough.

Across the park, there's a woman and her daughter. The little girl is cute as a button. Her socks are pulled up, one higher than the other. She stops to draw it up as her mum wipes a smudge from her shoe, then straightens her flowery top before flattening a bump in her hair. From behind, a little boy comes running, all grass-stains and grubby hands. No one tells that little boy to clean himself up. The mum ruffles his hair a bit, and that's all.

At a bench opposite, a woman applies her lipstick before making a video call. Adjusting her hair, angling herself so she's in the best light.

I glance to my right. The symbol is there, then again to my left and spot three places where it's been painted. The symbol of women.

Vandals, crude, man-hating, all the lies the papers churn out, whereas they never give a shit about the cock and balls painted on bus stops and the gang symbols on street corners.

How about empowering, creative, equality-seeking. I Google the paper, and unsurprisingly, its editor is a man from a wealthy family. His title allows him to say what he wants and sway the masses to his line of thought. He is, after all, important. A somebody. A role he was born into.

I look at his picture, at the arrogance oozing from it like dripping ink. There's fear in his words, however much he tries to hide it behind entitlement and bravado. There's a typo missed by the proofreader. Then I spot two more, like his shaky hands hit the wrong keys, his fingers trembling when they tapped at his keyboard. I hope he's gone into hiding, doing his work from a nuclear bunker, too terrified to leave his house.

On second thought, I hope he is still parading around in public, looking for a woman to catch off-guard and not decline consent, for one he can pounce on before she's had the chance to say no. I want to see him in person, to lure him closer. He would look fantastic strung up in my piggy sty.

I tear at the paper, then pound at it until it's the smallest ball it can be before chucking it in the bin beside me.

I should go and see my piggy tonight, whip his bare body, maybe carve some symbols into him with a bread knife. I could make pretty patterns, maybe engrave the symbol for women into his butt cheeks and the soles of his feet. My piggy needs looking after like a houseplant, requiring feeding and watering.

I want more though. I want to turn that old barn into an entire forest of piggies, all strung up and stretched out like old trees.

Then, with the most perfect timing, my phone pings with a message from Christopher Morely: How about a date tonight?

I wet my lips and reply: perfect.

Chapter Forty-Five

Katarina

All my other piggies were easy kidnaps. They picked me up in their fancy cars, and I suggested a make-out spot, saying I'd always wanted to make out there, since I never got the chance as a kid. I'd complement their car and swoon over all the fancy gadgets. 'Look,' they all said, 'I can even monitor it from my phone, along with all my other cars.'

They'd show me the app, and as we arrived at whatever make-out spot I'd selected, I'd simply spike their drink with a sedative. Once they were asleep, I'd turn the tracker off along with their phone, which I'd bury. Then, I'd drive their fancy car to the barn, drag them in, then tie them up and change my clothes. I'd take their car to some dodgy estate and leave the engine running—plenty far away enough from the barn. Someone was bound to nick it, joyride it, then trash it.

Christopher Morely may be a little more tricky.

He has a driver. Whether that's usual or a new addition over his safety concerns, I don't know.

The only option I can think of is to drug them both, but as the driver would see me, he'd be an undeserving piggy.

This does not sit well with me. I pace the flat, drinking a gin and tonic, hoping the fizz will stop the sinking feeling in my stomach. Christopher Morely's driver is probably a poorly paid minion, probably treated like shit like all minions. He likely doesn't deserve that. I can't even research him to justify it, since I have no idea who he is. And I'm only assuming it's a he.

My one hope is the driver is a properly nasty bastard. Wife-beater, something along those lines. Sadly, for him, he'll be guilty until proven innocent.

I text Christopher Morely and tell him to pick me up from the tube station. There's a spot around the corner where I'm sure CCTV doesn't reach. There are blind spots everywhere when you know the city. I arrive there in black gym clothes, then strip them, revealing a fitted jumpsuit underneath. The gym stuff goes in a bag in the bin. No one bats an eye at my activities. This is London. It won't even register as unusual.

The car pulls up, a huge ostentatious thing that would comfortably house a family of five. Why would the likes of Christopher Morely be concerned about emissions? He's far more important than the environment. I resist scowling at the car as I slide in. Despite the space inside, our legs touch.

'Hi,' I say, and he hands me a glass of champagne as the car rolls away, smooth as if it were gliding. 'Phone off. I'm not being watched again.'

He takes it out and makes a show of turning it off before leaning in to kiss me on the mouth.

I take another sip of champagne after and wince. 'Yuck. This is not my favourite.'

'It's Crystal.'

I shake my head. 'Overpaying doesn't make it nice. It tastes like old arse.'

'You're hard to please,' he says with a smirk. 'Jake,' he shouts through to the driver. 'Pull into the Majestic. We'll get something more to the lady's taste.' He turns to me. 'What would you like?'

'You chose. Something less fancy and more fun. Something to remind me of being a teenager again. I want to go to a make-out spot I knew as a kid.'

His eyes sparkle with mischief. 'All right.'

He gets out of the car, leaving his switched off phone still on the seat. I send him a load of 'Thanks for standing me up' messages. Just to erase the trail.

He returns with a six pack of WKD, and I laugh as he opens one. 'That's more like it.'

The driver follows my directions to a secluded industrial estate. The drugging bit is easy, I've practised this sleight of hand a hundred times. I act drunk, playful, and insist the driver has a can for old times' sake. It all goes like clockwork. Within minutes they're both passed out, dribbling, ready to play.

The car is a huge chunky thing for me to drive, especially as my arms are tired from heaving whatshisface onto the passenger seat. It's over half an hour to the barn from here, down a few narrow country roads, so I crank the air con up as well as the music. In the rear-view mirror, Christopher Morely continues to dribble and snore.

I get the car as close as I can, and then still have to drag them both across part of a field. It would have been nice if he'd picked me up in a 4X4 so I could've parked closer. I groan and grit my teeth as I heave them across the grass, the bottom of my jumpsuit trailing in the mud.

It's a warm night, and I pour with sweat by the time I string up Christopher Morely, using the ceiling beam as a pulley to take his weight, then tying off the rope to leave him dangling like a piñata. I then cut his clothes off right down to his birthday suit. He fidgets as I do, rousing too quickly, and his knee gets me on my cheekbone.

My hand goes to my face. 'Ow.' *Prick.*

His eyes start to focus as I tie the knots around the driver's wrists. The strength of his aftershave makes the barn smell less damp, and I smile when I imagine the metallic blood aroma that will soon fill the place.

'W. . .what. . .?' His glazed eyes harden when he looks over at me. 'You? What the fuck?'

I smile sweetly and blow him a kiss. 'Were you expecting someone else?'

He looks at Jake's ropes, then up at his. 'Is this some sex game? If it is, the answer is no. This is fucked up.'

I should have given him a top-up dose. He's not groggy enough for my liking. But, oh! He's just the most glorious piggy. I'm going to make sure he stays alive for days. As long as possible.

The driver's knots are tight, and when I start hoisting him up, he whimpers. *Dammit.* I didn't use enough sedative on him either. No matter. I hoist quickly, groaning with the effort, and my hands chafing from the rope. He's dangling nicely by the time his eyes are fully open.

'Jake,' the piggy says. 'Jake, what the fuck is going on? Did you put her up to this, you worthless piece of shit?'

Jake's crossed eyes come into focus, and I tie off the knots. He tries to say words but they come out as a slur.

'Morning, sunshine,' I say. 'Sorry you've been caught up in this. I really am. Collateral damage, I'm afraid.'

I don't cut his clothes off. That seems too undignified for someone undeserving. I consider ending his life quickly rather than the long torture the piggies go through. That might also terrify the other one, showing him I mean business.

'What the fuck have you done now, Jake?' he says. His voice gravelly and stern. 'I knew hiring you was a mistake. Serves me right for taking pity. What is this, some homo game? You owe people money? After all I've done for you.'

Jake's head lollops from side to side as he slowly regains consciousness. 'W. . .what? I don't know. . .what's going on? Where am I?'

I shuffle on my feet and turn away so I'm not looking at Jake. I need to ignore the guilt and think of the bigger picture. It's a shame for him, but it is how it is.

'He'll explain.' I poke the one that's been here a while. He barely groans, so I remove his gag and blindfold, then give him some stimulant and water. Funny how even though he probably wants to die sooner rather than later, he still accepts the drink. 'Wakey wakey.'

The new piggy turns this way. 'Andy? Is that you? What the fuck?' His eyes widen so much, they may bulge out.

'Come on,' I say. 'Tell them what we're doing here.'

His head hangs low, not even glancing up to look at the new piggy. Rude. 'This. . .' He speaks with little sobs. To think of how lovely he was just a couple of days ago! A bubble of snot bursts and dollops on the floor. 'This is the abolition of the patriarchy.'

'Andy!' the new piggy says. 'Andy, don't you put up with this crazy bitch. Help will be here soon.'

'P. . .please,' Jake says. 'I haven't done anything wrong.'

'Bollocks,' the new piggy says. 'This is definitely some set up. It'll be a loan shark thing. You've been borrowing money again, after I took pity on you and gave you a job! I could have hired anyone, but I hired you. That will teach me for doing a kindness.'

Jake leans into his arm to wipe his face. 'I only borrowed money to help out my mum, I told you. She's not been able to get a job, and my little sister needs looking after. That's the only reason I got in debt.' He looks at me now and I face him. He's all red-eyed, his bottom lip trembling. 'Listen, lady. I never borrowed money off anyone bad. I just got a normal bank loan, that one time, and I'm working three jobs to pay it back.'

'Save your fucking sob story,' the new piggy says. 'Listen, crazy bitch. How much? Whatever he owes, I'll pay it. You only have to let me go. Do what you fucking want with that waste of space.'

'Interesting,' I say. 'Jake, what other jobs do you do?'

'I'm a dancer, at a club, twice a week.'

The new piggy scoffs. 'Fucking homo.'

'A. . .and I help out at an old folk's home. Caring and that. I did have a better job, but it got—'

'Taken over by AI.' I finish his sentence, the answer too plainly obvious.

He nods and sniffs a little. 'My little sister. She's not able to work or study or anything. She had a head injury. My mum has to look after her all the time, so I have to earn enough for all of us.'

'Yet I'm the one strung up here,' the new piggy says. 'Sounds like that family needs putting out of their misery.'

A little grizzle comes from the old piggy and I consider killing him right now, simply so the new piggy is scared rather than just angry. But then I glance at the driver.

Jake isn't a piggy. He just isn't. And he shouldn't have to witness that.

I pace a moment, chewing on my cheek. The new piggy tries to speak a few times, and I put up my hand to silence him. My barn, my rules. He can shut the fuck up a while and let me think.

I stop pacing and face Jake. His innocent, teary face tells me I'm doing the right thing, so I step closer. 'Here's what's going to happen, Jake. I'm going to let you down. I'm going to give you a dose of sedative to take with you. You are going to drive far away, take the sedative, then when you wake up, you will call this man many times. Obviously the call won't go through. You will then call the police and say your client—' I point to the piggy, 'this dickhead, is missing. You will say that you don't know what happened, that he picked up some woman off the street, some blonde, though you didn't get a good look at her. And the next thing you know, you were asleep. You now feel woozy, you think you were drugged. Understand?'

He nods.

'I'm really sorry this will mean you don't have this job anymore. As you will never see this prick again. Do you understand why?'

'A. . .all those missing men, them ones killed, it's you?'

Jake clearly is smarter than his employer, who's still tutting and scoffing, as if his disapproval will save him.

'There are many of us,' I say. 'And I know your name. I know where you live. So you understand how important it is that you do exactly as I've instructed?'

He nods again. 'I do. I promise, I do.'

'You are not the sort of man we're aiming to eliminate, so I don't want to have to hurt you. I will, for the cause, if it comes to it. But I'd rather men like you are on our side and help with our cause.'

As much as he can from standing on his toes, Jake thrusts his chest out and rolls his shoulders back. 'I'm all for the cause. I think what you're doing is brilliant. The Clarity Directive is awful. My sister, she can't say no. She's non-verbal. She can't refuse consent. She's been groped loads of times. She's in a wheelchair, but they don't care.'

I smile and press my hands into my chest, inflating with the wholesome goodness of Jake's words. 'Okay. I'm going to let you down now. You remember my instructions?'

'Yes, but, no. Can't I stay? Whatever you do to him, to all of them. I want to stay. I want to help.'

'Sorry Jake, not this time. We need to cover our tracks and so my instructions are the way to do that. That is how you help us.'

'Fine. Okay. I'll do everything you said. I'll help any way I can.'

Inch by inch, I lower him, then cut the rope from his wrists and I take a leap back. Tears brim his eyes as he steps closer to me, but I back up, throwing the bottle of sedative to him.

'Drive away, park, take that, then do exactly as I said.'

I don't have to tell him twice. He legs it, and I'm left with a knot in my stomach, worrying I've just done something stupid. Although there's a part of me, the part that's likely still linked to

Layla and Isobel, that gleams with pride. I'm not a bad person and this proves it.

'He'll go straight to the police and bring them here,' the piggy says. 'No man, not even a lowly one like that, would follow instructions from a woman. Not if it means harming his own.'

I turn to face him and smirk. 'That's a shame. I was hoping to let you suffer for ages, but if you think the police will be here soon, I'd better make this quick.'

I take the knife, and my fun begins.

Chapter Forty-Six

Isobel

As a child, my parents took me to the aquarium. I remember being mesmerised by the fish. Their underwater dance was magical. It was the cuttlefish I liked best, the funny way its body rippled, the way its colour changed. It could blend in however it liked, change its appearance as simply as breathing. I gasped when I saw it, my young eyes filled with awe, my little fingers touching the glass. Imagine being able to just change like that, to be whoever was best at any given moment. As striking or as drab as you wanted.

Instead, I was just me. Plain old Isobel.

I wake with an ache on my cheekbone. I rub it but it's tender to touch, then check my reflection to find a purple bruise. I must have hit myself in my sleep, perhaps. I raid Katarina's makeup stash to try to cover it up. It takes a considerable amount of concealer and blush to blend it in and still it shows. At least I look a bit less tired now with a full face of makeup. If only I was that cuttlefish and could make my bruise disappear.

My walk to work is slow, my desire to be there non-existent. I'd rather stay among the pigeons pecking at the pavement than be in the office. Or even better, I'd stay in bed, alone, curled up under the duvet and deny the real world exists. Instead, my commute is busy, and I have to push away wandering hands several times. It doesn't rile me like it should. I walk with heavy footsteps, shuffling along. I find myself sighing at every inconvenience, everything too much effort.

The afterimage of the simulation is still with me. The despondency of knowing that it's not real, that my workplace is nothing like that, still rests heavy on my limbs. It was idyllic. Too many what ifs and why nots come with me on my commute. Why can't it really be like that? What if it was? Imagine getting out of bed every day knowing I didn't have to shout no at so many men, that I was valued at work, that there was a career path to climb. Respect. That's what I felt in that game. Something so incredibly alien.

Real life is nothing like that. It's chaotic and demeaning and stressful.

***

As I sit at my desk, Hugo stands at the glass wall of the office upstairs and peers down. A half-smile spreads across his face. I want to shed my skin, to scratch off every part he's touched, and in that simulation, I've no idea what he was up to. I was his plaything. Is a perverted avatar better than a perverted person? I suppose only a pervert in real life would do such a thing. His hands in real life are borderline inappropriate. In a game? I shudder to think.

I don't collect any more evidence today, not able to get a moment to myself without Hugo Baxter watching. I have quite a bit of footage and photos already, but more would be better. My letter is drafted in my head. It'll take minutes to type, but I don't want it living on my computer any longer than necessary. It's safe in my head. IMAtech can't tap into my thoughts yet. I've been searching for the right person to send it to, there's some influencers, some journalists that aren't bound to big companies, a few who haven't been bought.

Any day Harry's supplement swap will kick in, so that will help too. I think. Although, I can't help feeling awful about it. The work zombies are all completely emotionless. What will the swap do to them? Will it be like Christopher Morely's hack and send them into fits and choking? Will they all fall asleep or go hyper, be too buzzed when they get home and not be able to rest? It seems like a stupid plan now. I should have considered how dangerous it is. The ends don't justify the means.

***

I walk past the evidence of Katarina's antics. Newspaper headlines, the news on my phone, a trail of what my body has been up to, or, inspired others to do. I see visions of my DNA everywhere, sprinkled all around London as if it's the smoggy air. I'm everywhere. Flesh has memories like a mind, I'm sure of it, and with every picture in the paper, every story of a man missing or found dead, my skin tingles. There are so many now I've lost count.

There's a texture in my hands always, my palms too warm, as if they're grasping limbs. I don't smell the exhaust fumes of London anymore, my nose burned with the smell of blood instead.

I need to take more action, take more control of my life. I need a friend, and the only one I can talk to now is Layla.

I tidy the flat when I get home, just a bit so it doesn't look quite so much like a tornado has passed through. I do the dishes, pick clothes up off the floor, then spray some air freshener about. Layla thinks I only call on her when there are chores to be done, so I need to prove otherwise. Perhaps the smell of furniture polish will reassure her before she arrives. Dinner is also on, filling the space with a homely aroma. Shepherd's pie, enough to leave some leftovers for whichever one of us is eating tomorrow.

If anger helps me summon Katarina, it's anxieties that make Layla turn up, and I have plenty of those. Layla's presence was once a reassurance in my life, a rock, making me believe everything was going to be okay.

To me, she looks the same as she always did, the same as she did the last time I saw her. A little dishevelled from our night together, plain clothes, an efficiency in her wardrobe, fuss-free, no makeup. She always thought she was so plain, but to me, she was everything a woman should be. Organised, career-driven, natural. Not bogged down with aesthetics, but still totally captivating and affectionate. She was so meek and hardworking, a people-pleaser. The good girl my dad always wanted me to be.

She died because of me, and I'm partly her because I couldn't let her go. The world was a better place with Layla Daley in it. With me masquerading as her, I'm not so sure.

She sits on the sofa, leaning away from me and tucking her chin in a standoffish pose. Not the receptive, enchanting Layla Daley I once knew. My mind creates a poor representation of her.

'What?' she asks in a tone that matches her posture. She looks around though, and I'm sure she's noting the tidiness of the flat. 'Feeling lonely without Harry?'

'Just thought we could catch up.'

'Why?'

My insides clamp up at her sharp edges. I slide along the sofa a little, and she leans back farther.

'Thank you for that work you did the other day. That was a ton of emails you replied to. And writing those reports up was a real help.'

She nods, still with her chin tucked in.

'Okay, if you don't want to make small talk, let's talk about Katarina.'

She rolls her eyes and huffs. 'Shoot.'

I wring my hands out on my lap a little, rehearsing the words before I say them aloud. 'She needs to be controlled somehow. I know this. I don't know for sure what she's been up to, but she terrifies me.'

'You?' Layla scoffs. 'She terrifies you? Why?'

'I think she's killing people. Don't you?'

'And that's what terrifies you?'

'However bad these companies are, she can't just go around murdering people.'

Layla's eyes narrow. She has scorn in her features, more so than I've ever seen before. I needed a friend tonight, but she's looking at me with more disdain than love.

'And who are you to decide what's right?' Her voice hisses, a simmering hatred that makes me draw my own head back. She's never used such a tone with me before, however much I've annoyed or upset her. She loves me. 'I know what you did,' she says, over-enunciating every word. 'I know why Katarina is here, and I know you're going to find it impossible to get rid of her. She's under this skin so much, we'll never be free of her.'

I shake my head and rub my temples. 'What are you talking about?'

'I went into your memory safe. I saw what you did all those years ago when you were at school with the real Katarina. And I know you'll never stop being influenced by her.'

The air freezes in my lungs. I knew she'd been snooping, but I had no idea at what. My eyes dart from side to side as if I can see what she saw. But it's still locked away for me. I look up and meet her gaze, my watery eyes locked on hers.

I swallow back my dread. 'Show me.'

Chapter Forty-Seven

Isobel

Walking home past the corner shop, the other kids shouted their usual taunts. 'Freak! Weirdo! Dyke!'

I ignored them as I always did, shut off the edges of my vision and focussed only on what was ahead of me. A lamppost, a crossing, another pedestrian. The insults blurred into background noise as I picked up my pace and made it home. In the kitchen, my mother was preparing dinner. It smelled like meat, despite me always saying I no longer wished to eat meat.

'Saw Florence Mckenzie today,' she said.

I poured myself a glass of water. 'Oh?'

'She's not a bad boss. Her daughter, Katarina, such a pretty girl. And so bright. Why aren't you two friends? She'd be a good influence on you.'

If a good influence is someone who called me names and made fun of me, then that would be right. I didn't say this to my mother though. There'd be no point. Instead, I shrugged. 'I'm going to my room.'

'Video games aren't going to help you at school, Isobel. You're nearly sixteen years old! It's time to be responsible. Video games aren't going to help you make friends.'

I ran up the stairs, away from my mother and her never-ending scorn. She'd go on for hours otherwise, chipping away at me, pointing out my lack of friends, every flaw I had. I didn't need friends when I played. It was pure escapism. They were the only thing that could hold my attention for more than a few minutes. That and nature. I could spend hours with animals, but not even ten minutes with people. Or more accurately, they couldn't spend ten minutes with me.

I stayed up late, too late as always, dimming the screen when my parents went to bed, then turning it up again when I heard their bedroom door close. I played for hours like that. Same every night.

The next day, walking to school, there was a little bird. A sparrow. It had flown into a shop window and knocked itself out. My eyes welled when I saw it. I crouched, and slowly I scooped it up. It rolled in my hands, dazed, so tiny and delicate but alive.

'What's that?'

The voice startled me so much, I almost dropped the bird. It was Katarina McKenzie, peering over my shoulder.

'A little sparrow,' I said. 'He's dazed, I think.'

'How do you know it's a he?'

'Look in its underwear,' I joked.

Katarina laughed. She actually laughed, and my face flushed. 'You're funny,' Katarina said. 'Aw, he's cute. Hope he's okay. I love animals.'

My heart skipped a beat. Katarina McKenzie was the most popular girl in school, and she was talking to me, and we had something in common. My brain ticked at a hundred miles an hour. I had not a second to waste, and I seized the opportunity. 'There's a badger set over at Southdown's common. They come out after dark if you're quiet. I could show you, if you want? There's a whole family. They're super cute.'

'Yeah,' Katarina said and smiled. 'That would be really cool.'

'Tonight? We can meet by the bus stop and I'll show you.'

Katarina nodded. 'Sure. Seven?'

I could have jumped with glee. Excitement fizzed inside. I was always distracted, but that day at school was even worse. I daydreamed out of the window, tapped my foot, dropped my books, and went to the wrong classes twice. The day just couldn't go fast enough. I ran home after school and wolfed my dinner down so quickly I almost choked, not even moaning that it was meat again. I changed at record speed, throwing on all black clothes so I could blend into the night and not scare off the badgers.

I was at the bus stop at six-thirty, just to be sure. And I waited. And waited.

I tapped my foot, hummed to myself, recited the names of my video game characters, anything to pass the time and to stop my mind wallowing in what was plainly obvious. When eight o'clock came, I gave up and walked home, wiping my watering eyes on my cuff.

Stumbling by the shop was Katarina. My breath caught in my throat as I hid and watched. Katarina was making out with some boy. I recognised him. He was from a wealthy family across town. He didn't go to our school, but everyone knew who he was. His dad was some famous shipping billionaire and his mum an actress. He wore the sort of clothes I had no idea where to buy, so exclusive they were. He pressed up against Katarina and pinned her to a wall. She pushed him away, then told him she wasn't going home with him, and he shouted insults at her. Katarina told him to fuck off, called him a leech, gave him the finger, then staggered off, bumping against the wall as she did.

I followed, hot with rage. I'd been stood up for that boy. She'd ditched me for some booze and a grope from that fucker. She wore a little skirt and heels and a bright red top, not the sort of clothes to wear looking at badgers. She'd never intended to come.

Anger burned inside. My muscles tensed, and my nostrils flared.

A little park with a couple of swings was a few hundred metres past the shop. Katarina plonked her drunk self onto one of the swings, rocking back and forth. She was mumbling to herself, drunken ramblings, followed by a few hiccups. She took a bottle of what looked like spirit from her handbag and swigged from it. I hid behind a bush, debating confronting her or running home, my hands balled into fists at my sides.

A rustle to my side made me jump, and I ducked lower, then peered around the side of the bush. That boy was back.

'No one tells me to fuck off, bitch.'

'Piss off then. How's that? Better?' Her words came out mixed up from booze, but they were clear enough.

He yanked her by her hair, and she almost fell off the swing as he leant over her. 'Watch your fucking mouth.' He then yanked harder and with a yelp, she fell off.

I watched from behind that bush, hugging my knees as he forced himself on her. Then, when she tried to fight back, he picked up a rock and smashed it into her head.

She stopped moving then. All her limbs were still. A trickle of blood pooling in the gravel caught the moonshine. The boy said something, panicked, then ran away.

My breath shuddered in my lungs as I stayed sitting for a while, then pushed myself from the ground. I stood over her perfect face for a moment. She was so still; her eyes only half open, the tarmac below as red as her top. Then, I ran home.

When I got to my bedroom and closed the door, I loaded up my games console and played video games. I forced the memory away, shutting it out. Instead, I was a swordstress, a hero, fighting others, winning games.

I played and I played and I played.

Chapter Forty-Eight

Isobel

They're both with me, one of the rare moments the three of us are present across some watery plane of reality. I don't know why Katarina is here. I didn't call her. I'm not angry or drunk. Perhaps she feeds on despair too. Layla's face has softened slightly, concern knitting her brow as tears brim my eyes.

'I. . . I. . . I was so scared,' I say. 'You felt that too, right? I was so afraid.'

'She died,' Layla says bluntly. 'You didn't even try to save her. You did nothing when he was pushing her to the ground. You could have shouted or tried to stop him. But you let her die. You could have called for help or called the police, but you did nothing.'

I look at Katarina. She's barely present, an outline really. Despite the poor resolution she's smug, her pouting red lips smirking as I squirm. She says nothing but winks at me, the sort of I-know-you-too-well wink.

'I didn't kill her,' I say. 'It's not the same as killing.'

Layla's features harden again. 'You go on about how you fight for what's right, that you care about people. Yet you did nothing as she was molested and killed. You never even told the police when they called for witnesses. You let him get away with it.'

A lump forms in my throat and I shuffle away from her, shaking my head. 'I was a kid. Just a kid.'

'You were old enough. Katarina doesn't make you do bad things now. You have always done bad things.'

'No,' I look at Layla again. There's so much disappointment in her face, so much shame. All the good parts are in Layla. There's nothing good left in me. 'I made you.' I cry. 'And you're all good. So I can't be that bad.'

She hugs her body tighter, a million miles away from me. My Layla was never so distant. She would always fall into my arms when I needed her.

'Then why are you pushing me away?' she asks. 'Why do you listen to her and not me?'

If she's distant, and I'm pushing her away, then the chasm between us is my fault. My chest aches as I reach for her, but she's still too far to touch. The air next to her is cool and biting. I snap my hand back.

I look at Katarina again, she's more in focus now. There's devilry in her eyes, more than I've seen before. The darkest of twinkles, daring me to act. Was that what she looked like when she saw that sparrow? Was her face filled with mischief rather than care? I'm little more than a dazed bird and Katarina's showing me how to fly. What was that perfume Katarina was wearing that day? A body spray that was so popular back then, but of course, she doesn't smell like anything now because she isn't really here. All I can smell is the furniture polish and the flowery air freshener.

'The police said you were drunk and fell off the swing,' I say to her, the Katarina I've conjured. My limbs tremble with chill as I see her dead. In my hands I still feel the damp earth where I crouched, still hear the crack of her skull.

She shrugs. 'Well, only you and he know that's not true. That prick's father made sure any evidence was lost, no doubt.'

The memory now is as clear as anything. I remember it as well as I remember seeing Hugo Baxter at work, like it was yesterday. Perhaps that's how it works with memories. If you shut them away for long enough, they emerge shiny and new. The constant re-remembering wears away the edges, distorting them, warping them into something else.

A tear tracks its way down my cheek. 'Why are you so okay with this?' I ask her.

Katarina grins now. The wicked kind of grin I used to see her make before she gave the finger to some boy she was telling to leave her alone. 'Because I'm not really her. I'm you, your darkest side. I'm the part of you that knows you should have done more and is now determined to get justice for all women, whatever the cost.'

Katarina takes her place, bold and clear, her presence heavy in the air. I can smell her now, I'm sure of it, that sweet musky body spray from decades ago, from the day I watched her die. She's as intoxicating now as she was then.

Layla fades away. I can't keep her here. It's like she has no purpose, and if I can't resist Katarina, why bother trying?

Katarina licks her bottom lip, her eyes glinting with wickedness. 'I'm every time you wish you'd stood up for yourself but ran away. I'm every bad thing you've ever done or wish you'd done. I'm your scapegoat, and you need me more than you know.'

Chapter Forty-Nine

Katarina

Oh, so what? Original me is dead and Isobel did fuck all to stop it. This shouldn't be a big surprise. I'm the vengeance and anger she wishes she had back then. I'm what guilt does to a person over years and years. It eats you from the inside and spits out the bitter aftertaste. That sums me up pretty well. Isobel can't run away from her rage forever. Even in my high heels, I'll catch her up. The fact it can be fun is just the cherry on top.

Isobel has always had this wicked side. She tells Layla she was too scared to act that day, but really, it was because she wanted me dead. The popular girl, the one who called her names, the one who got all the attention. She watched someone else enact her anger, watched Christopher Morely do the deed she wanted to. She's figured that out by now, that it was that prick who killed the original Katarina. I'm Katarina 2.0, and I will not make the same mistake.

Fear and excitement elicit the same responses in the body. Adrenalin pumps, muscles tense, saliva flows. When I watched that memory, it wasn't fright I sensed from Isobel. She didn't even cover her eyes. There was jealousy in her heart when he touched my breasts, when he picked up that rock, when he felt my skull crack.

If she was scared, it wasn't of him, but of her own desires.

I knew she's more like me than Layla. That's why she enjoys my company so much more. We're two peas in a pod, while Layla is the fibrous annoying skin that you have to pick from your teeth.

My piggies swing from their ropes. The one I've had for longer looks almost dead now. His body doesn't react to the momentum. He's like strung up meat. I press my finger into his sinewy neck. His pulse is weaker, but it's there. His body is cold to touch, despite the summer air temperature. His breath, though, is hot and fermenting. I recoil as it's gone past the stale stage and is now like rotten roadkill. Sickly sweet as infection takes hold. The bruising all up his shoulders and arms is beautiful. I trace it with my nails, a slight tickle he doesn't respond to. A glorious purple bubbling in strands like thick rope. I'd paint my walls that colour. Wasn't purple a regal colour once? He doesn't look so regal now. Or smell regal.

'You're so fucking dead,' the newest piggy says when I remove his gag. He looks alarmingly healthy still, despite the art I carved across his torso. He was healthier to begin with though. All those hours at the gym are only making him suffer longer. I take a step back and admire him. He was beautiful to start with, even better now with the engravings. I can already imagine what he'll look like when he's pale and drained of blood. He'll make a lovely corpse. I hope his last words are something similar to what he just said. I laugh at the thought. Oh, irony! It would be perfect.

He's still rambling on, swearing and calling me all manner of names. Rude. I'm saving the world, and this is how he speaks to me? I blow him a kiss, then laugh until my stomach hurts.

'You're fucking dead, you crazy bitch! Dead!'

He's shouting so loudly, I tut and shake my head. I'll be sure not to give him any water today. Let that throat desiccate. I didn't sedate him when I went away. I want him awake always, to live every last second he has until I burn his eyeballs out.

'Silly, piggy,' I say. 'If I die first, you'll die here of exposure or thirst. If I stay alive, I'll carve you up piece by piece. Don't you see? You're dead whatever.'

'Jake. He would have gone to the police. I know—'

'Sh.' I step forward and hold my finger to his mouth. He tries to bite it. 'Save your strength. Might as well try to stay alive as long as possible, to really have the chance to consider all your regrets.'

'You—' He splutters and spits as I squirt dissolved stimulant into his mouth.

'Good. Take your medicine.' I've brought an apple with me, and I shove it in the mouth of the other piggy. 'Bite that, fat little piggy!'

It falls to the floor, his teeth barely making a dent. And here I was, thinking he might be hungry. Ungrateful prick.

I poke him with a stick, but he doesn't groan. *Dammit.* I want him to be more responsive than this. I take some more of the pre-diluted stimulants and squirt it in his mouth. It dribbles out, so I tilt his chin up and squirt some more. Perhaps I should have used a needle on this one. That would be quicker. I'm not in a rush though. All of London forever seems to be in a rush, dashing from job to job, home to home. For him, no doubt he rushed from a billion to two, always in a hurry to see how quickly he can get richer, or rather, how quickly he can make everyone else poorer. How quickly he can sleep with women a lot younger than him, poorer women who feel they have no choice, then how quickly he can cover his tracks.

I grit my teeth and squirt some more stimulant and slap his face. 'Wakey wakey!'

That's the difference between the piggies and me. My cause is gaining momentum, and I'm not in a rush to see that through. I know the art of savouring something, of relishing in a feeling instead of trying to jump to the next one.

He groans a little as he wakes up, the stimulant kicking in nicely. His pupils dilate, his mouth moving up and down like a fish.

'How are you, piggy?'

His response is an inaudible slur. There's tension, muscles tightening across his chest and arm. His breath rasps and pants before his eyes lose focus again. His left arm spasms.

I scowl. 'Are you having a fucking heart attack?'

Another inaudible slur.

'Oh, fuck. Help him for God's sake!' the other piggy cries. 'He's a great man in charge of a great company! You need to help him!'

My eyes bulge and I stamp my foot. 'No! Fuck that. I will not waste your death on a fucking heart attack.'

I cut him down and he flops to the floor like a sack of shit. I take my knife, then trace it over his skin, gouging out chunks, twisting the blade to be sure it hurts more than whatever his heart is doing, concentrating on the most painful parts, his armpits, ball sack, kneecaps, his eyeballs. Some noise comes from the other piggy. Little whinnies of protest that only make me gouge deeper. There is something simply divine about sticking a knife into an eyeball, like chomping a grape between your teeth.

I give him the kiss of life and thump my fist against his ribcage to try to keep him going, squirting some more stimulant into his mouth, then a little more. He's choking on it. I'd rather drown him than let his heart decide it's time.

With a final splutter and a groan louder than earlier, my efforts fail. He's dead. His bloody eye sockets stay open, his limbs twitch before his soul leaves for hell. My shoulders slump. That wasn't what I wanted. He didn't suffer enough. He wasn't afraid enough. He just succumbed.

There's some more cries and groans from the other piggy, something like, 'Oh, God. No!' I'm not really listening. I sit cross-legged next to the dead one, then fold my arms and allow my sulk to take hold. That was my penultimate piggy, and he's all finished. It's not fair.

I glance at his body and poke it. It's not yet inflated, still spongy. His death won't be for nothing, even if it was quick. His torso being so intact gives me a decent canvas to continue my carving, and rather than just the money signs, I opt for a phrase. It takes a while. I carve with such care, with tension across my forehead and mouthing the words as I write. It's important and needs to be legible.

When I'm done, I stand, hands on my hips, and nod at my handiwork. All the letters fit perfectly.

Death to the patriarchy.

I look at the other piggy and point at it. He's babbling now like a baby. 'Shut the fuck up!' I yell. He's squealing, which is actually quite delightful. His horrible cock dribbles some piss. 'You see, don't you? You see what you deserve.'

'I don't. I don't deserve that.'

I shake my head and click my teeth. 'You definitely do. I know what you did all those years ago. I know you're the worst piggy of them all.'

His weeping eyes look at me now, glazed yet focussed. I know he sees Isobel. This is her body after all, her face, her tits. But I'm the essence of Katarina McKenzie. The girl he murdered because she wouldn't give him what he wanted. Soon he'll see. When he's dehydrated and delirious, he'll see past the skin, and he'll know it is me haunting him.

I turn my back on him and once again admire my handiwork on the dead piggy. It's quite neat. I've no idea how rigour mortis will affect it, or if it will stay legible, but for the time being at least, it's a beautiful sight. Now where to dump the body?

I can't dwell on that for long as I have a more pressing matter. I resume my sulk, sitting on the floor cross-legged, pondering how to overcome the problem of my lack of piggies. Perhaps the other women who are taking action have their own stash. I hope so. Imagine if there were barns and sheds and garages all over the country with rich men strung up to show them how worthless they are.

As much joy as that brings me, my own lack of piggies still makes me sigh. One isn't enough. I want more.

After a wash down with some bleach, I plastic wrap the latest dead one (I put the apple back in his mouth, just because), then I go home and shower.

There is still one piggy I want more than any other. I just need a plan.

Chapter Fifty

Layla

Isobel is hiding herself away. As I sit alone in the kitchen, I stare at the front door and imagine she'll walk through it any moment, then my heart sinks when she doesn't. My eyes sting, but I sniff any tears away. There's a chilling vibe in the flat, cold and unhomely with so much misery hanging in the air.

I didn't mean to be so harsh. I'm just mad at her for not stopping Katarina, for fucking Harry Baxter, for never listening to me. She must have been terrified to have done what she did. She was just a kid, and she's spent her life trying to make up for that mistake.

Katarina isn't her. She's the worst bits of her under a magnifying glass. Katarina is all uncontained impulses. Everyone has bad thoughts once in a while. Evil thoughts, ones you'd never say out loud. Katarina's thoughts with no filter, no reins. She's what happens when the good is too quiet.

I grab my handbag and leave for work, but as soon as I start walking, my pace stalls. My heart rate speeds up as I think of somewhere else I'd rather go first. It would make me late, which has my skin feeling like it's on too tight. But why have I always got to be the good one? Why can't I do something for just myself?

I've not been able to get Amy out of my head. Every moment I'm not reeling from the news or worried about this body, she's on my mind. Her face dazzles my thoughts.

I take a taxi. Such an expense makes me wince, but I have to be as quick as possible. It drops me off right outside Baxter Pharmaceuticals. I recognise her car, and she's still sitting inside, looking at something on her phone. Upset is how I read her expression. Her downturned mouth looks kissable, even in sadness.

When we last met, and she was telling me about her concerns, I listened, in awe of her voice and presence, but it's only occurring to me now how open she was, how willing to talk and ask questions. I crack my neck, suspicion stiffening my muscles. Did she want to talk to me or was it some sort of test? I look down at my rubbish clothes and push my unstyled hair back, tucking it behind my ear. It was stupid to think she wanted to get to know me. I am not Katarina.

I hold my breath as she gets out of the car, and a hot wave of panic combined with desire hits me. If I don't speak to her again, I'll never know if a drink with me was just some work assignment.

It's stupid. I should be able to speak to her. Just a hello, some small talk, though walking over to her feels like it would be more like walking the plank than approaching a human. I tense, wracking my brain for what to say, how to act until I find myself wondering, what would Katarina do? What would Isobel do? They're both better in social situations than me. I'm the worker, the studious one. I like being organised. This sort of interaction is way out of my comfort zone. There are too many variables. It's too unpredictable.

But when she looks at me, my bones turn to mush.

'Isobel.'

My heart pauses, and it takes a second for my voice to work. 'Amy. Hi.'

She walks over. Her smile natural as it reaches her eyes, barely noticing the hair blowing in front of her face. Once again, I glance down at the state of me and inwardly kick myself for not making more of an effort.

'I'm so glad you're here,' she says, and my cheeks burn. 'I didn't even get your number the other day before. . .'

My cheeks are ablaze now, an inferno of inadequacy making my neck sweat. I look at the ground, cursing its inability to create a crevasse on demand. 'Yeah. . .sorry. I. . .I just came by to say sorry.'

'Want to get a coffee?' she asks, seemingly not hearing what I said. 'The canteen in here makes the worst stuff. It's so bad you should try it.'

After a second, I replay what she just said. It sinks in by replay number three, and I dare to look up from the ground. 'Sure. Okay.'

We walk through the entrance, and she signs me in. The echoey halls lead us to the canteen and if the coffee tastes as bad as it smells, she might be right. We sit at a table, and she grimaces as she pushes a cup my way. 'It really is awful, but gets me through a day more than anything else.'

I take the cup and recoil from its scent. 'Thanks.'

She smiles, then sips her own. We sit in silence for a few seconds as I stare into the cup. It's as thick as tar.

She looks at me now; her hands just a few inches from mine. 'Don't feel weird about the other day. It was nice. I would have said so if you'd given me the chance.'

How can anyone be this relaxed and confident? Though, in her presence, I find my awkwardness filtering away.

As I should be replying, I choose instead this moment to take a sip and almost choke. 'God, it's like. . . Eugh. Burned mud.'

'Ha! Yeah, I warned you.' She laughs. 'So, tell me about yourself. You must be pretty tough to survive what you went through.'

Her compliment takes my breath away. But it's not a compliment, just an observation. She's being polite. 'Well. . .my mum died in front of me when I was a teenager, fell and banged her head, and my dad's been sick forever, so I guess I'm used to being dealt a shit hand.' I slam my mouth shut. That was oversharing. Why did I spill all of that? Poor Isobel. I'm nothing more than a gossip.

'Oh, I know all about shit family,' she says as she grimaces through a sip of coffee. 'My parents pretty much disowned me because I wasn't pretty enough. Just after I got my job here, they tried to make me have a nose job so I'd look better in family photos. Now I just avoid them as much as I can.'

My eyes bulge. 'What? But your nose is perfect.'

Her cheeks flush now, I think. It could just be the lighting in here. Women like Amy don't get embarrassed by compliments.

'Well, not according to them,' she says. 'And not as good as my brother's, apparently.'

I nod. 'Oh, I know exactly how it feels to be the least favourite child.'

'Sounds like we have a lot in common.' She smiles. 'I shouldn't care about it. At thirty, all that childhood crap should just go away, but it doesn't. My brother is always in trouble, which my parents just ignore, and I have to pick up the pieces. But he's had severe mental health issues, so I guess that's why.' She sips her coffee and winces through the bitterness. 'Sorry, I'm always being told I talk too much. I could blabber on forever. So, was there someone you wanted to see here?'

I lick the coffee off my teeth, taking a moment to answer. 'Not really. Well, this time I just wanted to apologise.'

'But before. When you came last time, there was someone you wanted to see.'

I inwardly kick myself again. I'm so stupid not to plan ahead! I spin my coffee cup, staring into the black whirlpool for inspiration and fidget on my seat.

'I'm just worried,' I say, elongating every syllable to buy time. 'About the supplements being sent to WIT. I'm worried they might have been mixed up, somehow, what with the people being hospitalised.'

She sits back in her chair, and I look up as she knits her brows. 'I don't know how that could happen. But I'll do some tests, if that would put your mind at ease. How about I take your number?'

What's the collective noun for butterflies? Whatever it is, that's what's happening in my tummy right now. I stiffen, reminding myself she only wants my number for this purpose. She's obviously not asking for my number like a date. That calms my nerves slightly, sending the butterflies into hibernation as I type my digits into her phone, remembering only at the last second to save it under Isobel not Layla.

'Thanks,' I say. 'I really appreciate it. And, not to put you in a difficult position, but my boss doesn't know I'm here. He won't accept any question about the system not working.'

'Hugo Baxter? I'm not surprised. The man is the worst.'

She talks then with a hushed voice, leaning in, about some cost saving issues at Baxter Pharmaceuticals, bonuses being skimped on, the usual stuff we all go through. Her voice is like music and I smile, then nod. It's so nice to chat with a real human. Especially to someone like Amy, whose chat fills every second. I can't think when the last time I really talked to someone was. My colleagues are all zombies, Isobel and Katarina aren't real. I hadn't realised how lonely I've been. As I chew through the last drop of horrible coffee, I find myself stalling, not wanting this moment to end just yet.

She checks her watch. Of course she does, no doubt this wonderful woman is counting the seconds before I'm gone. 'I really need to start work,' she says.

'Yeah. Course. I do too. I'm definitely going to be late.'

'It was really nice chatting with you. And, well, I'd like to see you again, if you have some time?'

I try to speak, but what comes out is a slur of vowel sounds when she gives me a peck on the cheek.

'Speak soon,' she says as she walks down the corridor towards the labs, and when my shaking has stopped, I stand and float on a cloud all the way to work.

***

My late arrival goes unnoticed by everyone except IMAtech and I find myself, for once, not giving a shit about that. My hormones are at the other end of the scale today. Too much of everything, apparently. I grin as I know the cause.

Work is slow, no meetings with the board, just the zombies for company. I've really not got much to do besides clearing up after Isobel. All the stationary is mixed up, paperwork left at a haphazard angle, and there's muffin crumbs in the drawer. Her timesheet hasn't been filled in, and the diary has some rough notes I can't understand. I swear, when she's at work, she does literally nothing. The office manager's job requires a bit of initiative and self-motivation, but Isobel would be better working under guidance with instructions.

I lose myself in my daydreams for a while. My cheek is still warm from her kiss. The sound of her voice still rings in my ears.

For the billionth time, I take out my phone to see if she's messaged. Of course she hasn't. She said she'd test the supplements and get in touch. Plus, I saw her an hour ago. But I find myself holding my breath, my belly still fluttering with the aftereffects of hope.

I should stop it. It's no good to obsess. There's definitely work I should be doing. I scroll through to the diary on my phone in case there's some reminder there that Isobel didn't put in the correct calendar—wouldn't be the first time—then I check emails.

Any fluttering left in my belly stops, knotting instead. My neck and face heat, and slowly, I hunch my shoulders, creating a visual barrier in case one of the zombies looks this way. There's a draft, ready to send, complete with attachments. The address bar is empty. A quick read through the mail body and my heating face reverts to a chill. Isobel is doing something stupid. Really stupid.

I brace myself, then open the attachments.

My hand goes to my mouth as I watch each video and photo. There are videos of the staff, photos of emails and data, all painting WIT in the worst light possible, all ready to expose what happens here. In breach of secrecy contracts. Isobel, me, we, will lose our job for this.

She always goes on about how worried she is about the staff, but this is such a risky move. Firstly, it's pointless. The press are on IMAtech's side. And, secondly, even if it did get some traction and the company tanks, everyone loses their job. It's a lose-lose.

How like Isobel to try to do something without thinking it through. My muscles relax as I think, at least I'm finding it now. At least she hasn't done this yet.

Chapter Fifty-One

Katarina

Another abandoned building, an old office where staff once worked before their jobs were all handed over to AI. I approach it just after sunset with a brief look up to see the cameras aren't functioning, hanging off their hinges, some smashed glass on the floor below. I look over each shoulder, disguise it as swatting a fly—there are plenty of those around. It looks like the offices cleared out the contents of their staff room and left it all in the skip to ferment over the summer. I give the skips a wide berth as they smell like landfill.

This building is soon to be turned into flats by the same developer who built the last place I met these women. The same wealthy developer that gets no reprimand for ripping people off. More housing is needed, the men in power say. Who cares if they're unsafe and derelict from completion, is what they don't say. Providing housing is a vote-winner, the quality of the housing is not.

The sign says they'll be affordable homes, though what's affordable to a multimillion-pound developing company, and what's affordable to the average Londoner, whose job has been taken over by a robot, is like comparing the contents of that skip to fine dining.

There's no board to push out the way this time. The front door is open. My shoes crunch over more smashed glass and inside, in the gleam of torchlight, graffiti decorates the walls.

Fuck AI!

Corporate wankers!

CEOs can die!

Fresh paint marks some areas. I step up to it, stroking the words and design with one hand, the wet paint staining my fingertips. My other hand clutches my heart. It's the same art springing up across London—the circle with a cross underneath. The symbol for women. Along with the three words I spent so long carving into that piggy's torso: *death to the patriarchy.*

I walk through the lobby, then down a darkened corridor. It's cold in here, the heat of the summer never getting this far inside. There's a conference hall. Their muffled voices beckon me towards them, a homing beacon for my tribe. There are more now. Desperate women, angry women, women who have nowhere else to go. Women who had more rights as an embryo than as a living, breathing female.

With the increased numbers there's a disjointed atmosphere, huddled groups and little space between, wide eyes searching other faces for answers and direction. I don't wait this time. As soon as I arrive, I stand on a desk, kicking away the detritus of a career that once was. Conversation lulls to an expectant silence as all eyes are on me.

'It starts with our daddies, when we are little girls with ringlets and smiling faces and we think our daddies are the strongest men in the whole world, that they would never do us harm. Then it's our brothers, who yank our hair and throw our dolls just because they can. Just because they want to be stronger than us.

'And we are told: boys will be boys.

'Then we have boyfriends and crushes who think we're expendable, replaceable. They feed off our misery because us seeming powerless makes them feel big and powerful.

'Boys will be boys.

'Then we have bosses who pay us less than our male counterparts, who pass us over for promotions because we dare to have children, who stop us progressing unless we repay with sexual favours, who place their hands in areas they shouldn't, who direct their eyes to areas they shouldn't, and once again we're told, boys will be boys.'

There are murmurs of agreement from the gathering. In the gloom there's the outline of nodding heads.

'And they've justified this for generations, because why?' I continue, more riled now, throwing my voice farther. 'Because Eve ate a fucking apple? Because we birth the entire world, and they think they own it?

'We should not be the subservient, pretty, silent gender they think we are. We should not let those with fatter wallets tell us how to behave when they wouldn't dare to the males.

'Boys will be boys? Well, I say, let women be women!'

There's a cheer like what I would expect at a music gig, a festival of delight, air punching and war faces, a battle-cry of female energy. My heart is full to bursting.

In the back of the gathering, a couple of taller people stand, hoodies covering their faces, but it's clear even from where I stand they're men.

My stare is clocked by some of the others, and they turn around to face them. Every woman stands upright, feet planted solidly on the floor, arms tensed like coiled springs, ready to pounce.

One of the men holds his hands in front, defensive, then pulls his hood down to reveal his masculine face. 'We don't want any trouble and we don't mean to offend.'

Whispers among the women, 'Men, here! Invading!'

'We came because we want to show our support.'

'Really?' one woman says. 'You, a man?'

I step off the edge of the desk, walking through the crowd towards the men. They're lanky with gaunt cheeks, tattered clothes, and badly shaven. A far cry from how the piggies looked before I strung them up. 'Let him speak!'

He still has his hands in front of him, but he lowers them, his chest rising with a deep breath. 'The Clarity Directive, we hate it. So many men do. Most, actually. And we don't believe women caused the market crash and whatever other bollocks those rich pricks say just to dish out blame.'

'I've got two sisters,' the other says. 'I understand how wrong it is. Both have been felt up by arseholes who think they have the right. We're here because we're on your side.'

'I worked here,' the first one says, sadness in his eyes, a glint of moisture. 'In this block. I lost my job after the crash. The head of the company is three times richer than he was before, while I got my house repossessed. And he thinks he should be rewarded with shit like the Clarity Directive. It's not right. It's all broken. It's not men versus women, you know. It's all of us against a few of them.'

My mind goes to Jake. Not all men are piggies. It's important to remember that. These two men, in their eyes, their faces, I see nothing but hurt and kindness. They're respectful men, just the sort we need on our side.

'Welcome,' I say to them. 'Anyone who's against the patriarchy is welcome here.'

The women nod, though some take longer to do so than others. I remind myself of what many of them have been through. Trusting men doesn't come easily.

'Death to the patriarchy!' One woman cries and then the men, followed by the rest of the women, all repeat.

'The only way to end something strong is to make them feel weak,' I shout. 'Together, we can make things right.'

There's a glow in everyone's eyes. They stand close to each other now, bonded, nodding, rocking on the balls of their feet, ready for action.

They disperse out onto the streets, out to be strong, to make the powerful powerless.

I watch them leave with my chin high, feeling tall and inflated. These women are an army, a force for good, all off to round up more piggies, I'm sure, ready to put things right, to address the imbalance from the top down.

My insides swell and fizz with pride.

The success of this meeting makes up for my own lack of piggies, but there's still that one piggy I want.

Left behind is one woman. Her head still hangs a little low but when I approach her, she meets my gaze. I freeze, stifling a gasp. In the stillness we stand together, a silent conversation passing between us. She's not someone I expected to see, though her presence makes absolute sense.

'I need your help,' she says. Her voice is meek still, not yet empowered, desperation in her eyes. 'You know why I need your help, don't you?'

I nod, then step closer to embrace her. She's thin, weak. If I squeeze too tight, she might snap. But she hugs me back with a warmth I would never have known her capable of. It once seemed like her husband had rid her of all warmth, leaving behind a cold shell. I see now there is so much more to her than that.

I leave that meeting with a plan. Clear and concise.

When I get home, I put on Isobel's comfy clothes, scrub my hands, leave my makeup underdone, then tie my hair up in a messy bun.

After I take a sip of water, I take out my phone and call Harry.

Chapter Fifty-Two

Isobel

There was a time at school when another kid was crying. I forget her name now. She had glasses and braces and carried some extra weight. Some boy at school had been unkind. This young girl's tears were of self-pity, self-loathing, an apologetic tone to her sobs. She nodded along to the insults, her hands covering her face as if to spare the nasty shit the pain of looking at her.

She didn't retaliate as she should have, didn't say a single bad thing about that boy. Instead of hating the nasty kid for what he said, that young girl believed it. She believed she was as worthless as the school bullies made her feel.

That worthlessness is how I've felt on so many occasions. Filled with the all-consuming knowledge I'm not enough. Not good enough, not pretty enough, not smart enough.

I didn't do enough to save Katarina. I did nothing. Layla was right about me.

I can't hide forever. How long has it been since I was in control? It's a weekday, I know that much. The traffic reminds me. The heat tells me it's still summer. There's the stickiness of a looming storm not yet begun.

With sluggish limbs, I get ready, dressing in the most comfortable clothes I have, no hairstyling, no makeup, not bothering with breakfast. My body aches, deep muscle cramps, and throbbing temples. My vision is getting worse. I squint to see out of the window, dazzled and blurred. My waistband has some extra room. If I were thinner, maybe that would make me feel more worthwhile. In the mirror, I practise a smile, wider, lifting my chin up more. It doesn't fit right, like it's someone else's face. Perhaps, if I laughed louder, faked some effervescence to my personality, changed my hair, I would find happiness.

If I was more like Layla and Katarina, both of them, I would be pretty enough and smart enough. I would have the best of everything. Instead, useless me cut those bits of myself out and made them separate. Neither of them are perfect, but the three of us together must be better. They would dilute the me that's left.

On my way to work, pigeons fly out of the way and clear my path. How wonderful it would be to be a bird, to just fly away whenever I want, to see the world from a distance if I desired, instead of being stuck in the middle of it all the time.

Whenever I get to work after Layla has been in, there's a sensation of having been spied on. Layla must sit at this desk after me and sigh with its disorder. When I arrive after her, my cheeks flush with shame at the amount of tidying she's done. I should be used to it by now, but the way my desk is organised

— too tidy, too ordered, with every piece of stationary arranged neatly — it's like every placement of every object is some passive aggressive frown, her disapproval shining through.

It would irk me normally, but as I sit and open my desk drawer, I smile and my knotted gut unfurls. There's a packet of muffins there, blueberry, my favourite, with a jobs list and diary sheet printed to help catch me up.

I haven't sent my email yet, still not sure who to send it to. Hugo is due in shortly, and I manage to take a few minutes to film the staff arriving, to say hello to them, only to get zero responses back.

Hugo's security arrives seconds before him. Two of them walk around the building before taking their stations by the door. I place my phone on my desk, still recording,

Hugo bends behind me, his hand going to where my neck meets my shoulder.

'How's my best girl today?'

Where his hand touches is so blazing hot, I dip my shoulder down away from him, away from that crawling sensation coming from his fingertips.

'Just preparing the latest data results,' I say.

'Good girl.' He rubs my back. His touch radiates all over, boiling my blood. 'Well, Christopher Morely will be in later. He'll be delighted with how hard you're working for us. I suspect he'll think you're due some reward.' There's a lilt in his voice, something mocking.

'Of course,' I say through my teeth.

A pat on the small of my back now, and it's all I can do to not punch him in the face. 'Meeting is after lunch. Be up in the office at one.'

When he's out of sight, I check my phone. The footage is all there, though its interpretation may be questionable. My face is red, tense, but I don't push him off. I don't call him out on being inappropriate. The hand on my back is obviously not in shot. He could claim he was being friendly, supportive, that I should have said something if I was uncomfortable.

The laws these days state as much. The Clarity Directive would say he hasn't broken any rules. Remove ambiguity, the supporters said. And Hugo's actions would be in that murky grey area of inappropriate but not unsolicited. My flinch may not pass the test. But to speak out and risk my job?

I'll have to next time, just a polite word, an excuse me, but I'd prefer no physical contact, as opposed to the kick in the nuts I want to give.

I wonder if Harry knows how much of a sleaze his dad is. Perhaps I'll tell him when I meet him for lunch today. I messaged him on my way in, suggesting his favourite brunch place. Breaking up with him will be easier over some eggs Benedict. He hasn't responded, but the tick tells me he's read it.

When my stomach growls at midday, I leave my desk, scraping my chair legs along the floor, making the kind of screech that irritates my teeth, like nails down a blackboard, but the robots don't notice. I spot the odd fidget of discomfort during the day, the odd rolling of a shoulder and stretching of a neck.

The drugs must include some pain relief or anti-inflammatory, but nothing can make nine hours of constant desk posture comfortable. I make a mental note to zoom in on the swollen knuckles next time I make a video.

Hugo's security dominates the space by the exit, and I have to squeeze past them to leave. Beavis and Butthead don't even have the manners to move aside. They look me up and down as I step outside. From their twisted expressions, I'm not sure if they're suspicious or perverts. Both, probably.

A hot soup of body warmth and stuffy London air greets me as I make my way to the restaurant. It's usually only a couple of minutes' walk, but my pace slows, as on the way, I pass countless spray-painted symbols for women. I bristle, every hair standing on end, that creeping feeling of eyes on me, suspicion all around. I look straight ahead, force a semi-smile, yet guilt flushes my face. How hard it is to feign innocence! Katarina's handiwork is everywhere, and this body knows. Not her direct hand, maybe, but her inspiration, the ripples from stones she cast into the river.

I turn my head to look. Everyone else is anyway, not looking looks worse than staring. Some of the symbols are separated by a strange messy Y shape. People stop and take photos, women posing in front of the graffiti, showing off their biceps and scowling down the camera, a far cry from the usual pouting faces and plastered on smiles of selfies.

One woman is making a video and I pause to listen.

'Will be.' She points at the messy Y shape. 'That's the middle symbol, in shorthand. This reads, women will be women. The boys will be boys excuse has lasted for too long. Women are taking ownership of themselves. Women are giving themselves free rein to act however they see fit, as men have been doing since the Clarity Directive. . .'

I hurry my pace and get away. That woman sounds so much like Katarina, it's as if Katarina's sent out a memo.

As I approach the restaurant and text Harry to say I'm here, I wait.

I check my watch, pace the pavement, but I get no response. Waiting for a while, staring into the mid-distance, I think, this is probably his way of dumping me. Simply ignoring me. After I call him a few times, leave a voicemail, I put my phone in my bag, then slouch on my walk back to the office, grabbing a takeout sandwich on the way.

I don't care. Of course I don't care, I was going to break up with him anyway, and I don't even know if we're still together, but as I approach the office, I take out my phone and check his socials. He's probably met someone else already, probably been out having fun. I tilt my head as I look through his Instagram and Facebook, my eyebrows rising as I search. By the time I'm at the door to work, my walk has ground to a halt.

There's nothing on his socials—for over twenty-four hours. That's so unlike him. Unheard of, actually. Even from his hospital bed he posted at least daily.

My lungs fail to draw breath as my mind goes to dark places I wish it wouldn't.

Katarina.

She wouldn't hurt Harry. . .would she?

I call him again, leave another voicemail, still no response. I must sound like some paranoid, possessive girlfriend, or ex.

I shake my head, then take a bottle of water from my bag and gulp down most of it. He's fine. He's definitely fine. Just asleep, at an appointment, something mundane and ordinary.

At work, I can't concentrate, can't get comfortable. I fidget and rearrange the stationary, pace the room, then tap out a messy rhythm on my desk.

He's fine. He's definitely fine.

I go to the toilets and try calling again, still no answer, still nothing on his socials. Inch by inch, my veins turn cold and sweat collects in every crevice. I try to will Katarina to come talk to me, but she's not there. Why would she come? I killed her. She wants revenge.

Except, she's obviously not the real Katarina. The original is dead. But does that part of my mind want revenge for what I did? Fuck knows if it works like that.

There's a knock on the toilet door, and I jump so much I almost drop my phone.

'Isobel?' It's Malorie Baxter. It's maybe only the second time I've ever heard her speak. 'Is everything okay? You've been in there a while. Who are you talking to?'

'Just on the phone,' I say.

'Okay. Well, you know, IMAtech.'

Fucking IMAtech. 'Won't be long.'

I call Harry once more. Still no answer.

I leave the cubicle and avoid looking in the mirror over the sink as I don't need it confirming I look a state.

Back at my desk, I check my voicemails. Perhaps he left me a message to say he's had a change of plans. For the hundredth time, I check his socials. Still nothing.

I sit, frozen, staring at my phone for a minute. When my eyes sting, I blink, but the screen still looks the same. There was a call last night from my phone to his.

That wasn't me. I didn't call him then.

Katarina.

There's a message from him I hadn't seen, from that night also, when I was asleep. When Katarina took over. All it says is: *Ten mins.*

Ten minutes until what? All the blood drains from my face and my stomach heaves. *Shit.*

Tingles of dread cascade through me, a numbness of denial. She wouldn't have. She couldn't have, surely. She did not.

She would. She could. Surely, she did.

My hand goes to my throat as I dry heave. I need her back. I need to find out what she's done with him.

I email again. Check his socials again. There's nothing. With my hand still over my mouth, I shake my head and stand, stepping away from my computer like it's about to explode, like Harry's absence is toxic. It's her. The chilling of my bones tells me it's her, and she's gone too far this time. She's hurt him. Or worse.

'Katarina!' I scream, she has to answer! She has to tell me! 'What the fuck have you done, Kat?' None of the zombies pay me any regard, not that I care. 'Kat!'

'Oh, dear.' Hugo appears, an impatience about him. 'It seems you're having another meltdown, sweetie.'

He looms over me as my muscles fail me and I fall to my knees, still screaming her name. 'Katarina! Get here now!' I squeeze my eyes shut, thumping my temples with my fists, trying to force her into view, but she's not there.

Layla appears, a wispy figure fighting her way through to the conscious plane, shaking her head, full of disapproval. 'Don't anger the big man,' she says, in that goody-two-shoes voice. Along with, 'I told you so.'

Bit fucking late, mate.

'Katarina!' I scream again. 'Come here. Now!'

There's a hand on my shoulder, yanking me up or pushing me down, I can't tell. I don't want it. I shake it free.

Layla's voice is louder still. 'Don't anger the big man, don't anger the big man, don't anger the big man. Be a good girl, be a good girl, be a good girl, be a good girl.'

'Shut the fuck up!'

The room spins. Me, in the office, zombies all around, Layla's shaking head, trails of her spinning around.

'Don't anger the big man, don't anger the big man, don't anger the big man. Be a good girl, be a good girl, be a good girl, be a good girl.'

'No!' I shout to no one in particular, to the floor, to the empty space, to myself. 'No, I need to know where she is, what she's done!'

There's a throbbing in my head more than I've ever had before. I'm being ripped in half, in thirds, like they're both trying to break free of me.

'The pills, Malorie. If you wouldn't mind.'

Hugo's voice comes through like I'm underwater. There's another hand on my forehead, the nape of my neck, a rubbing on my back. I elbow it away. *I do not consent to this!* He's going to pin me down and make me take those things. I can't. If that stops Katarina coming, I'll never find Harry.

I jump to my feet and back away, looking over my shoulders, my eyes darting side to side like Katarina's going to pop up in the corner of the office somewhere.

'Katarina!'

There's a man dressed in all black. A huge guy, his hands in front of him like he's trying to tame a lion. 'Come on, love. Calm down now.'

'No. No, leave me alone! I need to find Kat. Where's Harry, do you know?'

I turn around. Hugo's face is all raised eyebrows and slow nods. 'I think what's needed is a nice calm down. Cup of tea, maybe?'

I press my hands into my temples, then tug on my hair. 'Fuck. Oh, my God. What has she done?'

Chapter Fifty-Three

Isobel

I'm in a doctor's office. Not Doctor Cottrell, some other one, a cleaner one. It smells of disinfectant, not a whiff of cigarettes. The walls are white instead of the orangey hue of nicotine. They must have sedated me. I've no memory of getting here or else one of the others took me here.

Even the other parts of me think I'm insane.

My hands shake as I check my phone. Still nothing from Harry, just a message from my dad. Oh, God. My chest tightens as I know I'm letting him down. I'll get the sack. I've not stopped IMAtech, and who knows if Harry did what he said he did with the drug switch. Everyone is still a zombie, so I'm thinking he didn't, or it didn't work.

I'm useless. I'm nothing.

I'm not good enough at work to be Layla. I'm not stopping all the bad things like Katarina. I'm the worst of us.

Katarina. She's still not here.

'Isobel Harrison, please come through.' A female doctor, her voice like silk. She's smartly dressed, clothes crisply ironed, with the sort of kindly authority I can't say no to.

I follow her through to her office where we sit. It's a proper office, not some dingy room at the back of her house. She speaks clearly and doesn't cough. I sit on a sofa, her on a chair.

She looks at me with a face filled with warmth. 'My name is Doctor Ansari. Let's talk about how you've been feeling,' she says.

I'm sitting upright, tension pulling across my shoulders and back, still searching the corners for Katarina. 'Why am I here?'

'Your boss recommended it. It sounds like you need someone to talk to.'

Shame burns my cheeks, and I squint in the brightness of the room. It's like I'm under a spotlight, being interrogated, dissected. 'I've angered my boss. I can't do that. I haven't fixed anything.' I was meant to be like Layla, to be a good girl, a good worker. It's all gone so wrong.

'Just relax,' she says, her voice like a lapping shore. 'It sounds like you try too hard to please people. Why is that?'

Do I? Layla's the people-pleaser, isn't she? She's the good girl. I'm the useless one, the one that never gets anything done. I can't say that to this shrink. She'll take me away in a straitjacket.

'My dad, and my mum,' I say. It's the truth, and it's what she wants to hear. It always starts with the parents, doesn't it? That's what they say. 'They always said I had to make something of myself. I was never good enough.'

'I see,' she says. 'Let's tap into that. Now, sit back, close your eyes, and try to relax.'

I swivel around on the sofa and lie back, but relaxing is a million miles away. I'm as rigid as I was when I came in.

'Try to remember when you were a child,' she says, 'and didn't have to please anyone.'

I sit bolt upright again. 'No! I can't. I don't look back, just forward.'

'It's important to confront your past, Isobel, to see if there is anything there that has scarred you.'

'There isn't,' I snap. 'I locked it all away. Forgot it all.' My wide eyes glare at her, and her face twists slightly. I can't read her expression. Pity? Concern? Fear of being in the same room as a proper nut-job?

'Isobel. I think you must be bottling something so deep inside, it's stopping your mind working properly. It doesn't work to just forget your past. That's not effective. We can't run away from our problems.' Concern, I'm sure it is. Her voice is soft and inviting, luring me in.

Katarina said that Doctor Cottrell was a cowboy. Maybe this doctor is right. If I confront whatever I've locked away, maybe I can get rid of Katarina. Maybe I can access her mind space and figure out what she's done. I have to do this—for Harry.

I lie back, then close my eyes.

'Good, Isobel. Just listen to my voice.' She goes through some breathing exercises for a moment, and I hang off her every word, allowing her lapping shore voice to carry me away. 'I want you to remember your childhood. When your parents started to expect so much from you. Is there a point in time when this was emphasised?'

I take some deep breaths and think of my parents, my mum's nagging, always wanting me to do well at school, better than I was capable of being. Dad's voice comes through louder, a quality he doesn't have these days. He was always more encouraging than nagging, assuring me the bad times will be over soon.

I don't picture the safe. It doesn't seem necessary. I'm in my childhood home with its textured wallpaper and smeary windows that overlooked a garden no one ever had the time to look after. There's a breeze, as if I'm inside and doors have been left open. I'm travelling through doors that have been closed for such a long time, the decades whooshing past. My dad's face is there, chubby, like how he was years before his stroke stopped him being able to eat properly. I can smell the takeaways.

'My dad,' I say. 'He always said I had to be his good girl, to not anger the big man.'

'Who's the big man?' the doctor asks.

'Just. . . It's an expression, I guess.'

In the scene is dad's neighbour, Scott. He's huge, even as an adult now he seems big to me.

Dad's voice sounds, clear as day. 'Be a good girl, Isobel. Don't anger the big man.'

The room is dimly lit, orangey lighting, not full daylight, some curtains are closed. I shake, afraid. I'm small, young, too young to understand.

'No,' I say, I think, aloud, maybe?

'Isobel,' the doctor says. Her voice in my memory comes through the walls, the floor, transcending time. 'You need to confront this. Tell me what you see.'

'I can't. I need to be a good girl. That's what he's saying.'

The breeze is stronger now, and it's cold here. It's my dad's house, but it's different. The living room, the furniture, it's all wrong. All pushed to the edges, there's open floor space where the coffee table should be. There are biscuits, my favourite. I know I can't have one yet. Not until. . .after.

'Be a good girl, Isobel,' he says again. His hand is on my arm, my back, nudging me towards the middle of the space. Scott is there, a menacing grin on his face. He licks his lips. 'Good girl, Isobel. Make him happy now.'

I need to wake up. I need to stop this. This can't be my memory. It just can't.

There's someone else there. Doctor Cottrell, he's standing to the side. I can smell him, the cigarettes. He coughs, and as he does, the camera he's holding wobbles.

'It'll be over soon, Isobel,' my dad says. 'Go on, now. Be a good girl.'

I need to wake up I need to wake up I need to wake up.

My chest tightens, and my throat constricts with the burn of bile.

I need to wake up I need to wake up I need to wake up.

I squeeze my eyes shut, but the image is in my mind, my memory. I can't shut it away. It's all playing in front of me. I scream and scream for it to stop, but they don't hear me, they only hear the little girl who does as she's told with the softest of whimpers. Where's the safe? I need to put this in there, lock it away. I can't relive this, I just can't.

The image blurs, going grainy and pixelated. I feel myself going under, deeper, yet my body stiffens so much, my muscles tense in anger. It's hot rage, burning more than I've ever known. I'm going to sleep, but this body isn't. This body, fired-up and fuelled by wrath, is waking up more than it ever has.

She's here now. It's her turn. Her rage. Her consequences.

The body is conscious. But it's not me. It's Katarina.

I've set her free.

Chapter Fifty-Four

Layla

I jolt with surprise when I wake. It's not a slow transition to consciousness, but more like cold water on my face. I'm nearly always at the flat or work. It takes a while for my vision to clear to a soft focus, like I haven't got my glasses on, and it clears one patch at a time. I'm at Dad's. Well, Isobel's dad. It's the smell I recognise first, his general uncleanliness, the bag that his catheter decants into. Only this time, it has a sharper undertone. I rub my eyes and my vision clears some more, the grey splotches fading away. There's breakfast TV on, so it must be morning. I stand in the middle of the living room. His neighbour Scott is on the chair, his face frozen, looking directly at me. I turn, and Dad's on his usual chair. He's asleep, by the looks of it. The breakfast show is playing, the volume up really loud, the live audience laughing at some joke I don't catch.

'Dad?' I ask, then lower my gaze slightly. My breath freezes, my chest turning to ice. Down his torso is blood, trickling like a river. 'Dad?'

I turn back to Scott, note the pallor of his face, frozen in surprise, the puddle of blood beneath him. It's impossible to tell which wound killed him. He's more holes than flesh.

She's here. Katarina, next to me. She's not smiling like last time. She's panting, spent, still erupting with rage. My shuddering breath now matches hers.

'Jesus Christ,' I whisper. 'What the fuck have you done?'

She snarls. 'Only what was deserved.'

My knees weaken then, but I can't kneel. The carpet is soaked. Isobel is here too, looking more upset than me. She would be. It was her dad.

'Isobel. Oh, my God. I'm so sorry.' I move to hug her.

She leans away. 'Don't.'

I swallow, my eyes still unblinking, though I wish I couldn't see. The smell is like raw meat. I glare at Katarina, then at Isobel. 'Katarina needs to go.'

'No,' Isobel says. 'I let her do this. I even watched.'

My jaw drops and I hold my stomach. No. She couldn't have. Not Isobel. She wouldn't do such a thing. Just because she watched Katarina get killed years ago doesn't mean she would do this. I have to somehow stop them, I have to—

The memories hit me like a hot poker, my hands flying to my forehead. There are no walls up anymore. The memories have been released like a dam and our mind has collapsed. I'm swimming in them. All the badness. So much trauma. Worse than I saw in her safe. I choke as it hits me like a torrent.

I cover my eyes. I don't want to see. The visions are in my mind, so it doesn't help. It doesn't stop the tears. 'No,' I cry. 'Stop it, please. Wall it back up.'

'We all need to see,' Katarina says.

'Please,' I beg, when the images won't go away. A dimly lit room, that huge ogre of a man, the doctor, the camera, Dad. . . 'No. It's better forgotten. Make it stop.'

'No.' Katarina snarls. 'You want me gone, then you both have to cope with all of this. Wait until you hear his final words.'

I uncover my eyes to look at her. She still faces the body, her arms tense like she's not even done yet, like she wishes she could kill him again. He's not dead enough to her. She still wants to rip him apart.

Isobel turns away then and wipes her eye.

The recent memory hits me.

She killed Scott first, making Dad watch on helplessly. Then she cut him. Small wounds at first, then bigger and bigger. He's bleeding, begging for his life, a disgust for the daughter he loved so much.

'After all I've done for you,' he says, blood dribbling from his mouth. 'You were always evil. I should have known.'

Katarina hisses at him. 'You did nothing for me. Pervert! Paedophile!'

He wheezes a final breath. 'I forgave you. I covered for you after what you did. After you killed your mother.'

Chapter Fifty-Five

Isobel

Through my mind safe that memory hangs, tucked away behind layer upon layer of denial, but all of that is stripped away now, leaving me with the bare bones of the truth. I'd hidden it for so long, like the Katarina-memory. It emerges shiny and new.

My mother's voice sounded from downstairs, calling me with that tone of disapproval, and I didn't even know what I'd done wrong yet.

'What?'

'Come downstairs, now, please.'

The please was unnecessary. She said it to make a point about manners, not to actually be polite.

I padded down the stairs, and she tapped her foot when I got to the kitchen, her arms folded, my school report in her hand.

'What's for dinner?' I asked.

'Steak and kidney pie.'

'I'm vegetarian.'

'No, you're not. You are what I say you are.' She still hadn't stopped tapping her foot and shaking her head in case her disapproval didn't come through from her tone alone. But it did. It always did. 'Are you going to explain?'

'What?'

'Don't be rude. You know damn well what. Your school report.'

My shoulders slumped, and I sat at the counter. 'It's not that bad.'

'It's also not that good.' She slapped my hand when I reached for a grape from the fruit basket. 'Daydreamer, it says here. Easily distracted. Doesn't concentrate.'

'The grades are okay.'

She tutted so loudly I thought she might rip the roof of her mouth. 'Yes. Okay. But they're not all As, are they? You're not taking those pills. The ones to help you concentrate.'

'They make me feel weird.'

'Feeling weird is better than being like you are normally. What else does it say? Bit of a loner, it also says. You won't get anywhere in life being so unlikeable.'

'It hasn't done you any harm.'

The slap across my cheek stung my pride more than my face.

'It's about time you grew up, knuckled down, got your head out of the clouds. This isn't one of your computer games. This is your life, and you can't go around being this unfocussed daydreamer. You need to change, Isobel. This attitude you have is simply not good enough. You need to start trying to make me proud.'

I shrugged, then reached for a jar of olives. She slapped my hand again and they fell to the ground, smashing on the tile floor.

'See what I mean? What have I done to be cursed with such an idiot for a child? I see girls at your school all with their groups of friends and good grades. Why do you have to be such an oddball? I always thought having a daughter meant girly sleepovers and crushes on boys. God, sometimes I even worry you're a lesbian.'

My rage burned hot, consuming me. An asphyxiating, all-consuming anger prised to rip out of me.

She went on and on and on. 'So many girls go on to be lawyers and doctors. What use are you going to be if you can't apply yourself? You're going to end up with some pervert supporting you forever if you don't do well in life. Why can't you at least try to fit in, to be normal, to be—'

The shove was meant to get her away from me, temporarily, not forever. The olive brine from the jar on the floor was slippery, and her feet went from under her. It was so quick, she didn't even put her hands out. There was a step that went down into the kitchen, a square edge to the hard tiled floor. The cracking noise her skull made sounded like porcelain. A broken vase. Her eyes stayed open, judging me until the very end.

In the doorway was my dad, his jaw hanging open. My hands went to my mouth, tears streamed down my cheeks, and my stomach caved in. I didn't mean to do that. I just wanted her to shut up for a minute. Just a minute.

The blood gushed underneath her, snaking its way towards me.

'Isobel,' Dad said. 'Come to me now. I need to make a phone call. This way, be a good girl.'

Chapter Fifty-Six

Isobel

My hands cup my face as the scene plays in my head. The memory was too clear, every bit of detail visible, fresh and untarnished. 'No. No, I didn't. It was an accident. I didn't mean it.'

Katarina smiles now, her chin tucked in, her narrowed eyes still staring at my dad's body. 'Don't sweat it. She was a cow. Good riddance.' She disappears then, her cackling laughter lingering longer than her image.

Layla remains with that head shake she has, and I know who she reminds me of now, more than the real Layla. Always criticising, always disapproving. 'Katarina didn't make you bad,' she says. 'You just were.'

'No! They did.' I point at my dad's body, then snap my hand back as I almost nudge him. The blood flow has slowed, his face pale and drained. 'They made me bad.'

The blood on the carpet is starting to dry, turning brownish and crusting. I hold my stomach as I wheeze. He's dead. Oh, my God. He's dead.

I killed them both.

I hug my chest as the room shrinks, closing in. I step away from him, but somehow he's closer. The space between me and everything else is being sucked away. I can't breathe. I need to get out.

'Wait!' Layla says as I turn to run. 'I'm not rotting away in prison because of you. You can't just run away.'

I freeze, forcing a few breaths. 'What else can I do? I didn't think this far. There's so much mess.' I scan the room. Everything is red now, it's all I see whichever direction I look. There's so much blood, I can taste it.

'Hugo Baxter gave you pills,' Layla says. 'Before you saw that shrink. Just after lunch yesterday.'

Yesterday? What did Katarina do in the meantime? I shake my head, focussing on the here and now. 'So?'

'So.' She tuts, the same way as her, her foot starting to tap. 'They messed you up. You reacted badly. Blame them. Let him and all his money fix this. Tell him he needs to or else you'll tell everyone it's what IMAtech made you do.'

I nod, wiping sweat from my brow, but some gets into my eyes and stings. The room is foggy and blurred. Layla is closer, her face inches from mine, and she repeats what she just said. It comes through clearer this time. Yes. Yes, I can do that. Two birds with one stone, really, since Harry mixed up the meds anyway.

Harry. Shit. I forgot about him. One problem at a time.

Focus Isobel, for once in your fucking life, just focus!

I look around the room. It spins as I turn my head I locate my handbag. After wiping my clammy hands on my trousers, I take my phone, then dial Hugo Baxter.

I don't need to feign hysteria, and I don't need Layla to take over. All the panic explodes into a shower of expletives and alarm. It's raw and uncensored.

'What fucking drugs did you give me? You made me do this! IMAtech made me do this!'

I imagine he's my dad, my mum, their ridicule and perversions. I remember his hand on the small of my back, on my shoulder, too familiar. I was too accepting.

'You fucking monster!'

I should have screamed no at him. I should have fought back. I never should have been a good girl.

He's saying something on the phone, but I can't compute what. My ears are ringing. My IMAtech buzzes. He's locating me. It gives me the option of turning the tracking off. It's a safety feature, the popup says. I let it go. He can find me here. He can find me among the blood and the chaos and all the gore.

Perhaps I'll kill him too. He's as much of a pervert as any.

Katarina was right. Fuck the patriarchy.

Chapter Fifty-Seven

Isobel

A black SUV rolls up outside my dad's house. I sit in the corner, pressed against the wall, hugging my knees. The blood has all dried and the summer sun is burning its rays through the gap in the curtains. I should open a window and get some air in here but, besides the odd shake, I'm unable to move.

Layla has gone. It's late morning now. I left the doctor's in the afternoon yesterday. What Katarina did in the meantime has been concerning me.

The front door is unlocked. They knock, wait a minute, then come in. The warm wind rushes through the house, stirring up the smells I'd been adapting to. They hit me again, awash with fresh tinges of rot and stale piss. I curl into the smallest ball I can and bury my head into my knees.

Two people's footsteps pad along the grimy carpet and into the living room. I don't look up to see who they are. Their shadows cast a shade over me as they stall when they get to the doorway. A gasping breath from one, a gag from another, then they walk the final few steps in.

Hugo's voice rings loud and clear. 'Isobel, sweetie. Step this way.' His tone is tense, every word strained.

I don't want to be close to him, but he puts that hand on my shoulder, gripping hard. I don't tell him no. I need to play the good girl still. He yanks me up by my shoulder. 'There, there,' he says in that unsoothing way he does as I keep my head low, meek and obedient. I need this covered up. I need to have never been here.

'What a shame you arrived home to see your dad like this,' he says, his arm around my torso now. I lean on him a little, let him think he's my rock. 'We only just got here, didn't we? We were just stopping by to tell your dad about all the good work you've been doing. Isn't that right?'

I nod, and his hold tightens.

'About how you're a true ambassador for IMAtech. How wonderful the new game is going to be. We were all ready to tell your dad about the speech you're giving at the conference next week, where you'll be saying how wonderful IMAtech is for all the staff.'

There's a man, one of Hugo's security, standing next to me and he passes me a top. I recognise it from my wardrobe upstairs. A summer top that's pink and yellow, too cheery for today. Too much like sunshine. Hugo watches as I lift my arms and remove my bloodied shirt. His eyes stay on me as I stand, exposed for a moment, before redressing. His security takes the dirty top away.

'You shouldn't have hugged your father when you came in here. It's made you such a mess, but it's understandable why you did. Did you touch anything else in here?'

The knife is on the coffee table. A long, serrated bread knife. I remember how heavy it is, how cold it was at first and how it got warmer in this hand's grip. I look over at it.

'Good girl,' he says, and he nods at one of the men.

I bristle and swallow as he goes and wipes it down, then he steps back the way he came, waiting at the edge of the room with me.

Blue lights flash through the window. It's a game show on TV now, one of my dad's favourites. He always knew the answers. The live audience laughs.

Chapter Fifty-Eight

Isobel

I'm sitting on the floor again, curled up in the corner by the time the police arrive. The game show still plays on TV. No one wants to touch anything to turn it off or down. The laughter and catchphrases and jingles muffle the sound of the police officers' boots as they walk through, though their shocked curses ring as loud as the blood rushing in my ears.

No police officers have looked at me yet. Hugo has done all the talking. In the corner, I'm a fly, caught in a spider's web, disregarded and unimportant. I shake and sob while Hugo tells them we just got here and found them like this, that I've been hysterical since. I'd been with Hugo Baxter on the drive here, the business tycoon billionaire they've all heard of. It's the perfect alibi.

Hugo refers to the detective by his first name, shakes his hand like they're old friends. Hugo tells him the story he has crafted. If there is a hint of doubt, he tells them he'll personally make another financial gift to the station—placing careful emphasis on the word *another*—for their time and compassion. No one questions when money talks.

He thanks all the police officers. He'll arrange therapy for me, and the family liaison officer thanks him. They all shake hands again, as if it's nothing but a business deal.

Back in the SUV, behind its blacked-out windows, he takes my phone and checks my IMAtech.

'Your levels aren't too bad, considering,' he says, then puts my phone back in my bag. I reach for it and check my messages. My chest hurts. Still nothing from Harry.

But the mental walls are down. I must know what she's done as my mind space now traverses hers. If I can stand to see it for myself.

I close my eyes and press my hand into my forehead, searching her side of the mental divide, flicking through pages of horror. It's all in the soft focus of a dream, faceless people, the hint of sounds, the smell of a butcher's shop. There's a barn somewhere in Surrey. I can smell the damp wood, the same metallic undertone as my dad's house had. There's plastic sheeting, a similar-looking knife.

I see men, dead and cut up, the knife scoring in those symbols, the words that were on the news. None of these men are Harry and I hold my breath as I allow a little glimmer of hope to trickle through me. He's alive. I'm sure of it. I need to get to him.

'Put your phone away, Isobel. You don't want to make any silly mistakes,' Hugo says, while scrolling through his own.

'Have you heard from Harry?'

He doesn't look up. 'My son? No. He's probably on some bender somewhere.'

'You can see where he is from his IMAtech, no?'

'My son's ridiculous affairs are not my concern.' He still stares at his screen.

His indifference makes me wonder how he would react if Katarina has killed him. Rid of a burden, maybe? Boost business deals by playing the sympathy card? I wouldn't put it past him.

'Now relax,' he says in his there-there voice that gets my back up. 'We'll be back at the office soon. We need to start planning your speech.'

His phone rings, and he exhales a heavy sigh before answering it. 'Darling, what is it? I'm busy… What?… What the fuck?' He hangs up and groans. 'Lance,' he shouts through to the driver. 'Step on it will you? We need to get to the office.'

He sits back in his chair, one clenched fist grinding into his other hand. 'It seems one of your colleagues has decided to do something absolutely crazy today. Fuck. Can't I just have one easy day?'

My breath catches. The meds. It must be Harry.

Hugo shakes his head and jabs at his phone with his finger. 'You'd think my wife could handle things for five minutes while I'm gone. Bloody women. Useless.'

I grit my teeth as the car speeds along, recklessly weaving through traffic, and I think it could crash now. A horrible crash that sends the car somersaulting and crumpling. Such a simple way to go. Just a statistic. A way to end it all. Maybe it would damage my brain, two sides of the divide, but not the third. Only one of us would survive. Which one of us do I want to make it? Because, right now, I'm not sure I would be my first choice.

After over an hour of sitting, knuckles bleaching as I grip the seat and we race around corners, Hugo and I sharing the kind of silence that makes me want to shrivel up even smaller, we arrive outside WIT.

The driver gets out to open Hugo's door and I don't wait for a second chance. I can't get side-tracked by whatever's going on in the office. One problem at a time. My body moves before I've time to think it through. I climb forward into the driver's seat, and as soon as Hugo is out, I pull away. I've not driven in years, but I remember. Of course I remember. Someone else who shares this body has driven very recently.

And I know where to go.

Chapter Fifty-Nine

Isobel

It's over an hour to the barn, but I know the way. This body has been there so many times before it's as if I'm on autopilot. As I approach each bend, each landmark, it's like a jolt in my brain, telling me which way to turn.

The air con in the car is on full blast, yet still I sweat. Rummaging through the dash, I find a packet of biscuits and a can of Sprite. It's not much, but it'll do for now. The sugar hits me like a spark of electricity. God knows when this body last ate.

I park down a dirty lane, brown dust kicking up in the air, misting my view for a moment. When it settles, I cut the engine and look out into the field at the old barn. The afternoon light shines on it, making it appear less ghastly than I know it is. The dilapidated and shoddy construction has a patchy ceiling with some tiles misplaced or littering the ground below. Wooden planks that make up the walls show evidence of rot and tractor accidents over the years. Outside, some machinery is rusting into nothing.

There's no one around. No one would hear the screams.

There's a blackbird calling, a bleating sheep in an adjacent field. I take a moment to summon some courage. I've seen the blood, the gags, the blindfolds, the excrement, the plastic sheeting, an apple—that relevance of which I can't place. They're all faceless people, unidentifiable in my soup of a brain, like remembering a film I half slept through.

With the engine off, the car heats quickly. The hot weather threatens to break. There's a closeness, like static as dark clouds collect overhead, the sun piercing its last shards onto the field before the clouds envelop it completely. I doubt there's any lighting in the barn. It's going to get dark and wet in there soon.

I get out of the car and the mugginess hits me as I walk across the field. I can't remember the last time it rained, but the grass is wet. The dampness soaking through my shoes is familiar, the squelch these ears have heard so many times before. This field sits in a ditch. There are the remnants of a stream cutting through the middle, a couple of yellow wagtails scratching out a living in the grasses. It could be in that simulation of a perfect countryside scene.

Some crows caw in the browning horse chestnut trees at the perimeter. A murder of crows. The clouds rumble in the distance, and I shiver on my approach.

There's no lock on the barn door, just a wooden plank wedged between two rusted slots. I heave it out of the way. It's exactly as heavy as my arms expect.

I open the door, then walk in. The sunlight cuts slits through the gloom.

There's a beam across the ceiling where ropes were once tied. I know this because Katarina tied them. The rope was scratchy and coarse. I rub my thumb and forefingers together. My hands have a roughness, with dirt dug into the cracks.

There's a bench across the back where a knife once lived. I know because it was Katarina's knife. Grimy and blunt.

The floorboards are spongy, and every step pushes up the smell of bleach.

At the far end of the barn, there's some sheeting. Muslin sacks piled on top of some large and lumpy items underneath. A few flies buzzing around.

Wind cuts through the gaps in the walls, carrying with it the scent of manure from the local pig farm. Or is it sheep? In my head, it's pigs.

I take a step towards the pile. It's about two metres away, but the last couple of steps are a monumental effort. I pause, take a breath of the fusty air, my hands not ready to leave my sides just yet.

There's the squelching sound of more footsteps on the grass. I snap my head around, freezing a second, then run back towards the entrance and hide behind the door, my heart hammering in my throat.

They're closer. Two sets of footsteps. Polite conversation between the people, discussing the weather, the looming storm. I sag against the wall when I realise who the voice belongs to. I want nothing more in this moment than to hold him.

I step out from behind the door, and he pauses on his approach. He looks so handsome in his casual joggers and T-shirt, even his scars barely show. His eyebrows shoot up above his sunglasses when he sees me.

'Katarina, did you get him here already?'

My body tenses, and I scowl at him. His expression morphs from acknowledgement to busted.

'Oh,' he says. 'Hi, Isobel.'

The person next to him looks equally confused. Pale-faced and wide eyed.

'Harry, what's going on?' I ask. 'Why were you expecting Katarina?'

The grumble of tyres sounds outside. There's dust kicking up from the dirt road, and Harry peers over his shoulder, then they both step behind the door, into the shadow.

'Never mind,' Harry says. 'I'm sure Katarina will be here in a minute.'

Chapter Sixty

Katarina

Isobel calls to me, wanting answers, ones she's too afraid to really seek. This body has been riddled with fear lately, and such emotion leaves it depleted and weak. I push my way through to the conscious plane. I still have work to do. She can watch this bit, bodiless and out of control from the sidelines. It'll be a good spectator sport. I almost wish I was in her position, like in a movie. I'd want popcorn. She'll enjoy it all, I'm sure.

Harry, *eugh*, looking so fucking smug, is already here. I hate that grin of his, that million-dollar smile shows him for the entitled prick he is. It's a shame the bar explosion didn't burn his lips off.

Still, it's good he's here. It's the old saying: if at first you don't succeed, try, try again.

His posture relaxes, which tells me he knows Isobel's gone for now, though she screams in my ear, demanding answers, telling me not to hurt him. I could block her out if I really tried, but it's good she sees this. It's about time she knows everything.

I should kiss him or fuck him right here in the barn, in front of her while he screams my name and begs for more, just to show her how loyal this dipshit really is. With her voice in my ear, it would be like the most perfect threesome. In the half light he looks hot, defined. I remember those biceps were rock hard.

The car has stopped. We've no time for such antics. The driver is coming. Only one set of footsteps approaches, accompanied by grunting and moaning.

'I'm done chasing after you, girl,' Hugo says as he storms into the barn. 'What the hell do you think you're doing, stealing a company car and coming all the way out here?'

Sweet Isobel wasn't to know his cars have trackers. She did exactly what I wanted her to. I take a step back, and he takes another forward.

'Sorry, Hugo,' I say, in my most pathetic Isobel-like voice. 'Just needed some fresh, countryside air.'

'What sort of mess are you getting yourself into? You are a representative for the company, remember?'

'Oh, I know.'

There's a jerk in my arm, my muscles twitching, an itch up my spine. It's Isobel, trying to control me. I don't want to talk to her in front of these people. They know about our situation, but demonstrating the crazy is a whole other level.

Layla is screaming at me too, but she's always weaker. I can block her out like white noise. I try to reply through our minds only, but that takes concentration, and I'm so excited I can barely keep still.

Too late, Isobel. You set me free, remember?

'Time to go,' Hugo snaps. 'Back to work. How many more seconds do you want to waste? You trying to cause another market crash? Bloody women. Every day I think the lot of you need to be sedated and I'd only hire men. I need to give a speech to the press right now about the benefits of IMAtech. You need to come with me right—'

The thump on his head echoes through the barn. I jump, but grin as his face freezes there a second after the metal bar lands squarely on his head. He stays standing for a moment, lingering between awake and unconscious, before his eyes look towards his nose and he splutters a little laugh before falling to the ground.

Behind him, arms still shaking, her body convulsing with her breaths, Malorie drops the metal bar.

Chapter Sixty-One

Katarina

Lightning cracks through the sky above and thunders through the valley. It's nice. It drowns out Isobel's whining for a moment.

'Nice to have you back, Katarina sweetie,' Malorie says. I've not seen her since the last meeting with all the other women. She was so quiet and weak then, but now, she has a power about her. Still skinny and pale, but she's finally fighting.

I hop on the spot, rub my hands together like Hugo does when the staff are all zombies.

My piggy is here. The one I've been wanting.

Hugo groans on the floor and rolls from one side to another. I make my way to the pile in the corner, pull back the sheets, then grab some rope I stashed among all the other fun knickknacks.

Layla screams in my head when she sees under the sheeting. Christopher Morely's body is there, tidily wrapped in plastic sheeting, awaiting disposal. Weird how he still looks handsome even when dead.

His death was simply beautiful. As I pause a second to remember it, I know Isobel will be seeing it too. I cut off his balls first, then his tongue. His dick was so shrivelled after that it was like clipping off a toenail. It's in his mouth now. I put it in there before I drove my knife into his gut. Nice and slowly.

Another thunderclap halts my daydream and spurs me into action. There's no time to relive the glorious past.

Rain hammers on the sparsely tiled roof and the dribbles that leak through are turning into torrents. The barn is thrown into darkness, and I find a couple of torches in my pile of goodies, tossing one to Malorie.

'He's been drugging me since before I can remember,' Malorie says as she glares down at her husband. 'Years. Sedating me every day. The one time I told him I wasn't in the mood, he made sure I could never refuse again. He'd bring other women back, sit me in the corner and make me watch.' Her eyes don't leave him. There are no tears. Her tone is flat. So many years without emotion and it doesn't just bounce back. The anger is there though, tightening her features, clawing its way out.

'Shall we tie him up?' she asks.

'Sure.'

I show her how as he starts to writhe more, then point out the joist across the ceiling before stepping away.

'You're not going to help?' she asks.

I put my hand on her shoulder. 'You've got this,' I say, then leave the barn, running across the field as the rain hammers down, and I sit in the car.

I wanted him here so much. Having him there, suffering, the reality of his actions hitting him with the pain is simply glorious. But I've heard her story, her years of suffering. He's not my piggy. He's her piggy. The pleasure of his end should be hers alone.

Isobel sits next to me, bedraggled and silent. I don't drive away. We wait, in the rain, in the half-dark. He's not my piggy, but I wish I could hear his screams.

'You just going to sit there and judge?' I ask. 'You want to know what happened that night? With Christopher Morely and that prick? I'll show you. I'll open it up like a fucking gift and show you exactly the sort of monster he is.'

'No.' Her head is in her hands. 'No. . .I can't handle that right now.'

'And that's why you need me.'

She looks at me; her face twisted with emotions, torn between gratitude and disgust, I think. I take down the final mental block, give her a flash of the memory from that night. The quickest glimpse. When I was fucking Christopher Morely, just a fun, innocent shag, Hugo Baxter walked in and decided he was entitled to watch, to put his hands on me, one firmly around my mouth.

Isobel shakes her head, tears tracing down her cheeks. 'Those men are monsters.'

'Yep. They are.'

She looks at her lap, fiddles with the hem of her top. 'Thank you for not killing Harry.'

I smile. 'Who says I didn't?'

We jump from the flash of light from the barn, and my feet vibrate when the sound of the explosion hits us. The barn bows out like a balloon before sending shards of wood and tile shooting out. A loud thump against the car and we jump again. It's not debris. It's a person. He opens the door, then gets in the passenger seat.

'Just fucking drive.'

Chapter Sixty-Two

Isobel

Harry is shaking, but not enough, not nearly enough for someone who's just escaped another explosion. I suppose he's been here before, and he came off much better this time. My shaking is far worse. I squeeze the steering wheel as hard as I can, each turn an effort.

'I could hardly tell you anything,' Harry says as we drive back to London. He has a cut on his head, some rips in his clothes with red seeping through. 'Let's go to my Surrey place. It's really close.'

'I want to go home.'

'Don't be daft.'

The windscreen wipers are going at full speed, but the rain is so heavy the road ahead looks like a smudge.

'Let's go get cleaned up.' There's a tremor to his voice, revealing at least a hint of emotion. Still not enough though, not enough by far. Both his parents just died. He should be devastated, spiralling. He slaps the side of his head a few times, like he's clearing a blocked ear.

'I just want to go home,' I say, tears misting my vision. I tilt my head to wipe my eye on my sleeve. Katarina should be here. I call to her, begging her not to abandon me now. I glance up in the rear-view mirror and there's her outline, so cool and calm, that relentless smirk plastered across her face.

Be nice to my little helper, she says.

My lungs fail to draw breath for a minute and I shiver, the air con now too cold. My foot lifts off the accelerator as my mind replays that again. I look over at Harry. 'You've been helping her?'

He's rubbing debris from his head and pulls down the visor to check his face. 'She could hardly dispose of bodies on her own. You don't even have a car.'

My body turns to ice for a second, then heats again as nausea chugs up my throat, and I slow the car even more.

'Keep driving. Come on!' he yells. 'Hurry the fuck up!'

Shouted into obedience, my foot goes to the floor. I wince as he yells some more, ducking my head as if that will deflect the sound.

'Hurry the fuck up!' He screams over and over. I open my mouth to protest, but he shouts first, 'Shut up! Just fucking shut up!'

I'm silent, but he screams shut up again and again. My chin trembles, every sound cranked up to full volume as I stare un-blinking at the road. I eat up the tarmac, getting as far away from that barn as possible, from everything this body has done, to stop Harry shouting at me. He won't stop shouting.

I swerve around the narrow country lanes, aquaplaning through puddles and fiords that are starting to flood. It's been so dry for so long the rain just runs off the dirt and pools on the tarmac.

Harry has been helping Katarina kill. This body has killed.

'Hurry the fuck up! Shut up!' he repeats again and again, to no one in particular. My eyes dart to his direction as he reaches for a little baggie in his pocket and sniffs a bump of powder. 'This will make it shut up.'

The world swirls around me. My head is light and woozy. Staring straight ahead now, not at Harry and his ramblings, I keep my hands on the steering wheel as if it's a boat and I'm about to fall overboard, swaying with the turns.

He sits back in his chair. He's stopped smacking the side of his head, and instead, looks at his empty hands on his lap.

'You've been helping her. Why? Why would you do that?' My voice is shrivelled and pathetic. I want to cry louder, to bellow and scream, but I've nothing left.

He turns his head to face me, a sneer spreading across his face. 'You should be pleased. I was doing exactly what she wanted. Taking down the patriarchy.' His voice is cool now, too damned cool. The polar opposite from a moment ago, like he's flipped a switch. 'And with all those men out the way, there's more room for men like me. Good men, who can do great things.' He laughs, a crackle really, and I jump.

I fight for breath, my head swaying with the car as motion sickness continues to make everything spin. I need food, some sugar to take this shock away. 'You. . .you killed your parents.'

'I only helped. My mum killed them both. It's what she wanted. My dad was an arsehole.' He says this in such a way that he's implying I'm stupid for not knowing. 'Think what I can do with the inheritance though. It's like we discussed. All the good I can do with that much money.'

I take one hand off the wheel to wipe my eyes. They're streaming now, adding to the blur. He's so different. There's a coldness about him I haven't seen before, some mania in his eyes. He's not the Harry I've been dating. Not the Harry who holds me tight. I turn the headlights on as the storm clouds throw us into night.

'But you have so much.'

He waves his hand at me, as if what I say is worthless. 'Not enough though. Not enough to really make a difference. Come on. I'll make sure you're promoted at WIT. Come on the board! Or at Baxter Pharma. We can do so much good together.' There's a nagging to his voice now, a terrible impatience.

I lift my head, a new worry stiffening my back. 'WIT. Oh, my God. The drug switch kicked in today. I need to know how everyone is.'

'Relax. They're fine. I never switched the meds.'

'What?' My head snaps around to face him, the car yawing with it, and I fight to correct it.

'Pull over and let me drive,' Harry says.

I ignore him. 'You never switched?'

'Well, I was hardly going to tank my own company.' He laughs again, holding his stomach. 'Financial suicide is not the aim here.'

Layla is here. I see her in the rear-view mirror, shaking her head with that disapproving face she does so well. But she's right. He's just like all the rest.

Lightning cracks through the sky above us, and the thunder that follows is ear-splitting loud. The rain turns to hail, like gravel pouring on the car.

'You could have told me!' I say. 'I've been so worried.'

'Relax. Seriously. We're going to get everything we want.'

What *we* want? My mind ruminates on that for a second. We. Does that include Katarina and Layla, or just me? Really, it's none of us, only him, only what he wants. This Harry I do not recognise. This Harry that has done such bad things.

I need this to stop. The world, everything just needs to stop.

A thud comes from the windshield, a splattering of feathers. My body presses back against the seat as the wipers sweep the bird away. *No!* I slam the brakes and the back of the car skids out. My fighting with the steering is useless as we slue over puddle after puddle. My head smashes into the side wall and it all goes dark for a moment. The rain is silent. Nothing swims around me.

It's all just blissfully still.

Chapter Sixty-Three

Isobel

I wipe my hair from my face and it flops away from me, not tickling my neck like normal. It falls the other way, pulling at the roots. The slightest touch of my head sends shockwaves of pain through my skull. Everything is blurry and smudged. I reach to grab my glasses and they come away in two pieces.

Shit. What the—?

The pain comes in droves now, ripples starting from my neck and cascading everywhere. A scream erupts from somewhere deep inside, guttural, vibrating every organ. It's like someone else is screaming, someone else's view, someone else's panic. Because this can't be happening. Please, God. This can't be happening!

My hands and clothes snag on broken glass. I can't breathe, my diaphragm shuddering with the tiniest inhales, like there's no space, too much panic for there to be room for anything else. My heart hums, a ringing in my ears like a dog whistle. It's dark, the headlights lighting the slick road ahead, just two beams, the shadows of raindrops. To my left, I reach over and there's no one. More broken glass, some other debris I can't decipher.

My stomach cramps as I try to calm my breaths, my throbbing head not allowing me to think. Seatbelt. I undo that and my head hits the roof. More waves of pain, so much pain. I whimper, I think, though over the ringing in my ears I hear nothing. Something soft is in the way, the airbag. I push on that, then fumble for the door handle and pull it. Leaning back, I kick the door with my feet to get out. My legs are too weak and there's no room, just a scrubby bush that snags and catches my clothes and skin even more as I heave past. It's pain on pain.

Silhouetted in the headlights, he's there, pacing the width of the road over and over. He's talking, I think. To no one.

'Harry?' Did that make a sound? I'm not sure. I try again. 'Harry?'

It's still raining, pouring, his ripped clothes are soaked through. I shiver and don't dare look down at my own. Lightning cracks through the sky, highlighting his face, his wide eyes, manic. He looks more insane than I've ever felt.

I step closer. He has blood all down his top, and though looks my way, he doesn't see me. He looks past me, through me. 'That's right,' he says to no one, muttering really. 'I knew it. It's what I've been saying this whole time.' He's gesturing wildly, like he's conducting an orchestra, his head still bleeding. 'Fuck all of this. All we can do is kill them all. Fucking bitches. Kill them all!'

He's talking to no one, to the darkness, the shadows. A surge of adrenaline shoots through me. I step back, creating some distance as he rants and raves on and on. His head wound must be bad. Another crack of lightning highlights his clenched hands, one fist thumping the other hand.

I need to get away. The road is drenched, rivers meandering down both sides, the grassy bank turning into a bog. There's a hedgerow that's half dead, parched from the hot summer, a drainage ditch to the side. The rain abates for a moment. Ahead, the black sky ends, leaving behind a streak of pastel pink. Birds are calling like it's daybreak.

I step onto the grassy bank, my shoes soaking through, then push through the hedgerow. More snags. More pain. There's a road up there. I see the trail of headlights.

I head that way, away from him. Alone. I just need to be alone.

***

I arrive at my local train station with little memory as to how I got here. The world spins as I drag my sore limbs through the entrance, that pastel pink sky now less welcoming and more revealing. I must look a mess from the stares I get, it would be better if it was dark. No one asks if I'm okay. One of the benefits of living in London, everyone minds their own business.

I shuffle the walk to my flat. What normally takes ten minutes takes an age. My thoughts are of nothing but the pain. Every bit of motion is like I'm being punched all over or burned again. From my building, each step up to my level is like a mountain.

When I get home, I fall onto the bed, still soaked from the rain, bloodied and bruised. Sod the sheets, sod the mess. I'm too tired to care. Just so, so tired.

***

A shard of light fingers its way through the curtains and falls across the bed. I rub my eyes and they sting, waking me even more. My bed is damp. My wet clothes have soaked the duvet, and there are blood stains on the sheets. As I roll over, the room still spins, but less so than it did before, whenever before was.

Bit by bit, I sit up. The mirror over the vanity frames a person I don't recognise. Someone with the worst frizzy hair, impaled with leaves and twigs like a bird's nest, a black eye, clothes ripped and stained, purple bruising and lumps up her neck and shoulder, a split lip. My hand goes to my mouth after a moment when I realise it's me.

My other hand touches the bruises, gingerly. I wince as the pain is still raw and fresh. My hair feels like a doormat, rough and matted with blood. Nausea churns in my stomach and I hold on to the bed, taking some breaths as I wait for it to pass.

No chance I can run to the toilet. My body isn't going to work that quickly.

The night flashes before me, memories bombarding my mind, making my headache worse. Hugo, the explosion, Malorie, Harry, the crash.

My nose starts bleeding and I tilt my head back, but even that causes an eruption of pain. I should probably go to the hospital and get checked out, but my damp clothes soak more with sweat at the thought.

I caused an accident. The explosion.

When my nose stops bleeding, I locate my handbag, wet and filthy, but somehow my phone inside is intact. Harry didn't message. There's only a message from someone called Amy, saying tests are all fine, and do I want to meet for that drink. Must be a wrong number.

Grimacing with every step, I make it to the bathroom, then shower. The water runs brown, black, and red. Bits of shrub and scab clog the drain. Naked and soaked, every cut comes alive, telling me it's there, like the shower spits out salt water. The steam helps a little after a while, soothing and clearing the lump in my chest.

Wrapped in a towel after, I sit on the toilet and rest my legs. Even having a shower has left them wobbly and weak.

The doorbell rings and I freeze. No one would visit. No one cares about me. Who could that be? Any soothing effect from the shower is undone as I think it could be the police. I left an accident, the most minor of this body's crimes, but it's the one that, right now, I feel is the one most likely to get me caught. I heave myself to standing, put on a dressing gown, then walk to the intercom and take a breath before pressing the button.

I almost moan in relief when the voice says he's a delivery guy. My trembling finger presses for him to come up.

He recoils when he sees me. 'You all right, miss?'

I strain to smile. 'Yes.'

'Okay. . .' He stretches out the word, then takes a parcel out of his bag and hands me a tablet. 'Sign your name here, please.'

I take the tablet and stare at the box asking for my name. I swallow, the pen heavy in my hand, the box angry and glaring at me. My name. I have to sign it.

The room is a whirlpool as I search through my mind, my skull burning with the effort.

It's only one simple task, but I can't manage it. My hand won't work. The floor tips to an angle and then another as I try to think: what's my name?

Chapter Sixty-Four

Isobel

I know the smell of a hospital before I even open my eyes. I've spent enough time in them lately. Only this time, like a punch in the gut, it hits me: no one will be waiting for me to wake up.

I stir, groan, then try but fail to get comfortable as my limbs feel like they're on backwards. A nurse comes. She has the sort of kindly no-nonsense way of adjusting my pillow and checking my vitals without a hint of fluster.

'Are you feeling sick at all?' she asks as she checks my pulse.

I shake my head, then wish I hadn't. It's like a thousand ball bearings are ricocheting inside.

'Doctor says you're going to be fine. Just a concussion and a lot of bruising. That's a nasty bump on your head.'

I reach up and touch it, and again, wish I hadn't. My eyes stream and roll back as the pain makes me gasp.

She inspects the bump with gentle hands. 'You got anyone we can call for you?' It's not really a question. She means who should she call, what's my next of kin's number.

I look around the room, glaringly white and empty. I choke back some tears when it's clear there isn't anyone.

When I look down, my drawn face reveals the answer, and she gives me a pained smile. 'We need to take some details from you. You didn't have any ID on you. What's your name?'

The nausea hits me then, and she grabs a bowl just in the nick of time.

'It's all right,' the nurse says. 'Get it all up. You'll feel better soon.'

***

There's a little TV next to my bed, the channel choice is news or game shows. I opt for news.

My jaw drops when they play the headline. Malorie Baxter's face fills the screen. It's her profile picture she uses on social media, from days when she used to smile and engage. She looks twenty years younger. Radiant and happy. Lack of smiling over the years hadn't saved her developing wrinkles. She had lines digging deeper from other experiences. The story is about a video that's gone viral several times over. Malorie Baxter's suicide video. Her murder explanation.

She holds nothing back.

I turn the volume up and lean a little forward, entranced by her story. Every sordid detail of her marriage is exposed, telling the world exactly the sort of man Hugo Baxter was.

She was dying, she reveals. Untreatable cancer that was eating away at her insides. She wanted her death to mean something, for her end to end the tyranny. I cry as I listen to her recount her misery. Her husband had his hand over her mouth, always. As she tells her tale, it's like it's my mouth she's talking about. The pressure from his fingerprints left their mark on my face. My neurones remember.

Malorie Baxter was respected in the world of business, the news says, came from a good family, bolstered by her father's money. How had Peter Ward described her once, 'An example of a good woman'. Her confession is more damning than that of a thousand nobodies. She was somebody. A rich somebody. That counts for so much more.

I go to speak to one of them, on autopilot, so used to having one of my friends with me for company when I needed it. I open my mouth to discuss Malorie's story, to share in my shock and horror at her revelations, as well as my awe of her strength. But there's still no one else here but me. My thoughts echo in an empty mind. No walls anymore, but also no one else to fill the gaps. I gaze across the empty room, at the garish white, the walls creeping farther away from me as I shrink into insignificance.

***

I wake the following morning and tell the nurse I'll call my family. Using their phone, I dial nobody, and tell the dial tone I'm in hospital, fake some responses, then hang up. The nurse smiles, satisfied as I tell her what she wants to hear. I pretend I'm someone loved and cared for so the hospital will discharge me.

Loneliness leaves me hollow, my voice flat, and I avoid eye contact. It's getting harder to pretend.

When I get home, I kick off my shoes, leaving them scattered by the door, then raid the fridge for whatever I can find before showering and climbing into bed. I'm dodging the painkillers they've given me, not wanting to feel any foggier. My whole body hurts, an all-over ache with some indeterminate cause. Shock, relief, a splitting headache that never seems to ease.

I check my phone for the hundredth time. It's a habit, a generational thing. Of course there are no new messages. I should probably at least email work and tell them I'm sick, but thinking of such practical things only makes my headache worse.

I recite this body's name as I lay on my bed staring at the ceiling. Over and over I say it, for in all likelihood, no one will ever say my name again.

I say it like I'm forcing it to fit, like I'm squeezing into a pair of shoes that are too tight. If I say it enough, it'll loosen and give and envelop me like it should.

Isobel. Isobel. Isobel.

When I sleep, I dream of them, of us, of the best friends I ever had.

***

I sleep for so long, it's afternoon by the time I wake. I sit on the sofa with a cup of tea and turn the TV on. The news still plays the Malorie Baxter story, but after, there's a story about WIT. The journalist, Kammy Parsons. I've seen her on TV before. She tried to stand up to the Clarity Directive ages ago. She never made a difference, other voices were louder, but at least she tried.

I blink, then rub my eyes a few times as I watch the footage. I almost drop my teacup when the screen fills with photos and videos showing all the staff at WIT, working like zombies, taking tablets every couple of hours. There's a picture of one, their eyes blurred out to hide their identity as they lie on the floor, foaming at the mouth.

I know those images.

Looking through my phone, they're gone, wiped. An email in my sent items shows they were shared by someone using this phone and email account. It must have been one of the others. I wish I could hug them. Instead, I wrap my arms around myself and squeeze as tight as my injuries allow. It's their body too. I hope they're still inside somewhere so they can feel it.

There's talk across all channels, more than there ever has been, condemning the Clarity Directive. The only difference is fear among men. No man is willing to defend the Directive now. Well, hardly any man. If such a directive leads to drugging wealthy wives, to men being brutally harmed, then those powerful men suddenly feel powerless. Women everywhere have been fighting fire with fire, only now it's a supernova.

There are other videos, ones that warm my heart. Perhaps it's tiredness or the pain or I'm still in shock, but tears once again wet my cheeks, though these come from a happy place, overwhelming me with an inner sensation of joy. There are journalists reporting from Trafalgar Square, from outside Parliament, and other cities too across the country. Women are taking to the streets, shouting for justice for all women, for the end of the Directive. Not just women, men too. The Clarity Directive only sought to serve an elite few. Those with so much money, they thought they owned everything. Most never took advantage of it. There are more good people than perverts. The wealthy, who have stood on their mountain for so long, are falling from the landslide.

I have an inkling to join the marches, to stand with them, but I'm in no shape to do that right now. I'm bone tired. My headache eases as I lie on the sofa, listening to the TV, to the voices of justice and worth. Just before I dose off, I whisper into the night to both of them, and to all those people marching the streets, 'Thank you.'

Chapter Sixty-Five

Isobel

I debated not going to the funeral, but then, how would that look? I'm still meant to be playing the part of a grieving daughter, at least for the father he was meant to be.

I wish I could turn those memories off, but that safe won't close. The door swings open, loose on its hinges, the slightest wobble has them pouring out.

Flashes come back when I least expect it. I've dropped three coffee cups this week when an image startled me. I change my top twice daily when sweat soaks it through. Every noise makes me jump.

I've visited Doctor Ansari several times, and she says it will take time. I wish there was a definite number to that, like I could say three weeks on Tuesday my mind will be healed. Doctor Cottrell's method at least offered me peace for a while. Now, I don't know if I'll ever recover.

There are so many memories, like a jigsaw, and none of the pieces fit, shattered images and conversations all out of place.

I remember the blood though. I remember how he looked when he was dead. And, worst of all, I remember why he's dead. It's that why which plays on a loop as I try to sleep. Any pain eased rips through me again when I curl in a ball and wish him to stop. He never does. My imagination isn't what it once was. I can't change the visions of the past.

The funeral service is simple, cheap and poorly attended. A couple of carers, my brother and his partner and me.

The police have put the double homicide down to a business associate or vigilante. They found videos, hours and hours of videos. Half the planet would have killed him if they knew what sort of man he was. I'm never named as a suspect. The one good thing Hugo's money ever did was sway the police that day.

Doctor Cottrell was arrested, and Dad's assets seized. They were considerable, apparently. The humble life he led was mere subterfuge for the cash he was sitting on. His sordid empire reached across the globe. Mum would have been proud of his business acumen. They have leads, the police assure me. There will be more arrests. There will be justice.

I nodded and thanked them when they called with the latest update. What am I meant to feel about it? How should my tone of voice be? Somehow, being me doesn't really fit. My emotions are out of place, improper, not as the police would expect. It's hard to play a role when I have no idea what that role should be.

No one says a eulogy at the funeral. The celebrant doesn't say much, just some standard waffle I don't listen to. If it were up to me, there would have been no funeral at all. Dylan arranged it. No flowers or music. It's as dreary as he deserved.

Dylan walks over to me after the coffin goes through to the crematorium. He looks so much like him. 'Pub? Might as well have a pint.'

'Sure.'

It's Dad's local, where he used to frequent before mother nature served a semblance of just desserts and rendered him housebound from a stroke. Dylan has no idea it was me in the videos, as per my request to the police. Maybe he was in them too, but I wouldn't know.

'To the old prick,' he says, and raises his glass.

I give a cheer but keep my gaze low and don't drink.

He sips. 'So,' he says, the froth sticking to his top lip. 'How're things? Still at WIT?'

'Yeah. Well, I guess so. If the company survives.'

'I'm sure they will. Sounds like they're really on to something with IMAtech. A few tweaks and it would be a game-changer.'

'A few tweaks?' I ask, then instantly regret it.

'Just minor things. Like, it's only women's hormones that really need monitoring. What's the point in monitoring mens'? That's all just natural man behaviour. Our hormones make us faster and stronger. Women are the ones who need, let's say, fine-tuning. Isn't that right, dear?' He turns to his partner, who gives a small nod but says nothing. She has the sort of face that looks like she's never spoken, the sort of posture that looks like she's never stood straight. As much as the marches show solidarity with fellow women, there are some still cornered. I want to hold her hands, to embrace her, to whisper words of revenge in her ear. Instead, I sip my pint and listen to the same shit I've heard so many times before.

'It's like all those sports women who win races by having more testosterone,' Dylan says. 'Proves it's not a bad thing, doesn't it?'

I gulp my beer, hoping the sound of my own swallowing will drown out his voice.

'And now there's all these men scared of simply being men. Scared of the consequences of just being themselves. The world's gone mad.'

I neck the last of my pint. 'Nice to catch up, anyway. Until next time.'

I don't wait for a response. I grab my bag, then walk out of the pub, the fresh sea air of the coastal city blowing over me as I take a deep breath.

I'm alone again.

I've been alone since the car accident. No images of the others. Their voices aren't even a whisper. It's like the bump on my head killed them off. Or maybe opening the safe meant there was no need for all three of us. There's my own voice though. My conscience and confidence. Both shattered.

As I walk to the train station, my fingers twitch, empty, in need of something to grip. My thoughts spiral, thinking of what I should have just said to Dylan, of what I could have done if I was just a little more impulsive.

A tingle spreads from my ear down my neck, and my eyes glisten. I shake the thought away. There'd be no point in more violence. He's a nobody. No power, not rich, no one. I reason with my demons, explaining the killing would never end if I thought like that, if I acted like that. I load up my phone and read the headline, standing taller than I ever have, my lungs expanding to their fullest as I read the headline over and over: *Clarity Directive to be repealed.*

It's over, I tell myself. As I reach the station and buy my ticket, there's a queue, but I don't fear the men around me. I move along the line, unconcerned as to whether I'm in arm's reach, and a little bubble of satisfaction grows inside.

We won.

The bubble bursts as reality hits like a needle. Laws don't change views. Views don't change when the laws change. It's ingrained.

I take my ticket, then make my way to the platform, telling myself it's okay. One step at a time.

Chapter Sixty-Six

Isobel

I should stop watching the news. For every good story, there are ten worrying ones. Every time the news jingle plays it makes every hair on my body bristle, and an icy chill creeps over me, that sense that there are eyes watching. But I still watch, like an addiction. Some soap opera full of cliffhangers.

DNA evidence found, the reporter says on the breaking news article. On one of the bodies murdered and carved up. My heart jumps to my throat. My stomach knots.

That knot stays put all day and night as I stay awake, worry robbing me of even a moment of sleep or desire to try. It's been there twenty-four hours now since the latest update. I haven't left my sofa, keeping the curtains drawn like somehow that will stop them finding me. I've nowhere else to hide.

Today's headline: *An arrest has been made.*

Harry Baxter.

I shouldn't sneer at the footage, but I do. So much so, my eyes narrow. I lean in to watch, biting on the last of my nails, chipping away at the last of the red polish. There's a video of him writhing against his handcuffs, twisting his shoulders around one way then the next as he screams innocence. He still has that wild look he had in his eyes that night as he cries out her name, shouting down the lens of every camera in range.

'Katarina McKenzie! It was Katarina McKenzie!'

A history of delusions, the reports say. Harry was unstable as a teenager, spent time in an institution. The report rips apart his family, says how his parents were determined to make him the son they dreamed of. They mention his sister, how she is un-known, cast aside in favour of the more photogenic child. The medicated one, the one they learned in some way to control.

Katarina's — the real Katarina's — photo fills the screen and I choke on my own breath. She was so young when she died, and picture-perfect. Harry described her in detail, like he really could see her. Perhaps his madness is why he could always tell the difference between us. Takes one to know one.

This proves his insanity, the papers say. Katarina has been dead for years.

The police call me in for questioning, since they've figured out we were dating. Harry has never placed this body anywhere, always saying it was Katarina. Out of loyalty or insanity, I guess I'll never know. The questions are routine, mundane. Was I aware... Did he ever give any indication... Have I ever seen this Katarina McKenzie?

'No,' I say, over and over. 'Of course not.'

My shock is genuine.

Socials are awash with conspiracy theories that the real Katarina's still alive somewhere, that she was hidden away or kidnapped, that she lives on, fighting the good fight.

I wish that were true. She would love to see this.

***

Hugo Baxter's funeral was a secret affair, probably as dreary as my father's. Malorie's, though, they have to put fencing up and shut the streets. Flowers are thrown into the road as women watch, holding on to each other, faces etched with sadness and hope. Harry is in a limousine, a police officer sitting on either side of him. The news cameras get a better view than my position on the pavement, so I watch the live footage, his scarred face blotchy from whatever emotion he feels. I'm unsure what that is, anger, grief, sadness, a cocktail of negativity? The will reading wasn't what he'd hoped for, according to the press. Most of the family fortune was left to the Taylor Foundation for vulnerable women, something Malorie arranged before her death. Not that it will matter to him. It's unlikely he'll ever be released from the mental institution.

I remember my conversation with Katarina after the explosion.

'Thank you for not killing Harry.'

'Who says I didn't.'

He may not be killed in the murder-sense, but his dreams are stifled, his freedom gone along with his ambition, his billionaire status, so in his eyes, the effect is the same.

I should be wretched with guilt, but beyond an ounce of pity, I feel nothing. He deserves what he gets. His intentions were evil, only thinking to serve himself. Katarina's intentions were for the greater good.

In this crowd, standing in unified silence, all holding hands in vigil for Malorie Baxter, I'm alone. But here, among these people, I find kinship.

My phone buzzes with a text from Amy again. She's asked me out several times. It's not me she met before. I've visited Layla's memories, though, and I know how she felt. I recall snippets of conversation between them. Amy never fitting in with her family, her desire to do good, her distrust of WIT. Amy's in a bar not too far away and I think, well, why not? I owe it to Layla. She's been gone since the barn. I've not heard from her at all. I don't miss her disapproval, but I miss her company sometimes. I wish I could thank her for what she did to help bring IMAtech down by sharing those pictures. I am sure it was her. However much she prioritised work, she put us first in the end.

I make my way through the crowds. They're dispersing now and bars are filling up, then into the Red Lion.

'Isobel!'

It still doesn't feel like my name, but I know to react when I hear it. I turn around to see her, my stomach fluttering just as Layla's had. 'Hi.'

She walks over and hugs me, then pulls away, noting the stitches on my head. 'My God. What happened?'

'I was in an accident. I'm sorry, it's affected my short-term memory, so I've been a bit out of it.'

She smiles. 'Well, I guess then we get to start over. Sounds good to me.'

Over some drinks, she tells me of our meetings, how she checked on the medication, and I find myself leaning into her, a familiar scent, a musical voice. I scoot my chair closer, breathing her in, my eyes darting between her eyes and lips.

'I feel awful,' she says, 'I always tried to be there for him. But I guess I didn't do a good enough job. Harry's my brother, and I couldn't save him from himself. I failed.'

Harry. Some of the jigsaw pieces fall into place. In her face, I see the similarities now. Strip away all of the bad and she's the kindness left over. I take her hands and squeeze. 'You would have done your best. Harry's broken. Some things can't be fixed.'

She leans in and kisses me, and I think then what I said was wrong. I was so broken, but with her kiss, I feel healed.

I hope Layla senses this kiss, if she is still somewhere inside this body. I lean closer, press my lips into Amy's again, breathing her in, my hands on her waist, skin-on-skin. If Layla's mind is still inside me somewhere, then I'm sure to let this kiss permeate every part of my thoughts, enjoying it enough for two people.

***

Doctor Ansari is teaching me to understand and to move on. Not to forgive, I refuse to do that, but to accept the past and to not let it darken my future. The safe door is wide open, and I don't hide from its contents. I am stronger now.

I cry more than I thought possible. My tears are for my friends who still haven't come back, for the void they have left behind, and for the pain of all women who fought against the Directive. There are even tears for the mother I never loved. Her words have played over and over, and that memory fragment now haunts me. There's so much hate eating away at me. Hate for the mother who was so awful, though I understand now she only wanted what's best. But she could have stopped him. She could have at least tried.

I've been off work for a while since my head injury. But when Monday comes, I feel well enough to go in, not really knowing what I'm about to walk into. The office staff are working, but without the help of the usual pharmaceuticals, the pace is slow. There's twitchy fingers and irritability, yawns, sore backs and arms. Some arrive late, flustered and panicked when they do. The dispensary staff are absent, the desk minus its stock.

The IMAtech displays are still up, and they show the collective seconds are slipping away, the hormone data swinging from one side to the other. I consider taking the charts down.

They serve no purpose now, but they're quite high up, so I email maintenance instead.

I walk around the office, asking the staff if they're okay, to ignore the IMAtech, just do what they can. Take breaks.

As far as I know, it's business as usual in designing the game. There are silent partners, someone will be taking over, even Harry's technically still a board member.

The tapping of keyboards is punctuated with the odd sigh and sound of people taking toilet breaks and sipping their coffee. Code and designs are being churned out at a reasonable rate, not the zombie-swiftness, but it's all progress. Ellen's character designs are stunning, better than anything I've seen before. I compliment her and she beams. It's so nice to see a smile on her face again.

Joel sits back, stretching his neck and back. His posture is so arched, it's like his chin is heavy. His misbuttoned shirt has the remnants of his breakfast down the front.

'Hey, Joel.'

He looks at me, pausing his typing for a moment. His eyebrows draw in, then blinks a few times when he sees me. 'Oh, hi, Isobel.'

'How's things?'

He rubs his eyes. 'I feel like the last few weeks are such a blur. The news is crazy, right?'

I nod.

He glances up at the IMAtech tally and bites his lip. 'I wonder what's going to happen to the company. I mean, look at the chart.'

'Don't worry about the chart,' I say. 'I think we just need to forget IMAtech.'

Throughout the office, there's a vague discussion about job security, of what the end of IMAtech will mean. They look to me for answers, as if I know. I wanted IMAtech to stop, but what happens next hasn't really crossed my mind.

'Will the company be better?' someone asks.

I shrug. 'Who knows? Maybe. But it's better to try to change things than to just accept how things are.'

'You know what this means though?' Joel says, glancing once again at the tally. 'We can't match the productivity of AI.'

'No,' I say, staring at Ellen's beautiful designs. 'But we are infinitely more creative.'

Chapter Sixty-Seven

Epilogue

6 months later

I miss my friends, and when I'm by myself in my apartment, I find myself talking to them, expecting to see or sense one of them with me. It still hurts when I remember they're not here anymore. I don't know if their minds absorbed into mine or just disappeared completely, though I like to think we are one person, a hybrid of the three of us.

At least I have other company now.

Amy and I hold hands as we walk to the restaurant Friday night. It's busy, the remnants of rush hour still lingering. I haven't been groped in the streets for ages, since it's now illegal to do so. There's even been some arrests of those who didn't get the memo, or who did get it but ignored it. No prison time for their actions yet. We're in a transitional time, the police say. People need time to change. The government has appealed for peace, for patience as we all adapt.

I've a few days off work, the entire office has, as a reward for getting the game finished. It's past its deadline by a couple of months, but it launches, and is as big a hit as anticipated. It includes all the AI that Christopher Morely developed. His dress rehearsal idea for those with social anxieties went down really well. It's not a game, it's a tool, the commercials say.

The Baxter Pharmaceuticals element was removed. The new CEO thought it best to distance the two companies. The new shareholder swooped in and bought the company, including Harry's shares, for rock-bottom prices. Baxter pharmaceuticals has a new board also. The stock market bounced back after all the killings, but Baxter Pharma is lagging behind in its recovery. It's tainted, some people say. They're probably going to change the name. Baxter doesn't carry the weight it once did.

I rub my hand over the scar on my collarbone where my IMAtech chip was cut out. Voluntarily. For some, they wanted to keep it, to know how much sleep they've had, to monitor heart conditions. These things may have their uses for some people. It's the choice we were after. Joel kept his, and on the days his levels aren't perfect, he can hold his nephew through the game. He seems pleased enough with that compromise. As does his sister.

The scar still itches. It'll take a while to heal, the nurse said. But I know, scars are more than skin deep.

As we sit in the restaurant, Amy pours me a glass of wine. She chose it, since she has the best taste. She knows what goes well with the food.

'You see that article yesterday, Kammy Parson's latest?' she asks.

I shake my head.

'It was a feature on some women, victims of the Clarity Directive, giving them a voice. There are women taking positions on boards again, saying they feel safe to do so. There are always some men saying it's too hard for them, that they don't want to be penalised simply for being men.' She scoffs, then sips her wine. 'It was funny, Kammy said, "You could always just keep your hands to yourself, women aren't playthings". You should have seen the look on that guy's face.'

'There will always be some,' I say.

She told me a while ago about the relationship she had with her dad. I always thought Harry was a disappointment, that he would have preferred some plain-looking swat to the dumbass pretty boy he is. Turns out I was wrong.

'I wasn't pretty enough for my dad to be proud of me,' Amy says.

I find that hard to believe. Sure, she's not someone who's going to adorn the front pages of some glossy magazine, but she is captivating.

'Not smart enough either. I gave up trying to spend time with him as soon as I was old enough to have a choice. I only wanted a job at Baxter Pharma so I could keep an eye on Harry, and to see what my dad was up to, to try to stop it. I vowed never to speak to him again after he went so public about his support for the Clarity Directive. What is it he said to me once? Behave. Of course, they all say that. But he said girls like me should know when to be quiet. The way he spoke to me, I just never felt I was good enough.'

I hold her tight and reveal a little more of my story. Not all. Maybe I'll never tell her everything.

'They always tried to tell me I needed to try harder,' I say. 'To work harder. I was never good enough. I always had to be better, to reach for the sky.'

She leans back a little and strokes my face. 'The sky starts where the ground ends. Whatever you manage to do, you're already there.'

I want to tell her I love her right now. But I won't yet. She can say that first.

'Doctor Ansari tells me I need to learn to accept my faults,' I say. 'She's right, of course. I've done things I'm not proud of. But I guess none of us are perfect.' I gaze into her eyes, at her girl-next-door features. She's enchanting. 'Except maybe you,' I tease.

She laughs, then jokes, 'Shut up.'

'It's what the world tells us, I guess,' I say, remembering one of Katarina's many life lessons. 'We're never pretty enough or sexy enough. We never dress well enough. We're not smart enough. We talk too much or not enough. We're too ambitious or too lazy.'

Amy nods along, then takes my hands again. 'But it's all a lie,' she says. 'You are enough. I was always enough. All of us, as we are. We are enough.'

Her words warm me, lift some of the weight from me so I'm relaxed, light, giddy with the truth of it.

My attention is snapped away from Amy, as across the bar, a woman shouts at a man for getting too friendly. My muscles tighten and I glare at him. I'm ready to react, should things regress. I may be able to relax in public, but complacency will never be the norm. How can it, after everything we've been through? Women everywhere can never take their rights for granted.

The man backs down. I smile and lick my bottom lip. I may no longer be able to hear or see Katarina, but her influence lingers.

Amy strokes my face, and as I look her way, my body simmers down. Doctor Ansari has been teaching me to temper my anger, and when my rage threatens to boil over, I repeat my name again.

Isobel. Isobel. Isobel.

I am Isobel. And I am enough.

A note from Emma

Thank you so much for reading Free Her. I really hope you enjoyed it. Scanning the QR code will take you to Amazon to leave a review. Reviews are so important for authors, and help other readers to discover books they'll love.

I quit a high-pressure corporate job a few years ago. It was a role in which every minute of my day was monitored. I'd spend all day in a windowless room, working my arse off with barely a second spare to take a toilet break. I lasted seven years in that job before I couldn't stand it anymore, and moved into my vanhouse and headed for the hills. I'm sure that kind of work pressure sounds familiar to so many people. I tired to explain it to my partner, describing it as being like a flower that had been dumped in a cupboard, forgotten, and left to wilt. IMAtech may not be a real thing, but in those days, it certainly felt like it. Those years inspired the IMAtech side of this story. The Clarity Directive came from other inspiration, and I'm sure so many others have stories that can relate to that.

If you want to get in touch, Check out my website and Facebook page.

Subscribers to my website receive a couple of free stories linked to my previous series.

I have a short story, See Her, featured in a thriller anthology, The Secrets of Lilypond Lane. See Her tells the tale of Katarina in her school days, and her inspiration behind her feminist ways. The anthology is on sale now and features some fabulous and thrilling stories by authors from across the globe.

Emma's other works

The Eyes Forward Series. This best-selling dark and dystopian trilogy is set in a world where the global population is too high, and extreme methods are enforced to reduce it. Each book in the trilogy follows the journey of women trying to survive in The Society, where women's fertility is deemed a dangerous nuisance, where every child is regarded as a burden, and every citizen is a spy.

If you are in the mood for some more twisted dystopian, my first series, The Raft Series, is also available now. In this world, the entire country has been sterilised and all non-human life made extinct. But poison comes in many forms and Savannah Selbourne must discover the truth.

Acknowledgements

Free Her would not be in print without the help of my wonderful betas and critique partners. Thank you to Keith, Alice, Jay, and Mia. . .and anyone else I've forgotten! Their time and honest feedback made this book what it is today. Thank you also to my editor Shannon K. O'Brien, for being so incredibly thorough, and Natasja Smith for her proofreading skills.

Thanks especially to my partner, John, for giving me the space and time I need to write, for his support, patience, and encouragement.

And thank you for reading it.